The Joshua Line

The Joshua Line

William A. Morgan

Northwest Publishing, Inc.
Salt Lake City, Utah

The Joshua Line

For information address: Northwest Publishing, Inc.
6906 South 300 West, Salt Lake City, Utah 84047
JC 2.8.95
Edited by Paul VanDenBerghe

PRINTING HISTORY
First Printing 1995

ISBN: 1-56901-304-7

NPI books are published by Northwest Publishing, Incorporated,
6906 South 300 West, Salt Lake City, Utah 84047.
The name "NPI" and the "NPI" logo are trademarks belonging to
Northwest Publishing, Incorporated.

PRINTED IN THE UNITED STATES OF AMERICA.
10 9 8 7 6 5 4 3 2 1

My thanks to those who helped me
with this book, especially Carole Morgan,
Stacey Morgan-Foster, Mildred Galinski and
Mark Stanleigh Morris.

Thanks also to James Hartsfield of NASA,
and two wonderful Great Lakes sailors,
ex-freighter Captains Baganz and O'Hara.

Prologue

The blast of a rifle flattens a deadly marauder on the rocky slopes of an island, the echo of one fired three thousand miles away and one hundred sixty years before. A young man, desperate to survive against the odds, has drawn upon his legacy from another young man, the progenitor of the Joshua Line.

Somehow, someway, a sinewy thread in the fabric of humanity has spanned the generations, connecting one dot on the pages of history to an as yet unwritten chapter, a chapter that may describe the future of civilization itself.

Why? How? Follow the Joshua Line and learn for yourself.

1
The Natural Thing to Do

It was midafternoon, and the October sun shone pleasantly down on the two riders and their two pack animals, warming them gently. The older one, in front, gray whiskers, dirty buckskin pants and jacket, hat brim pinned flat to the crown over his left eye, rode comfortably, one with his horse. While his long striding chestnut found its own way along the poorly defined trail, he kept up a constant scan of the surrounding terrain. The bouldery hills were sparsely landscaped with squat pinyon pines and tall twisted junipers and offered a thousand hiding places amongst the gulches and ridges. Not that they were expecting trouble, though.

His partner, a young man of nineteen, in hickory shirt, jeans, and broad-brimmed hat was currently interested in finding a more comfortable position in the saddle. He pulled his right leg out of the stirrup and hooked it over the horn. The lead rope running from the horn to the first of the two packhorses had been rubbing his thigh. The new position was a welcome change, and he grunted a satisfied noise to no one in particular. He was a rangy young fellow, and he had an honest look to his face that appeared clean shaven even with the three-day stubble of beard that he now stroked with the palm of his hand.

He was thinking about the stories his companion, Bill Bright, had been telling last night after supper. They'd eaten their biscuits and venison and had restoked the fire against the growing chill of the evening. Bill was a natural talker. Joshua Mitchel was just as naturally not a talker.

"Josh, my boy, we're pretty smart, you 'n' me to be headin' south this time of year. Even if your pa hadn't died, I think I'd have had to quit'im and move on anyway. But it's good I didn't leave afore. You'd a been on your own, and I don't think your pa would a been content to die thinkin' that. He was a good man, no argument there, but he didn't quite see you as full grown like I do. Just the same I'm glad you offered to join me."

That had been a little hard to follow, but Joshua knew that old Bill had trouble saying in words what was in his heart. In the past year he had come to understand and admire the mountain man a great deal. He hadn't been in Carson City with his father long enough to make any more trusted a friend so he had asked to join up with Bill when his father died of lockjaw. He had sold the wagons, mules, and tack of the modest freight business, and the two had outfitted themselves for prospecting in the southern Sierras.

Joshua had sat gazing into the flickering fire, blanket draped over his shoulders, as Bill recounted stories of his younger days as a trapper.

"I did indeed see me a lot o' new country in those days. Went inta Gila Valley first with Pattie and Young. Yessir, wasn't much older than you. Got run off by the Papagos and lost near ever'thin'. First white men ever in that country, unless ol' Coronado got there first. Ha, ha. Maybe that's why the Papagos were so downright unfriendly. Maybe Coronado traded 'em out of all their food with tradin' beads. Some o' those injuns sure do go for trading beads. Ribbons and rings, too, though I hear they be more for calico than trinkets these days.

"Any the way, the next year we went back and the Papagos jumped us again and killed seven of our party. Later on the Mojaves surprised us one night, near midnight, and killed two more. Jehosaphat! I never saw so many arrows come at once in my life. There must a been two hundred of 'em. And you know what? We never fired a shot in return during that attack. Never did see 'em. I tell you, I began to learn somethin' about injuns on that trip. 'Course we caught up to 'em next day and taught 'em what for.

"Those injuns. They sure do come in all sorts of temperaments. Take the Crow. Now they have a lot of ponies, dress fairly well and have a fine sense of humor. Very honorable. Yes, indeed. But mighty tough customers, too. The Sioux just the same they say. They been fightin' for years back in Wyoming. Against the Army. Just won't quit.

"Then there's the Apaches and Navajos. Horse stealers, 'Par excellence,' as they say. Fighters, the lot of 'em, but dirt poor. Like the Utes, Shoshones, and southern Paiutes. 'Course you know somethin' about the Paiutes from north o' Carson City. And the no account Digger injuns from California. Ha, ha, I remember once Kit Carson and a bunch of us buffaloed a whole village of 'em one time to make 'em surrender some horse thieves they were hidin' amongst 'em. Fired a volley and they were ready to surrender every lad in the place. Ha, ha," he had said, laughing to himself mostly.

"That Kit Carson, he's a real fence buster. He got treed by two grizzly bears one time and kept 'em from climbing up in the tree with 'im by cuttin' off a limb 'bout the size o' your thumb and whackin' 'em on the nose. First one up let out a bawl and backed down, then the other 'un took a turn. Had to find out for hisself. And he retreated with a bloody nose. A real catastrophe for a grizz, you know. They say a grizz's nose is so keen he can take one whiff o' you from half a mile downwind and tell what color your grandmother's weddin' dress was. Ha, ha.

"But the whole country is gettin' crowded. Look at California. And look at Carson City. There wasn't hardly a town there at all three years ago, and now it's the capital of a whole new territory.

"And look at Fremont's Lake west of Carson City. Kit and Fremont was the first to set eyes on it back in '44 and now it's got a sixty-foot schooner sailin' from one end to the other. Holy Moses! What's this world coming to?

"Hey, lad. Throw another chunk o' wood on there. I think I'll stay up long enough to smoke another pipeful."

He'd continued to talk as he refilled his pipe. "They tell me Kit's back in Taos now as an injun agent. Don't surprise me none. He married one once, don't you see. I've been pretty close to a couple of 'em myself," he'd said, winking at Joshua, and grinning broadly.

"Tell you what, though. The best gals are those Mexican gals. A way o' talkin' that bubbles like a brook, and bodies so round and soft. Long black hair and soft doe eyes. At least usually soft doe eyes. Ha, ha.

"Have you ever known a woman, Josh? I don't mean to embarrass you. Just say none o' your business, and we'll drop the subject, if you want." Joshua had been glad it was dark so Bill didn't notice his blush.

"No, I haven't yet," he'd mumbled.

"What's that you say?" asked Bill, cocking his head.

"No," he'd said again, a bit too loud that time.

"Oh." Bill had paused, then lit his pipe. "Well, let me tell you 'bout Santa Fe. That's the beginnin' of the Old Spanish Trail. Not too far from Taos. Quite a place. Quite a place. And those Mexican gals. Oh, I tell you. You could learn a lot from them," he chuckled.

"Fellers used to drive a lot o' horses and mules from

California back to Santa Fe. Most of 'em stolen, I reckon. Far as I know, they might be still doing that.

"You know what? After we get done pokin' around in the rocks looking for the next mother lode, you and me oughtta go to Santa Fe. Maybe go to Taos, too, and visit Kit. What d'ya say?"

The prospect of fun and adventure with Bill had caused a rush of excitement to rise in him that night as it had many times since he'd gotten acquainted with the loquacious old mountain man. "Sounds like a great idea!" Then, "Say, I thought we set off to do some prospectin'?"

"We did, we did. And we will. It don't hurt none to sow the seeds of fun early so's to have a rich harvest later on. 'Sides, half the fun's in the makin' o' the plan. Oh, yes," he'd sighed, and puffed on his pipe which had nearly gone out for lack of attention.

"Say, Bill, how long did you say you had that Henry rifle there?" Joshua had asked.

" 'Bout six months. And a fine rifle it is.

"Keep this in mind, Joshua." Bill was inclined to preachiness now and then. "A rifle and a horse are a man's most val'able possessions. Also his best insurance for a long life. Always get the best you can get for each. Take that rifle. First repeatin' rifle that uses metal cartridges I ever saw and shoots true. So I got it. With that rifle and those cartridges, I've got a big edge on most others. Most people shoot a patch, powder, and cap tool like you got. Or a paper cartridge. Single shot, 'cept for some as got a revolvin' rifle. Still they ain't got quick loadin' metal cartridges. No criticism intended, now. I've shot many a load from those others, but their time has past. This here Henry is one o' the few good things to come out o' this loco business called progress."

Old Bill had stared thoughtfully at the fire for a while, his features taking an unfamiliar set. "And another thing. This here is hard country. I wouldn't be nowhere else, but ya gotta be just as hard as the country ta survive. 'Comes the time, ever' now and again, when ya have to use your rifle or pistol or knife or even your hands on another man. Sometimes it's kill or be killed. Ya can't have no regrets. Man comes to take your scalp, ya kill 'im first. If it's a case o' survival, it's the natural thing to do."

Joshua was rousted out of his daydreaming by his partner who called quietly over his shoulder, "Come on up here, Josh! Not too fast though."

Nudging his horse into a quick walk, Joshua pulled even with Bill.

"We got company up ahead. See there?" said the old mountain man, his right hand sliding up to rest on his pistol butt.

Joshua, squinting into the afternoon sun, looked ahead for something out of place in the pattern of bare dun-colored soil and lush greenery of the pinyons. An Indian, naked except for ill-fitting trousers, his thick black hair hanging to his shoulders, stood partway into the trail, staring intently at the coming riders. He held a lance upright, butt on the ground, its iron point towering more than twelve feet into the air.

With a couple of more strides of their horses, Bill and Joshua could see four Indian men in all. From the looks of it, they were in the process of roasting a rabbit. All four stared impassively at the two white men as they approached. Two held bows and arrows, though the arrows were not strung on the bows.

Bill pulled his horse to a stop, saying "Hold it, Josh." Bill's horse nickered, and was answered by a nicker from beyond the Indians. A buckskin pony stood on the far side of the small clearing, tied to a low-growing bitterbrush.

"I only see four of 'em. How 'bout you?" said Bill, quietly.

"Four. Just four is all I see," answered Joshua.

Bill nudged his horse forward, and the Indian with the lance stepped across to stand in the middle of the trail. He was of medium height but very broad across the chest and shoulders. His face had taken on a somewhat belligerent look. When Bill's horse reached him, he took hold of the bridle.

Bill held his right hand up in a gesture of friendship. "Hello. You speak English?" he asked.

"You pay me," was the answer.

"What for?" responded Bill lowering his hand to his saddle horn.

"You pay me."

Keeping his eyes directly on the Indian, Bill spoke to Joshua out of the corner of his mouth. "Looks like he intends to charge us a toll for using this trail," he said, dryly.

"How much?" he said to the grim lancer.

"You pay me," was all the Indian said.

"Josh, reach in my saddle bag on your side and take out one o' those butcher knives I have wrapped in a piece o' buckskin. It's right on top. But just take out one and give it t'me," said Bill, evenly.

The young prospector, his hands sweating, did as he was told.

"Here," said Bill, leaning forward over his horse's neck, as he presented the knife, handle first, to the Indian.

The dark-skinned spokesman stepped to one side, still holding the bridle, but refused the proffered knife. "Horse," he said, pointing to one of the pack animals. "You pay me."

Bill flipped the butcher knife into the dust. "That'll be enough," he said, his eyes hardening. He then slipped his big Army Colt revolver out of its holster and laid it across the neck of his impatient chestnut.

Joshua, seeing Bill's move, fumbled to get his pistol out also, forgetting at first he still had the little loop over the hammer, the piece of leather that kept the weapon from bouncing out of it's holster when riding fast.

The Indian spokesman, seeing the display of firepower, stepped quickly backward and said something to the others. They stood motionless. Then he carefully bent down, keeping his eyes on Bill Bright, and picked up the knife. An insincere smile creased his dark face. He grunted and nodded, backing away from the little caravan.

Bill, still focused on the Indian, said to Joshua, "Go on

ahead, while I keep a eye on these coyotes."

Joshua complied, and when the last pack animal had passed him by, Bill fell into line, watching over his shoulder till they were out sight of the party of Indians.

"Knew those trading knives would come in handy on this trip," said the ex-trapper, sarcastically.

An hour passed. Bill and Joshua were traveling up the bottom of a little valley. On their left, an open gradual slope led up to a low ridge; on their right, scattered boulders interspersed with pinyon pines.

Bill turned in his saddle to speak to his young partner, "You seein' what I see up there on the ridge?"

Joshua looked up and saw four men, one riding a buckskin, the others walking along the top of the ridge, parallel to the route of travel of the two prospectors, about two hundred yards away. "Yeah, I see 'em. Looks like the four from back down the trail."

"So far they don't appear t'be tryin' to hide, but there may be others around. Don't look nervous, but give a look around and see if ya can spot anythin' else."

They rode for another hundred yards or so. The hair was standing up on Joshua's neck. "I can't see anything else but those four. They're keeping right up. Why don't we just hurry awhile? We can leave 'em behind."

"No. Surprise ya how fast an injun can travel on foot. And how far. 'Sides, I don't want 'em to think we're scared," responded the old mountain man. "They're definitely those Paiutes we met before. They must be mighty poor. Only one horse for the four of 'em. The rider must be the top dog. He's carryin' the lance."

They continued to ride along, while Bill cast an eye now and again toward the Indians who stayed abreast of them, still about two hundred yards away. "I don't know what they're up to, but bet it ain't no good. 'Spect they had second thoughts 'bout settlin' for just a knife back there. No doubt they'd like to catch us nappin' and make off with our horses," observed the shrewd ex-trapper. "I got a bad feelin' about them jay-birds."

"Got any ideas?" asked Joshua. "It'll be nightfall in about two hours."

"Yep, I think I have," answered Bill. "I think we better run 'em off. You come on over here on my left, and, when we get up to that little flat up yonder, let's just stop."

When they had done so, Bill remarked very quietly and deliberately, "I'm going to climb down off this horse and tend to my stirrups. Then I'm going to pull my rifle and get down next to that rock like I might have a job to do. They won't be able to see what I'm really up to."

He then dismounted, fussed with his left stirrup briefly, then went around his animal to the side opposite the Indians and slipped the rifle from its scabbard. "Now take my reins, and when I get set and say 'go,' start walkin' the animals ahead. But hold on to 'em tight. I'm going to reduce their numbers some. I'm going to put that rider down and his pony, too."

He turned casually away and walked over to a nearby boulder. When he reached it, he crouched down and lowered himself quickly to a prone position. By now, the Indians, still about the same distance away, were entering an open sage-brush hillside just below a saddle in the ridge line, the mounted one in the lead and studying the packstring below.

"All right, Joshua. Start movin.'"

Joshua clucked to his horse and walked all the animals ahead slowly, screening Bill from view until the last packhorse passed him by. Joshua's heart was pounding and he stiffened his back against the expected report of the rifle.

"KA POW!" The blast startled the horses, and Joshua missed seeing the Indian knocked backwards off his pony.

"KA POW!" again. This time Joshua saw the buckskin pony, head down and hunched up from a hit in the abdomen. It struggled to retreat but was barely able to walk.

"KA POW!" A rear leg was broken and it dropped to its haunches.

"KA POW!" This time it toppled over into the sagebrush. The three other men had scattered out of sight at the first shot.

Bill ran to his horse and swung aboard, grabbing the reins from Joshua. "Let's go."

They hurried away from the gunsmoke and dust, leaving behind the rumbling echos of the thunderstick.

Later, just before dusk, they pulled up where the trail crossed through a saddle sheltered by the rugged presence of several juniper trees.

"Let's make camp here," said Bill. "These animals are all tuckered out." He seemed nervous and fretful to Joshua.

"You pull the wraps off those packs and lift the top load and panniers off, but don't take off the saddles," ordered the older man. "Don't unsaddle the others either, just yet. I'm gonna study our back trail."

"Do you think they're following us?" asked Joshua.

"Don't know yet," answered his partner, who then picked off his canteen and strode over to a tree and sat down.

After a while, Bill called over to Joshua, "Break out some jerky and hardtack. Might as well eat."

Joshua did so and sat down next to him. "Here's some dried apples, too." And after a pause, "Seein' anything?"

"No, not a thing 'cept a coyote diggin' up a ground squirrel over by that little openin' there. See 'im?"

"Oh, yeah," said Joshua. "Guess he doesn't smell anything either from our back trail 'cause the wind's right for him."

"You're right, Josh, absolutely right." Bill was relaxing some now. He bit off a piece of jerky.

Joshua thought awhile, then asked, "Why did we have to shoot the Indian? Couldn't you just have scared 'em off?"

"Could have, maybe. But it was just the natural thing to do. I'd ruther dicker with injuns, if I can, but ya saw what happened after we tried that. They likely would a just up and took our ponies when we first met 'em, if we hadn't shown 'em they'd have a fight on their hands. I figure they was trying to spook us into make a run for it, maybe gettin' split up or losin' one o' the packhorses. They was lookin' for trouble all right. I learned a long time ago to make the first move in a situation like that. Couple things bother me, though. The one carrying the lance wasn't the rider I put down. They must a switched on us when we weren't lookin'. I didn't have time to pick 'im out. I had to fire. 'Nother thing bothers me. I had that first shot all lined up and touched her off just right. Got that redskin square in the chest. But I sure messed up when it came to downin' that pony. Gut shot 'im right off. I hate to see a critter suffer like that. I finally got 'im right, but I sure hurried the first two on 'im."

Joshua pondered that, chewing silently while he kept an eye on the coyote off in a distance. The sun was down now and shadow had covered even the tops of all the surrounding hills.

Suddenly the coyote, digging eagerly for his dinner, stopped, perked its ears and froze. Then it bounded away and disappeared.

"Bill, did you see that? That coyote caught a whiff of something! Did you see how he kept looking back up the trail when he spooked?"

"I got a glimpse of 'im. That's not so good. We'd better do some cogitating," replied the old veteran, concern knitting his forehead again.

"Should I load up the animals?" asked Joshua, rising to his feet.

"No. No. Just set down a minute while I think this out."

"Why don't we just go as soon as it's dark?" persisted Joshua, still standing.

"All right. I got an idea," said Bill. "We'll go after dark, but we'll let 'em think we're still here."

"How?" asked Joshua.

"We'll start a fire and keep it burning like we've not got a care in the world."

When almost dark, Joshua struck a match to the wood and tinder he had gathered. Bill reloaded the pack animals. Then they sat or stood around, talking little, waiting for darkness to descend completely.

Finally Bill made the decision. "It's about time. Remember, ya go as quiet as ya can. Down that slope the other side o' this saddle, through those trees in the bottom, then foller that ridge toward the east as far as it goes, then head due south till the next big ridge on the skyline. Then wait there at the base of it by that rock palisade. I'll be along after an hour or so."

Then he added a somber thought. "If I don't show up by midnight, keep going south. You'll hit the Old Spanish Trail eventually. I've told ya where. Then go east to Santa Fe. I'll catch up with ya along the way. And, if I don't, well, what's there is yours and good luck."

Joshua set off on foot leading his horse and the two packhorses, while Bill walked over to the fire. When Joshua had disappeared through the saddle, Bill tossed a couple more pieces of wood on the fire and paced back and forth in the firelight, talking to himself.

It had been about an hour since Joshua reached the palisade where he was to wait. It was cold, so he'd buttoned up his jacket and stood close to his horse, among the silent pinyon trees, looking back from where he'd come. He kept one hand on his six shooter which was buckled around the outside of his jacket.

When he heard the distant hoofbeats, muffled in the damp night air, he pulled out his pistol and waited expectantly. His horse grumbled nervously, so he placed his free hand over its nostrils to quiet it.

Bill's riderless horse came pounding up toward them, then slowed to a trot, till it crowded into the waiting group. It was sweaty and was puffing and blowing. Its eyes rolled with fear. The other horses milled nervously about, pulling at their tie ropes. What had happened?

Joshua strained to see into the darkness and backtracked several yards to hear better away from the rustle of the horses. Nothing. No more sounds.

Joshua waited till morning, hidden in the trees, both hands

gripping Bill's Henry rifle that had been still in the scabbard on Bill's horse. There was no sign of Bill or any other person. Some deer passed by at first light, picking their way carefully to an open hillside where they could await the warming morning sunlight. But no Bill. No companion. He half expected to see the grizzled old mountain man ambling along, cussing for having been thrown. But that didn't happen.

Joshua was made of pretty stern stuff to begin with and now he figured what his partner would have done. He would have gone back. That's what Joshua did. Leaving Bill's horse and the packhorses tied in the trees nearby, he walked his horse carefully back to find his friend.

In the grove of trees Joshua had first passed through when leaving the campfire, he found Bill Bright. The old trapper was crumpled up against the trunk of a juniper tree.

A lance, the shaft broken off a foot from the point, protruded from his side. Near his right hand was his big "Arkansas Toothpick," its blade bloodied from battle. There were great splotches of blood on the ground and the bushes.

The flies were beginning to gather. There were two parallel grooves from the heels of a body which had apparently been dragged away by others.

"They knocked you off your horse," murmured Joshua, fighting back the tears. "But you didn't go down easy."

"Ah, Bill," he said beseechingly. "Why'd you have to shoot that injun in the first place?" But he already knew why. It had been the natural thing to do.

2
Shadow

She can make it a little furthur, thought Joshua. *It won't hurt her too much. I have to be practical. I can't shoot her close to camp. I'd have coyotes and ravens all over the place. And on warm days she'd stink.*

"Yes, you would, old girl. You'd stink. Can't have that, can we?" he said out loud as he led the badly limping mare along the snowy trail.

She looked up at him when he turned to talk to her, pain and distress visible in her deep brown eyes. She was a trim animal, all black except for the one white left fetlock, the one on the broken leg. She hopped along on three legs, occasionally trying the injured leg and staggering when she did.

"I should have left you down at the meadows and taken the

bay. He's too ornery to get his leg broken." He turned again to pick the easiest route along the narrow game trail.

"Heck, I'd give anything if it was him not you, old girl. But he's down there now at Haypress Meadows, munching good grass. And this winter he'll eat hay, if the meadow grass doesn't hold out."

In his mind he pictured the big pasture contained within the trusslike structure of the buck pole fence in the valley down below. He'd left two other horses there to graze with the ten horses and six head of cattle owned by the Butlers. They'd be fed all right if the meadow grass got cropped off. The two Butler brothers had fenced in a big meadow and a section of stream the summer before for the livestock of their small ranch at the bottom of the east slope of the Sierras. At the edge of the meadow, several tall cottonwoods sheltered a small, one-room log house and an attached shed. A lazy river flowed peacefully by, a stone's throw from the cabin. The yellow leaves of fall were gone now and the frosty nights had turned the leaves of the potato plants to brown. The squash and pumpkins had been picked, except for a few the rodents had spoiled. They lay like corpses midst the withered vines, seeming out of place in the pastoral scene. The two brothers would harvest nothing more from the garden, but they were well prepared for the winter anyway. The root cellar was full, there were tins of flour and beans in the cabin, and a huge herd of mule deer was wintering in the foothills nearby.

The Butlers would feed the livestock hay from the supply they'd harvested from the meadows that spread out in all directions from the meandering course of the river. All Joshua had to do was pay them some gold dust from the placer diggings he'd discovered late in the fall. His was a decent find and yielded good pickings for a small streambed. There might even be a mother lode furthur up the mountain, but he didn't care. He figured he'd make enough right there to be able to have some fun and still have plenty left for a rainy day.

"With you gone, I suppose there'll be more grass to go around." He talked over his shoulder in the mare's direction so

BUSINESS REPLY MAIL

FIRST CLASS MAIL PERMIT NO 970 HOUSTON TX

POSTAGE WILL BE PAID BY ADDRESSEE

GORDON BETHUNE
PRESIDENT/CHIEF EXECUTIVE OFFICER
CONTINENTAL AIRLINES
CUSTOMER CARE – GTWCR
PO BOX 4607
HOUSTON TX 77210-9934

Continental

More airline for your money:

There's more than one way for an airline to listen. Just fill out this card, or call
1-800-WE CARE 2. Your comments help us make Continental better. ~ *Gordon Bethune*

Mr./Mrs./Ms. _____
(circle one)

Address _____

Date Of Flight _____

Flight Number _____

From _____ To _____

City/State/Zip _____

OnePass® Account Number _____

Phone Number (office/home) _____

Dear Gordon,

Let me help you improve Continental: _____

_____

_____

_____

_____

she'd be able to hear him clearly. "I was meanin' to take you back down there after a few weeks and let you spend some time in the good grass. You know that don't you?"

Guess it's too late now, he said to himself.

Joshua reached a spot where the slope leveled out some and trees parted, offering a view of the valley, a thousand feet below. It seemed a fitting place for a horse to spend eternity. He squinted at the sun, fairly low in the winter sky, even though it was just a little past noon.

He turned to the horse. "Shadow, you and me, we've covered many a mile, but this is the end of the trail. I'm sorry it had to end this way, but it can't be helped. You can't make it on that leg." He said it matter-of-factly but politely. The horse grunted in response.

He removed the halter from her head. He tried to avoid those brown eyes, the look of trust mingled with pain stabbing him in the heart. For a few moments he occupied himself with coiling the lead rope and scanning the scenery about him. Finally he shifted the rope to his left hand and drew his Colt from its holster. He had to look at her now.

He cocked the hammer and pointed it at her head. She was facing directly toward him, head up, alert. He held the revolver at a spot just above her eyes, in the middle of her forehead. He could look at her no longer. He turned his head away and pulled the trigger. She hit the icy ground with a thud even before the echo of the pistol's report returned from the nearby ridges.

Joshua's eyes filled with tears and his breath came in little spasms. Bleary eyed, he turned again toward Shadow.

What had been a surefooted, smooth-riding companion of ten years; a light of step, affectionate beast; his since it was a colt; was nothing but a black mound of flesh. He stumbled off toward his camp.

I'll go back tomorrow and cover her with rocks so the critters don't get at her, he thought, as he hunched over the fire at the front of his tent cabin. The structure at his back wasn't much, even compared to the crude cabin of the Butlers. There was a log wall on three sides, about waist high, with the canvas of the tent coming to a peak eight feet up at the center ridge pole. The tent flaps would close in the front, but for now were open to allow the heat of the fire to be reflected inside from the rock fireplace he had constructed under a canvas fly just beyond the opening. Off to his right, the stream splashed over the edge of a rocky fall about three feet high, with the fifteen-foot length of hand-hewn sluice box resting on supports so that water could be diverted into its upper end when he was engaged in washing gravel from the streambed. On the far side of the fire, ten yards away, was an elevated platform not much bigger than an eagle's nest, where he cached his food so as to protect it from bears. The platform was in plain view of his tent, a location chosen so he could keep an eye on it most of the time. Losing one's food supply was serious business in this place, especially in winter.

For the young adventurer, on his own for only a few months, this was one of the bad times. His dad, a man who didn't philosophize much, had once told him, "Son, there be good times and bad times in ever'ones lives. You'll do well to remember the good times 'cause the bad times will take care of themselves."

This time would pass. He knew it. His dad had died and he had gotten over it. Then Billy Bright. He was pretty much over that, too. There would be other horses. He glanced to his left to where his packhorse was dozing within a pole corral. A brown and white pinto, she was sturdy but had no character. She was just a horse. Joshua told himself he would get a special horse when he was done digging gold.

Just when he thought he had wiped it from his mind, the boom and smoke of the pistol against Shadow's skull jumped back into his head. The sensation, relived, was sickening, not like shooting deer or rabbits. When shooting deer, after a long stalk, outsmarting the elusive quarry, laying sights on the mark, and squeezing the trigger, there was a sense of satisfaction. Wham! The bullet hits home and down it goes. A job well done. Venison for the table. Not so with Shadow.

But he'd had to do it. She was suffering and the pain would have gotten worse. *Well, it was my job to do it, and it's done,* he said to himself.

Evening was closing in, the shadows of the great mountains behind his tent were stretching out to cover the valley below. Joshua decided to prepare something for supper. He rose up and walked over to his food cache.

Night had owned the mountainslope for several hours when Shadow opened her eyes. A half moon lit the openings, and because of the light skiff of snow, illuminated the area under the trees as well. Only where there was thick brush was the ground completely in the dark. Shadow, in spite of her inherent good night vision, could not see well. One of her eyes was caked with blood, and she had no way to wipe the sticky mess away. She rolled upright. With a great effort she lurched until she had her one good leg placed in front of her, and with the characteristic motion of horses, raised the front portion of her body from the ground. Then she gathered her hind quarters under herself and stood. She had no idea what had happened. The last she could remember, Joshua had been leading her from the camp. She didn't remember the gunshot sound or the impact of the bullet as it bounced off her forehead. She was in great pain. She would find camp. She would find her human.

Joshua was sleeping fitfully when something awakened him. He thought he heard a horse nicker. Yes, he did. From the corral. The pinto.

No, from out in front. Another horse. Someone was paying him a visit. There was the sound of movement just outside the tent flap. He shoved the top part of his bedroll aside and drew himself into a crouch as he felt around for his pistol. Rising up, he crept to the tent flaps, the ground frigid on his bare feet. Carefully he pulled one of the flaps aside and looked out into the cold night air, the barrel of the Colt leveled and ready.

"Shadow!" he gasped. There beside the fireplace stood the

horse, head down, facing him, grunting softly, its broken leg held up expectantly.

He went to the mare and put an arm around her neck. He could feel the warmth of her body through his long johns. *Oh my god, oh my god*, he said to himself.

It wasn't hard to figure out what had happened. The bullet had glanced off her skull. Maybe she had lifted her head as he fired. Maybe the load in the chamber was poor, damp maybe. Whatever, he had failed her. Now he'd have to do it all over again. But not now.

He went back inside the tent and got dressed, pulling on his high boots and his heavy wool jacket. Tomorrow he'd use the big Henry rifle, but for now he'd wait with Shadow for the dawn.

3
Stay Clear of Raven-Haired Beauties

Joshua Mitchel kept his footsore horse at a slow walk as he approached the odd collection of shacks, sheds, and adobe buildings that comprised the town he'd seen from a distance, almost an hour ago, while riding across the mesquite- and cactus-dotted desert. Several large cottonwoods lined the banks of the nearly dry riverbed, and an occasional dust devil rose from the hot plain. Joshua's pack mare, empty pack-saddle sitting lightly on its back, shuffled along behind.

He entered town and rode down the main street, his horses swinging their heads from side to side, sizing up the few local nags which stood listlessly, tethered on either side, flicking their tails at flies. Between the town and the river was a line of freight wagons, mule teams resting temporarily on their long trek from Santa Fe to Los Angeles. In the middle of town was a large plaza with buildings facing all four sides. Things were quiet now. It was siesta time.

His shaggy hair stuck out from below the broad-brimmed hat that shaded his whiskered young face, and his hickory shirt and jeans were dusty from many days on the trail. Outwardly he was a study of nonchalance, but inside he was wound up tight. His throat was dry, and the tightness in his belly was because he'd made up his mind to find a woman while he was in town.

He'd left Carson City a rawboned nineteen-year-old boy and spent five hard months digging for gold, alone. A fellow had lots of time to think during those long, lonesome nights while staring at the fire. The West was a great and wonderful place to be, and life was for living. But it was a man's life, and for a boy to be a man he had to have a woman. So he packed up his belongings, slipped his pouches of gold dust and nuggets into his saddle bags, and set off.

Old Bill Bright, a few days before he was killed, had told Joshua about the Mexican girls that one could find in and around Santa Fe at the far east end of the Old Spanish Trail. "Round and soft," he'd said, "with speech like a bubbling brook." Only now Bill was dead, killed by an Indian lance and buried far west sometime ago. Since then, Joshua had found a diggins in the southern Sierras, worked it, and now was making his way east to sample life in this part of the world.

First he had ridden south to the Mojave River section of the Old Spanish Trail, reprovisioned at Forks of the Road, and joined up with a group of teamsters returning east with four wagon loads of hides and casks of wine. The muleskinners were glad to have another armed man to help protect them from marauding Indians along the way, especially one with a modern Henry repeating rifle. With two sets of two wagons joined together with a two-wheeled caboose, they couldn't afford to lose too many mules. It took a dozen of those strong California hybrids to haul each of the heavy tandem rigs. Those teams plus ten spares and some riding horses presented a real temptation for the resident redmen.

They headed east toward Santa Fe. It had been a wet year. Water supplies were ample and grass was available at regular intervals, so the animals faired all right. However, the wagons had seen a lot of rough use, and the outfit had more breakdowns than expected. When a front wheel broke three days from Santa Fe, they were out of spares. Joshua volunteered to go ahead with one of his packhorses and pick up a new wheel, returning as soon as he was able. He had been told by his teamster companions that the next town was only a day and half ride from where they now waited after the breakdown, and it would have spare wheels available.

"Take your time. These mules could stand some rest. Try to be back in four days, though," they said.

There's no cleaner feeling than that following a hot lather shave after months of whiskers, thought Joshua. The bath was all right, too; but he wished he'd told the barber not to splash all that stuff on his hair. It made his hat fit loose on his head, and he smelled embarrassingly sweet.

Later he'd find a cloth and rub it out, but first he needed to make a stop at the trading post.

The burly trader wasn't Mexican but made the young prospector feel out of place anyway.

"Mine this yourself, boy?" he asked suspiciously, when Joshua presented a small pouch of gold.

"Yes."

"Whereabouts?"

"West, in the southern Sierras," answered Joshua.

After a grunt, the trader examined the nuggets, then weighed them on his scales. "Twenty ounces. That'll make three hundred dollars."

"Fifteen dollars an ounce? Is that the rate nowadays?" asked the young man, skeptically.

"It is hereabouts," declared the man, giving Joshua a challenging look.

"Awright, I'll take it," said Joshua, glad that he had not

brought his entire nest egg to cash in here. "Make it fourteen double eagles, the rest silver dollars."

"Fourteen twenties and ten dollars. Right?" asked the trader.

"No. That'll be fourteen and *twenty*," Joshua replied, with an edge to his voice. "I can just as well take this gold to another town, if you can't count," he continued, his hazel eyes flashing with anger.

"Whoops, sorry young fella. My mistake. Just misspoke myself, that's all," responded the trader, his manner totally altered. "Can I sell you a hat? That'un looks kinda decrepit." Right away he knew he'd made another mistake. A boy might take it, but you don't criticize a man's hat. Especially not an angry man, and this young fellow was looking more man than boy.

Joshua just stared at him coldly for a few moments. Then he bought two bandannas and some sweets for his breath and left.

Next he looked up a blacksmith and bought a wheel of the correct size, arranging to pick it up the next morning.

He whiled away the rest of the afternoon sizing up the town, feeding and watering his horses, and sampling the strange odors of the Mexican food cooking. It was a dry and dusty place. A couple of mongrel dogs sniffed around the doorways of the little shops. A plump *señora* smiled at him from the window opening of a *panaderia*, the bakery. Finally he tied his horses in front of the biggest cantina and took a table near the window where he could keep an eye on his animals.

The food was almost too spicy to eat. That and the red wine started a small fire in his belly, but it also rekindled his confidence. "I'd like a smoke," he asked of the proprietor, a middle-sized man with a thin mustache.

"*Que?*"

"A smoke, a cigar. I'd like a cigar."

"*Ah, un puro. Sí,*" he replied, and brought Joshua a long black one.

After a leisurely smoke, he called the proprietor back.

"Where can I find a woman?" he asked rather easily, the wine relaxing him considerably.

"*Una señorita*? You wish the company of a *señorita*?"

"Yes, a *señorita*," said Joshua. "You know."

"*Señor*, come back later. We have *señoritas* here later. Very nice. Much fun."

So Joshua paid for his meal and went for a stroll.

Later he returned to the cantina. The murkiness of the place was barely affected by the flickering light of the candles on the tables and behind the bar. There were more men there now, but it was not crowded. Some were playing cards. Most were drinking. Three pretty Mexican girls sat about the room with the men, laughing gaily and sipping dark drinks. A fourth sat on a bar stool next to a seedy old man who ignored her in favor of the friend he sought in the bottom of his glass. Two guitar players sang ballads near the end of the bar.

Joshua stepped up to the rail and beckoned to the bartender, the same man who'd furnished the cigar earlier.

"Eh, *mi amigo*," said the proprietor, smiling, and placed a tequila with salt and lemon on the bar in front of Joshua. Joshua placed a dollar on the bar and took a sip from the glass. He gasped at the strong beverage while the bartender laughed good naturedly. Joshua didn't know what to do with the salt or the lemon, and the bartender didn't presume to tell him.

"Marta! *Ven aqui*!" he called to the girl down the bar. "*Señor*, Marta will show you," he chuckled.

So Marta came and showed him how to drink tequila. Bill was right. She did talk in a manner resembling a brook. *Maybe even a little like a night bird*, he thought later on. And she did look round and soft. Her long hair, done up in ornate combs, was black and shiny as a raven's wing. Her cheeks were lightly rouged, not so obvious as the others in the room, and she smelled subtly of flowers. When she pressed herself against his shoulder, the softness of her startled him somewhat. She was as straightforward beautiful a girl as he'd ever met.

After a while she led him out the back door, along a

corridor between two buildings, and to a long, low adobe building. She opened a heavy door, one of several that opened onto a verandah, and led him inside. This was her home. He'd come nearly a thousand miles for what happened next. It cost him two dollars. Like drinking tequila, there's nothing to it, once you know how.

They had some laughs when she pointed out the shadow he cast against the wall, outlined by the cozy glow of a single candle sitting in a bowl on the floor. She was warm and understanding and held fast to his arm as they walked back to the cantina.

Joshua and his companion partied well into the night. He with an occasional tequila, she with the dark drinks the bartender brought over regularly. She later admitted it was tea, but Joshua didn't mind paying whiskey prices for them. She was charming, not at all like he had expected such ladies to be. The two of them played cards, danced, and told one another outrageous stories of who they really were: she, exiled royalty from the courts of Europe, he a United States official on a secret mission for the president. *El Agente Amado*, the 'Lovable Agent,' she called him. He liked that.

Past midnight, the other girls were gone. A couple of drunks were fast asleep at their tables, the balladeers were gone home.

"I want to spend the night with you," said Joshua, after beating around the bush for a few minutes.

She hesitated for just a moment, then, "No. No, *señor*," she said rather loudly. "Nothing is *gratis. Buenos noches*," she added, rising from her chair, as Joshua sputtered to explain. Then she leaned over as if to give him a good-night kiss on the cheek and whispered in his ear. "Come to my *habitacion* in one hour, *Amado*. I will be waiting. No more talk. *Adios*." She then straightened up and stepped back.

When the bartender looked away, Joshua nodded his assent, rose, and departed.

Later, she invited him, along with his rifle and saddle bags, into her little unlit room to resume their earlier relationship.

By snatches of whispered conversation, between caresses, he learned she was working for…no, more than that…was property of an enterprising Mexican named Vicente. One bad *hombre*, as she described him. He and his brother, Paco, and a bunch of other *vaqueros* cleaned up all the "loose ends" in the territory. They dealt in stolen horses, separated solitary prospectors from their excess gold as a territorial tax, and sometimes extracted tolls from passing wagons. Men or women who crossed them were dealt with harshly. By giving herself freely to Joshua, Marta was taking quite a risk. But, she explained, Vicente and his *compadres* were out of town and not to worry. After a while, they both fell fast asleep on her bed, naked, under a sheet and heavy woolen blanket to protect them against the chill of the night air.

The sound of a stool being knocked over near the opening door and the sudden light of a lantern jerked the young paramour from his slumber. He sat bolt upright, an unintelligible expletive on his lips, and stared at the dusty *vaquero* who stood in the doorway.

"Paco!" blurted the girl, grabbing for the blanket to cover herself.

Paco hesitated just a moment, then quickly placed the lantern on a windowsill. He drew a stiletto from his boot and came at Joshua, cursing viciously. Joshua leaped upright on the narrow bed and threw the blanket over the lunging cutthroat. Shoving hard, he knocked Paco to the floor, then jumped off the bed on the opposite side. His eyes fell upon his holstered pistol hanging on a chair beside him. Slipping the loop off the hammer, he pulled it free. He cocked it, while swinging it up to point in the direction of the furious Mexican, who had leaped onto the bed to get at Joshua with his knife.

There was no time to yell stop. Joshua blasted Paco square in the chest, destroying the deadliness of the attack. The lethal slug left the man crumpled and still on the floor, face in the dirt, booted foot caught in the leathers of the mattress suspension.

"*Dios mio!*" You kill him!" blurted Marta. "You must go. Vicente will tear you to pieces!"

Joshua was dressing, his heart pounding wildly. "How 'bout you? Won't they hurt you, too, if you stay?"

"No. Not if you go. I will be *sin peligro*. Uh...safe. If you go. *Rapido!* Hurry!"

"Okay," responded Joshua, scrambling to get his things together. By the lantern light he checked the magazine of his rifle; then, grabbing his saddle bags, eased out the door.

There was no one in sight, but someone several buildings away was calling, "Paco...Paco."

Turning to the girl who stood in the doorway, he whispered, "I've got to get my horses." Then, "Marta, I'm sorry."

"No," she replied, "It is I who am sorry." Then she reached up to pull his face down to hers and kissed him, hard. "*Andele!*"

When Joshua reached an alley to the street, he noticed the rosy hue of the coming dawn in the east. It was a long block to where his horses were corralled. Judging by the commotion in the back of the cantina, fifty yards to his left, he might not have much time to corner the two animals and saddle up. And the cantina lay between him and the corral. He started to cross the street to circle around the cantina through the plaza, when he caught sight of a horse, already saddled, standing alone to his right. It was a magnificent stallion, with a beautiful silver inlaid saddle, and it grunted softly when he untied the reins from the hitching rail.

Swinging up, he turned it west in the general direction from whence he'd come several hours before. He had to pull hard on the reins to keep the horse down to a fast walk so as not to be noisy about leaving the place. *Plenty of time to let it all out once I get clear of town*, he thought. *I'll stay off the road for now, so they won't know where I went.*

Ten minutes later, Joshua was riding along at an easy lope. *Like in a rockin' chair*, he thought, appreciating the easy gait of his stolen horse. The gathering dawn had lightened the sky and the landscape below, and he looked backward to see if anything could be seen on his back trail.

He thought he saw some specks back there, but couldn't be sure. Ahead of him lay a great expanse of flat, mesquite-spotted desert leading slightly upward to a range of mountains cut with numerous canyons and ridges. The tip of the highest peak ahead of him was just now being lit by the sun nearing the horizon behind him. He was transfixed by the golden beauty of the unveiling of thc mountain. When he turned again to his back trail, there was no longer any question. There were several riders coming hard for him, about half a mile away.

Joshua had managed to attach his saddle bags to the saddle earlier, but was forced to carry his long, Henry rifle in one hand as he rode. With a tap of the rifle butt on the flank, the horse accelerated into a long striding run that few horses could match.

The lone rider raced toward the mountains to the west, legs gripping the powerful stallion, shown to be jet black in color now that the sun had broken the horizon. Josh could scarcely make out the riders behind him with the sun at their backs, but he knew they were there and appeared to be moving nearly as fast as he. There were six of them, and they had begun to fan out along a line like a cavalry charge. Their sombreros were flattened back from the wind of their wild race across the cactus and mesquite. They knew the ground well, and they knew their horses. They also knew the jet black horse ahead. It belonged to Vicente, and it was he who rode in the center, cursing through his clenched teeth and shouting orders to his men.

Joshua saw ahead of him the reason for his pursuers' stretched out line. A long arroyo slashed across his path, a dogleg, one piece of which lay almost perpendicular to his direction, the other leg angling up into the mountains.

Either he plunged down its steep sides or he changed direction and tried to overcome the advantage of their angle by sheer speed. He headed the big stud more to the right, hoping to reach the corner of the dogleg before the riders behind him closed the gap too much and forced him up against the edge of the arroyo. If he was successful, he could continue upslope into the canyon from which the arroyo ran. Some trees in the mouth of the canyon offered the possibility of cover in which to elude his pursuers.

The slender horseman on the right end of the advancing line sensed Joshua's maneuver and spurred his powerful roan ahead, shouting something that was lost in the wind.

Josh could see that one or more of the men would easily be in pistol range before he turned the corner, so concentrated on spotting a place to cross the arroyo. Then he saw it. A narrow crack in the uniform edge of the gully gave him a chance to slide into it, but still he wasn't sure if he could get out of it on the other side. If he couldn't get out again quickly, he'd be trapped in it just as he was apparently trapped against its edge now. He'd have to force them to back off somehow.

He took the break down into the arroyo, horse and rider plunging into the gap, horse on haunches, rider far back and standing in the stirrups. It was only about twenty feet down, but many couldn't have made it. There was a stout bush at the bottom to which Joshua tied the lathered black horse.

With rifle in hand, he scrambled back to the lip of the gully and sized up his predicament. The rider on the roan was out in front about four hundred yards distance. The others were farthur back and converging on Joshua's position, six dust clouds altogether, boiling with anger, all rolling right at Joshua.

Resting his forehand on a rock, he carefully leveled the rifle in the direction of the nearest one. The blast of his gun loosed a puff of smoke and startled the black at the bottom of the arroyo, but the horse held its ground. A spurt of dust jumped up in front of and to one side of the oncoming horseman. He didn't pause nor did any of the others. Joshua fired again with the same result. Again and again he fired warning shots at the riders as they barreled toward him. *They aren't going to stop*, he thought.

This time he took dead aim at the nearest horse. He hit the roan squarely in the chest. The horse and rider went down in an explosion of dust. Neither got up.

Aiming again at a horse, Joshua knocked another combination out of the race; but this time the rider recovered his footing. It was Vicente. Shouting to his men, the bandit leader searched hurriedly about for his carbine with which to return fire. The others reined up and retreated toward Vicente where they dismounted and began firing at the spot from where Joshua's gunsmoke had issued.

But Joshua wasn't there. He'd already slid back down the side of the gully and run to the horse he'd stolen from Vicente. He slipped six more rounds into his rifle before mounting and hurried up the bottom of the draw toward the canyon.

The quick elimination of two horses and the temporary banging away at the shadow of a gunshot had cost the bandit chief nearly three minutes. But he was stubborn and determined to catch and kill the man. It didn't matter if all his men and their horses were used up in the process, he had to get him. He damned the gringos in general and this one in particular. First the Americans seize the ranch where he works, forcing him and his men away to live by their wits, and now one comes like he owns this place, too. And this one kills his brother and steals his, Vicente's, horse. A man's name was worth nothing if such an ultimate insult was not avenged. It was hard enough to make a living in this bleak land full of hostility without a name that commanded respect.

It was a quarter hour before Vicente and three of his men caught sight of the gringo again. He was a half mile away when they saw him scramble out of the arroyo and disappear into pinyon pines at the mouth of the canyon. Even with one down and badly injured and another behind with the injured man and without a horse, having surrendered his own to Vicente, the *vaqueros* were not overcome by caution. Vicente spurred his horse onward toward the pinyon pines. The first shot from the trees broke his horse's leg. The second shot broke the leg of his cousin, Francisco. The fourth and fifth shots downed Francisco's horse as Vicente was trying to mount it, having pulled Francisco violently from the saddle to continue the charge.

Vicente crouched in the sagebrush with Francisco and the other two *Mejicanos*. No one shoots like that. Especially not one shot after another. The man must have one of the new repeating rifles he'd heard about. Vicente was expert with his Sharps but hadn't had a target to shoot at. They would have to advance on foot, keeping in the cover, till they could locate the phantomlike rifleman. Vicente was not one to give up easily.

Twenty minutes of stalking brought Vicente and his two remaining *compadres* to the pinyons where they found only footprints. The man was gone again. They went back to their horses to regroup.

Joshua was worried. The Mexicans wouldn't quit. He was crowded into a canyon he was unfamiliar with and was not certain how to get out. He was hot and thirsty. And the lather-streaked horse, strong as it was, it couldn't last forever. It's a wonder the others hadn't done in all their horses, the way they pushed them.

As he made his way up the canyon bottom, he noticed an animal trail that led up a side draw and seemed to lead to a saddle on the ridge line far above him. There appeared to be a lot of trees in that direction to provide him protection, so he turned his horse upward.

After a half hour of climbing, Joshua was amazed to find a cool spring in a grove of aspen trees on a minor ridge leading to the top. There was a lush stand of bright green grass. He'd been hard pressed since before dawn and needed a rest. This looked like a good place. After studying his back trail, he returned to the horse, loosened the cinch, and allowed it to drink. Then he extracted some jerky from his saddlebag to chew on once he had drunk deeply himself. He stretched out on the grassy slope where he commanded a view of the slope below.

Maybe it was over. If so, he'd need to head northwest soon to retrieve his other animals and belongings where they waited with the mule train for his return. He doubted he'd go back after the horses and saddles back in that little town. That poor girl. So pretty and bright, and captive of those bandits. Probably they'd be hard on her. She was something special. Maybe he ought to go back and take her away from there.

He pondered that awhile and almost didn't see the movement below. There they came. Two men, broad sombreros shading eyes from the scorching sun, riding slowly up the trail toward the grove of aspens. Why didn't they quit? Twice he'd decimated their ranks. He had shot two horses out from under the one, but the man wouldn't quit. That must be Vicente. Gradually came the cold realization, the bandit leader meant to kill him no matter what. It was that simple and that certain. A boy would keep on running, but Joshua was no longer a boy. He thought of old Bill's advice, "Sometimes it's kill or be killed." So. He must kill the Mexican. He could no longer aim just for the horses.

Joshua cocked his weapon and waited. When the two made it out of the mahogany bushes and broke into view some two hundred yards away, he'd shoot Vicente. But Vicente didn't show. The other did. The man continued into full view, scanning the ridges above him. He came within one hundred yards. Joshua killed him.

A short while later, Joshua saw Vicente riding downslope alone, far out of rifle range. The bandit had finally had enough.

But Vicente had not given up. He figured that Joshua could not be caught from behind. The dangerous sharpshooter would have to be outsmarted. Vicente knew this country. The trail the slippery gringo followed crossed over the ridge and went back down an adjacent canyon. This Anglo would not likely want to stay indefinitely in the mountain canyons. He'd come out, and probably down that next canyon rather than return where he'd had several encounters. Vicente would be waiting.

It was the middle of the afternoon when Vicente heard a noise of clattering rock from up the trail. He had waited patiently behind a jumble of boulders with a clear view of where the trail crossed through a large flat of tall sagebrush. His horse was well hidden behind him. The noise could have been caused by a deer, but Vicente knew what it was. He felt deeply that what was going to happen had been ordained from above. The murdering, stealing, gringo would die here.

The hatless American rode out of the trees into the open, scanning the terrain about him.

"How young he looks!" thought Vicente, as his finger tightened on the trigger. The gringo pitched from the saddle as Vicente's rifle fired. Or was it just before? It happened so quickly. The American had looked directly at him as he fired. His, Vicente's, black stallion bolted away at the shot. The man was down, without a horse, and without his rifle, since it had fallen free of the horse to lay across a bush, in full view of Vicente. The man, however, could not be seen.

As he reloaded, Vicente stared intently at the spot where the Anglo had gone down. The shot may not have hit home; even so he had the murderer. His patience would be rewarded. After a long silence, Vicente called, "*Hola, caballero! Hablame*! Speak to me. My name is Vicente. I not wish to kill you."

A bush moved a few feet from where the gringo had fallen. There seemed to be an outline of a person there. Vicente fired, and a scream issued from the brush, a prolonged scream punctuated by a choking grunt, while the bushes shook.

Vicente put his rifle aside and drew his revolver. He rose from his hiding place and stepped carefully toward the spot where lay the American. Vicente had killed before, but never had he heard such a cry of anguish. The man had obviously held his own life very dearly, a gallant foe. The *Mejicano* eased slowly through the waist-high brush. One more step and he was before the bush which had betrayed the American. Leaning over the bush, he saw a long stick lying in the dust, but no gringo. He looked up in time to see the explosion of the young American's pistol but not in time to fire his own.

Joshua arose from behind a sheltering rock, unscathed, and gazed down at the vacant eyes of the dead Vicente. Then he began to tremble. He shook so badly he had to sit down.

Thoughts raced through his mind, disjointed, disturbing. *Three men in one day. Maybe four. How did that happen? A knife in the dark. What did I do wrong? Horses down. They started it. I tried to get away.*

There had to be a lesson in this calamity somewhere. He struggled to sort it out. *Stay clear of Mexicans...Well, maybe...But the girl, Marta, is Mexican...Then stay clear of girls...No, that can't be right. A man can't go through life avoiding women...Then stay clear of girls that belong to someone else. Right! That's it!*

Stay clear of raven-haired beauties with voices like night birds and skin like velvet, beauties that belong to somebody else. But not necessarily Marta. She doesn't belong to somebody else. Not anymore.

He was a day late, but Joshua delivered the wagon wheel on the back of his heavily loaded packhorse. He had a woman with him, who was riding separately on his other horse, as he rode the black stud.

"Now we know what kept ya," said the waiting teamsters. "Where'd you get her?"

"Same town as the wheel." Then he told them of Paco and Vicente.

They knew who Vicente was. "Good riddance," they said. "Are ya going back there with us? Probably won't be too healthy there."

"No, I think we'll go back to California," he answered.

"Well, then ya best get along and catch up with that freighter caravan that passed by a couple hours ago. You two don't want to travel alone back to California. They'll be glad to have ya. Tell 'em we said so."

So Joshua and Marta loaded their belongings onto his three packhorses and set off on the road back to California. Riding beside him, Marta smiled at Joshua, even as the sweat rolled down her forehead in the hot afternoon sun.

Joshua felt as though he was on top of the world.

4
Anita of Auburn

"Ma! Ma! Come quick! Rattlesnake!" Eight-year-old Alexander Sullivan bolted through the open doorway of the little three-room wood farmhouse in the sunbaked foothills near the American River.

Sarah Sullivan, her spare frame shrouded with a long gingham apron, her eyes wide with fear, scurried toward the side-yard door with Alexander and six-year-old Betsy scrambling behind. The words, "The baby, the baby," formed noiselessly on her lips. No sooner did she step down onto the dirt of the yard than she froze with horror. There, fifty feet away, coiled a huge rattlesnake. With tail buzzing angrily, it lay between the pigpen and four-year-old Anita, who stood a few feet away, next to an outspread rug, clutching the baby,

Eddy, to her stomach with both arms.

Anita was staring unwaveringly at the snake, her bare feet planted firmly on the ground, as though her flimsy cotton dress was armor enough against the malevolent serpent.

"Zik,zik,zik,zzzzzzzz," like shaken seeds in a dry gourd, the vibrating tail of the cornered rattler warned of the deadly consequences of coming closer. Its thick body flexing powerfully, the viper's fist-sized triangular head hovered above the ground, tongue flicking to get a better sense of its adversary. Behind the stout boards of the pigpen, the hogs snuffled and grunted anxiously, their flat noses punching through the space between the boards, their sharp hooves stomping up and down in the mud of the enclosure.

"Ieeeee! Anita, get away from there!" screamed Sarah. The youngish woman was petrified, not knowing enough about snakes to realize that the cornered reptile couldn't leap clear across the yard to where she stood. But she was right about one thing. Anita was too close. If the snake chose to escape in her direction, she and six-month-old Eddy were clearly in jeopardy.

Anita backed up slowly, holding tightly to Eddy around his waist, leaning backwards to maintain balance against the weight of his chubby body.

Alexander stood behind his mother. "Kill it! Kill it!" he hollered.

"Alex, go get your father from the orchard! Tell him there's a snake in the yard!" she said, beginning to recover her wits. Alex ran off.

Sarah haltingly advanced to Anita and Eddy, grabbing up the baby in both arms. "Anita. Go inside. You, too, Betsy."

The two little girls headed toward the house, but Anita didn't go inside. Instead, seeing the broom leaning against the siding by the doorway, she took hold of it and turned to size up the situation. Then she advanced toward the snake.

She looked for all the world like a miniature Joan of Arc, her long weapon held at port arms.

Sarah stood motionless, still holding a wide-eyed but

silent Eddy. She stared at the rattlesnake, a considerable distance away. She was thinking of retrieving the rug on which Eddy had been playing with Anita and Alex. In the intensity of the moment, she didn't notice Anita until the little dark-haired child had passed by on her left. "Anita! Don't!" she screamed.

Anita did not hear. She was totally focused on her task. She approached to four feet of the snake and pushed the straw end of her broom out to the snake. The dark reptile uncoiled and slid sideways. Again she poked it with the broom. Again it moved sideways, its tail intermittently sounding a warning. Again Anita pushed at the snake. It slithered away some more, angling toward the pig pen.

Sarah stood rooted to the spot, still calling, "Anita, don't. Anita, don't," but less loudly each time as the creature retreated from Anita's attack. The pigs continued grunting and shuffling, more excited than before, their sharp little eyes following the action.

Again Anita shoved the broom forward. The snake struck at the broom. Sarah screamed.

Anita poked at the snake again. It retreated some more. She poked again. The snake, trying to escape to the darkness and shelter of the small shed that made up one side of the pigpen, slipped under the pen fence. The pink skinned little piglets nearest the snake oinked excitedly. A huge liver-colored sow charged and pounced on the stretched out snake with both front feet. She stomped on the writhing snake again and again as it twisted and struck desperately. Then she bit it in half. The other pigs waddled in to consume the rest.

Sarah, no longer nailed to the ground, ran to Anita. She took her hand and hurried her back to the house, the broom trailing behind in Anita's free hand. Once inside, on her knees, Sarah hugged both Eddy and Anita to her bosom, rocking back and forth, saying, "It's all over. Everything is all right," as much to comfort herself as anyone else.

Alex returned with his father, Daniel.

"Where'd it go?" asked the smallish farmer, his weathered

face flushed from his hurried trip from the orchard.

"The pigs got it!" answered Sarah, still kneeling. "Anita chased it into the pigpen with the broom!"

Daniel looked down at Anita.

She gazed up with her big brown eyes and smiled. "Snakes are bad, Papa."

Later, that night, after dinner, Daniel and Sarah talked. The taste of a freshly baked apple pie was sweet in their mouths, the cooling evening air through the open windows foretold the coming fall.

"Sarah, did I tell you, Alex said Anita grabbed up the baby right away when the snake appeared?"

"Yes, Dan, you did."

"She maybe saved his life. She's quite a girl."

"Yes," agreed Sarah. "I wish our own children were more like her. She's so bright and lively. And a regular little mother to Eddy. Look at her now."

Anita sat on the floor next to little Eddy, a basket of cloth-covered, rag-filled, balls beside her. "Here, Eddy. Throw it to me." She placed one the size of a small apple in his hand.

He gave a little squeak, waving both hands and letting go the ball which rolled across the floor.

"Look, Mama. He can throw the ball." She patted Eddy on the head.

"I wish her real momma and dad were alive to see how she's growing up," said Daniel.

"Yes, so do I...I wonder what they were like, her folks."

"Brave, I guess."

"And gentle, too," added Sarah.

"Yes, that, too."

"Mama, is it my turn to wipe dishes tonight?"

"No, not tonight, Anita. I'll do them all myself tonight."

5
Adios, Joshua Mitchel

Sam Wheelright ran the general store over at Franklin's Bar, hard by the meadows where Grizzly Creek runs into the Salmon River. His wife, Amelia (Sam called her Amy), used to cluck her tongue at the rough-talking miners who came down from the steep, heavily forested canyon sides and up from the placer workings along the edges of the Salmon and who chided her and Sam for not stocking the whiskey they liked to include on their grub lists. They teased her some, knowing she was a lady brought up in San Francisco and a teetotaller. She expected Sam to abstain from taking spirits, too, which he did, except for a sociable drink now and again when he was away from home for a day or so. She loved the area, though. The youngsters, five in all, were all healthy and

41

strong. The schoolteacher was competent, and Amelia herself was well thought of by the ladies in the little community, dressing well and attending church regularly. She fancied herself a cultural leader of sorts and did so without offending the rest of the residents much at all.

Sam was the one everybody liked, though. Big Sam they sometimes called him, because he was over six-five and weighed about two-fifty. He was pleasant and helpful, though a trifle slow thinking. He had a genuine regard for his neighbors and his customers. The local population thought enough of his fairness and steadiness to elect him constable. The constable's job wasn't much. There was a deputy sheriff on the other side of the mountain in Etna who took care of the real serious legal work, but Sam used to make peace between het up miners over claim jumping and occasionally sat down on a drunked up soul so he wouldn't hurt himself. The jail, when it was used, which was hardly ever, was his spring house, and a set of leg irons chained to a rock wall made it secure. However, it was damn cold in the winter, which was only half over now.

There were only two saloons and no bawdy houses at Franklin's Bar. It was a law abiding place now, not so rough as a generation and a half ago when the gold rush first reached the area.

Frank Brooks, a sawed-off stub of a man with a close-cropped beard, was the blacksmith, and pert Mrs. Brooks, the schoolteacher. Frank was the one who first brought Sam the report about the murder. Little Charley Houston, an awful and frightful look on his little face, had come screaming down the road to the Brooks's place about an hour after school had let out. He'd found his mama dead and, even worse, all soaked with gore.

"Sam, we got to go up there right away!" demanded Frank. "That boy found something terrible up there and we got to go see about it!"

"Where's Charley now?"

"With the missus, but he can't talk anymore. He's just

sobbing away now and can't tell me or the missus anything more," said a highly agitated Brooks.

Amelia stood behind the counter, taking it all in. "I knew she'd come to a bad end," she blurted, knowing Mrs. Houston was a widow who appeared to have some of that hot Spanish blood in her and whose beauty caught the eye of most of the men in town.

Sam's face, blank till now, hardened real quick. "Amy, you hush!"

Amelia, flustered by that, went silent, nervously folding and refolding a new lace handkerchief.

"Should I take a gun, Frank?" asked Sam, his everyday, commonplace mind struggling with the image of that nice girl, bloody, and a screaming seven-year-old boy.

"Yes, yes, good idea," urged Frank.

Sam pulled out his Navy Colt from behind the counter where Amelia still stood. In his confusion he had a stray impulse to give her a kiss good-bye, but quickly dismissed it from his mind and hurried out the door. Frank had his buckboard outside, so they both clambered in. Frank wheeled the team around, and they galloped up the street, then off up the hill to the Houstons.

Anita Houston was a remarkable beauty, about twenty-five years old and a widow for two years. Her husband, Phil, had been killed in his own mine tunnel when a sleeper had exploded one afternoon. Phil should never have gone back into that tunnel till the next day, but he was a hard worker and an impatient man. Anita supported herself and Charley by leasing the mine and by doing embroidery which she sold to buyers who shipped to places as far away as Sacramento and San Francisco. She did excellent work, having learned it from her foster mother down in Auburn. She never remarried because she hadn't been receptive to courting for quite a while after Phil's death. And besides, now she was in love with Harry Sandiforth. Everybody knew it but Mrs. Sandiforth. Harry had leased the widow's mine for a while but quit when their relationship got too obvious. Anita was a good Catholic girl, reared by good Catholic foster parents, and not given to home wrecking. Still she was broad minded about the prerogatives of the male of the species. She was more or less happy and truly faithful to her lover, though lately a bit restless in a physical sort of a way. Harry Sandiforth, on the other hand, was just plain miserable most of the time.

The buckboard with the two anxious townsmen rattled to a stop in front of the low, two-room clapboard house. Frank went directly inside with Sam at his heels. The front room was a shambles. Chairs were overturned, lamps were broken, and the smell of coal oil was strong in the air. The door to the back room, the bedroom, was wide open. Inside, spread-eagled on the floor next to the bed, was a corpse. It was Anita. Her clothes were mostly off, a pair of scissors were in her right hand, and a knife was stuck in her throat clear to the hilt. It was an unusual knife, a fancy design was carved on the end of the handle, and letters "Mc" were embossed on the grip. The two men were silent, taking it all in.

Finally Frank said, "It belongs to one of the McLean brothers. The knife that is. It's Jake's. I fixed it for him one time. The end of the handle broke off."

Sam was still standing right where he had first stopped. He swallowed hard a time or two to keep from gagging. "We got to do something about this, Frank."

"Yeah, I think so, too," agreed the stumpy blacksmith. "Shall we get up a crew of men and go look for him?"

"I mean about the woman here. We got to clean…it up…or something. We got to get some women up here to help. She has to be buried. Her boy, you know, her boy Charley has to be cared for." The big storekeeper rocked back on his heels and sucked in a deep breath. "This is awful. This is all wrong."

Frank began to glance around, searching behind doors and under tables. "She put up a fight. That Jake is fair sized, too. And mean. I saw him beat a man near to death with a chair leg in Red's saloon down at the Forks. He's got the worst temper

I ever saw. 'Specially when he's been drinking. Only man I know that's nastier is his brother Luther. Goddamn! Whatever set him to doing this?"

The pole framed house with its cedar shake roof, the low hanging loft where Charley slept, the upset canisters, the smoldering fire in the fireplace, the torn bedspread, the busted water jugs, the coal oil smell, the blood, the grotesque body, all combined oppressively to smother the senses of the two men and they retreated out the door.

"Sam, let's go back to town and get Art and Fritz and Mr. Potter and some others and see what we ought to do," suggested the blacksmith.

"All right, that's a good idea," agreed Sam, who climbed back into the wagon. Frank joined him and swung the team around and down the hill. There was a trace of rain in the air now, the wind was chilly, and the road was still wet from the last rain. They hunched over and wished they'd brought their coats.

Just at the first bend, not one hundred yards from the house, they saw a rider bolt from the road and into the woods toward the creek. With a crashing of limbs and thudding of hooves, the darkly clad rider and his bay horse scrambled pell-mell away and disappeared from view. Moments later the horse, riderless now, pounded back up the creek bank and across a little glade.

"Let's go!" shouted Frank, while he leaped from the buckboard. Sam followed immediately, still clutching the revolver he'd carried since leaving his store.

They ran along, threading their way through the trees, totally without caution. They almost stumbled over the man.

He was stone cold out. He'd caught a low hanging oak limb smack on the forehead. It was Jake McLean. A knot was growing near his left temple; his face above his scraggly beard was marred by scratches, parallel grooves of recent origin; and he reeked of coal oil.

They carried him to the buckboard and swung him in, still unconscious. Sam climbed in after, leveled the Colt at Jake's heart, and Frank drove them back to town.

They gathered together next to the potbellied stove near the door to Wheelright's store, Sam and Frank and Art Lawrence and Fritz Hoffman and Mr. Potter and a couple of others, to decide what to do about Jake McLean. Jake had been affixed to the rock wall in the spring house by the leg irons. He'd scornfully kicked away the bread and stew offered him by Sam, always the conscientious one, but had shrewdly kept the blankets to pull around himself once Sam and the others left him alone.

Frank was talking now, "Sam, we got to get that man out of here. When his brother Luther comes back up river...Well I just don't think we want the kind of trouble he'll cause. Likely he'll try to bust Jake loose if he's still here. Besides, I'm not so sure that spring house of yours will hold Jake until the sheriff can come after him, even if Luther doesn't come up here." Others echoed agreement.

"I think you're right," agreed Sam. "And it's mighty cold in there now and getting colder."

"Why don't you throw him on a mule tomorrow and take him over the hill to Etna? One day over and back the next and Luther'll have to fuss with the sheriff's people instead of us," suggested Frank, full of fake confidence to mask the fact he was beginning to get the shakes thinking of having to help ward off Luther McLean. That was one trouble with Frank. He wasn't reluctant or fearful of much till he had time to think about things, then his feet got as cold as anyone's. He had good reason to fear Luther. Jake's older brother was woodswise and crafty. He and Jake were a double dose of the means. A fight with one was a fight with both. Trouble by the pair. Folks said Luther was down at the Forks working as a guard at one of the company mines there. Word traveled fast up and down the river; he'd know soon enough.

Sam's brow was crumpled with consternation. He knew his responsibilities and set a lot of store in doing what was expected of him, but he wasn't accustomed to dealing with a problem as thorny as this one. Unexpectedly he erupted with a tremendous sneeze, the vanguard of a cold, and pulled his kerchief to wipe his nose. Having used that slight pause to cogitate on the matter at hand he said, "I'll need an extra man to go with me, you know. Maybe two or three."

Before the slow thinking constable could direct his gaze at any one of them, Frank broke out, just a bit too quick, "Sam, you know if I didn't have all the little ones plus little Charley to look after while the missus teaches, I'd join you in that chore. Let's see who we can round up who'd be good hands. Art, how 'bout you?"

"Frank, the wife's got a bad case of the grip. She'd crown me if I were to take off, if only for two days. Besides, if Luther McLean shows up with a mad on, it'd be wise for men with families to stay and watch over 'em. Why can't you get some of the single men to go?" he offered, neatly extricating himself from any responsibilities in the matter.

All the others, including Frank, the blacksmith, nodded vigorous agreement. "I'll watch over Mrs. Wheelright, of course," he said.

"Fritz, how 'bout your oldest boy?" queried Sam; then said, "No, he's too young," answering his own question.

Frank said, "How 'bout a couple of the men from the Lucky Creek Mine. There's some pretty good men up there. We might have to pay them, though," he said, tailing off at the end of that comment. Then finally, "No, I guess not. Those men probably wouldn't want to have to explain to Luther McLean some night how they came to take his brother to jail."

That last thought was particularly depressing to Frank himself, once he'd said it. He was beginning to wish he wasn't such an impulsive person. He decided to keep still for a while.

There were several long moments of awkward, foot shuffling silence. Sam suddenly erupted with a violent sneeze. Then two more.

"*Gesundheit*," said Fritz.

"Yeah, thanks." Sam wiped his nose thoroughly again.

It was slow in coming, but the idea took form in Sam's

head and all at once seemed like the wisest thought he'd ever had. "Mitchel! How 'bout Joshua Mitchel?"

Joshua Mitchel, rugged and lean, in his forties, eyes yellow-brown and focused, always focused, like a cougar's. He had a small diggings by himself, making enough to pay for his supplies at the store with nuggets that Sam prized enough to save once in a while.

"Damn, why didn't I think of him," blurted the blacksmith again. "He looks like he could handle Jake by hisself. He says he's just a miner, but he don't look or dress like one to me. Wears buckskin shirts, like an old mountain man; and won the rifle shootin' contest last Fourth of July, as you remember."

They were all animated with self-congratulation and relief till Fritz asked, "You tink he vill go? He ain't done noddink for der town before dot I know uf."

"We'll pay him," said someone.

"He don't need the money," said another.

"He might do it for Mrs. Houston's sake. He kinda looked out for her, getting venison for her and such," said Art Lawrence.

"You sure? I never saw him do anything like that. He don't go to church neither," said Mr. Potter. "For all we know he might be a friend of the McLeans."

They debated the matter for a while longer, then agreed to have Frank and Sam go ask him anyway, right now, even though it was past dinner time and pitch dark and drizzly outside. The others had to leave for home, and set off—some borrowing lanterns from Sam to light their ways.

Sam and Frank were both in Frank's wagon when Sam remembered. "Hey, Frank, one of us has to watch over Jake. Here. Take my pistol."

So Frank disembarked, much preferring to have traded places with Sam, and returned to the shelter of the porch of the store where he curled up in his coat in full view of the springhouse.

Before dawn, Sam Wheelright was saddling his horse

when Mitchel rode up, no jingling of tack, just a soft clop, clip, of hooves on wet ground.

"Morning, Sam," he said expressionlessly. Then, "See you got the mules all set."

"Yeah, we'll put Jake on old Lazarus there, the black one on the end. The grub and stuff we talked about is on Lucifer."

"That was a heavy rain last night," remarked Joshua.

"Yeah, it sure was."

"I suspect it was all snow up on the pass. These animals have their work cut out for them today."

"You suppose it'll be too deep for us?" asked Sam.

"Only one way to find out," was the reply. Joshua swung down from the saddle, six gun in a holster tied to his leg in the fashion of the gunfighter.

They took a lantern and went to fetch Jake McLean from the springhouse. Jake had been squawking about the cold and damp of the makeshift jail, but had wisely toned down enough to eat a breakfast of biscuits and venison chops. He started off at the mouth again while Sam unlocked the chains, but stopped abruptly when he saw Joshua Mitchel. Mitchel was glaring at him with a look of cold contempt.

"What're you staring at?" snapped Jake.

There was no reply from Joshua. Instead he reached down and grabbed Jake by the scruff of his jacket and jerked him to his feet. Jake was half dragged to the mule and shoved up onto the big animal. He was somewhat subdued but still nasty enough.

"These stirrups is too long. They're damn near dragging on the ground," he exaggerated.

"Don't worry yourself, Jake," said Sam. "When I get these leg irons fastened to the stirrups, you aren't likely to fall off, or jump off for that matter."

Mitchel said nothing, but moved the lantern around for Sam to see by. Though the black night sky had taken on a gray tone, it was not yet light enough to work without a lantern.

Sensing the chill air, Sam tied the flaps of his heavy cap under his chin. He and Joshua placed boots into the stirrups and swung aboard their horses, almost in unison.

Within an hour after daylight, they hit the snow line. The wet snow clinging to the trees and shrubs gave a magical quality to the otherwise very ordinary forest of fir and pine. There was absolutely no wind. It was noiseless save for the muffled plodding and the puffing of the animals as they tooted steam from their nostrils.

The trail was steep in places. If they were lucky and the snow wasn't too deep, they could make the saddle of the high ridge to the east by noon.

Sam, in the lead with Jake's mule in tow, stopped, turned, and looked back past the prisoner. He sneezed violently, then said, "Mitchel, how do you think it'll be up ahead?"

"Judging from the look I had through that opening back down the trail, I'd guess the snow will be kinda deep this side of the saddle. Looks like the wind stacked it up some in there."

"Shouldn't be too deep otherwise, should it?" ventured Sam. "The trail was clear all the way two days ago, so I'm told."

"If the snow's too much for this mule you'll just have to turn around and come back," spouted Jake. "I ain't about to get off and walk with these irons on." Then, "Say, what if this mule falls down? How'm I gonna get clear?"

"Don't you worry, Jake. We'll get you there," growled Sam. "Ready to go, Mitchel?"

"Lead out," he replied.

Sam was beginning to feel a bit uneasy as he rode along. At first it had been comforting to have Mitchel along. He was strong and self-reliant. You could tell right off from talking to him that he was his own man. He was the kind of man you were glad to have on your side, what with Luther back there somewhere. But the storekeeper, rocking back and forth in the saddle for hours, eyes watering, and head starting to hurt, was beginning to fret about the situation. What bothered Sam now was he wondered if he could really count on Mitchel. The man didn't owe Sam or anyone else any favors. And he didn't have any grudge against the McLeans as far as Sam knew. He could just as well have turned Sam down when asked to help as anyone else.

But he'd said he'd come along right off when Sam had explained his need there in Mitchel's little log cabin. A strange thing, too. Sam thought Mitchel had looked particularly grim even before he was first informed about the situation, though he had revealed nothing of his feelings.

"No thanks," he'd said, when Sam had invited him for breakfast before they were to pull out. "See you at sun up," he'd confirmed as Sam prepared to take his leave. Then he had turned back to oiling the long-barreled Colt that lay next to the black holster on his bench by the fire. He was an impressive man. Still, when the chips were down...?

It was not yet noon when they reached the long open stretch that crossed the rock slide. Sam and Joshua had taken turns in the lead so as to give their horses a breather from breaking trail in the knee deep snow. The air was cooler at that elevation, and the snow was loose and grainy. The sun had climbed up and now shined full on the open slope they were traversing. The scattered trees, coated with the fresh snow, glistened like silver candelabra. Way, way up the sharply climbing mountainside to their left was a rocky promontory with an overhanging cornice of snow that marked the top of the ridge. Ahead, scarcely a mile on a slight grade, the ridge dived down to a prominent timbered saddle that served as a portal to the great valley to the east. Down the other side, maybe four hours away, was Etna and a regular jail.

Joshua's horse picked its way along, pacing itself as it broke trail under Joshua's gentle urging. Suddenly it lifted its head and stopped. It glanced upward toward the top of the ridge just as the others heard the sound and looked up also. A low pitched rumble that grew louder and louder preceded the puffy cloud of snow that took form high up at the head of the open slope.

"Slide!" shouted Mitchel. "Come on!" He swatted his

horse with the loose end of the lead rope to Jake McLean's mule. The horse lunged forward. Joshua's arm was jerked backwards as the trailing mule strained at him, trying hard to swing around and go the other way. Joshua dropped the rope and his black gelding plunged forward frantically toward the protective timber ahead.

Like a massive wave, the avalanche exploded down the mountainside with the roar of a freight train.

Sam, seeing Jake's mule blocking the trail turned his horse around and tangled with the pack mule. Still he traveled several yards before the swirling mass of snow caught him, knocking his horse off its feet and tumbling Sam helplessly down the mountain in a turmoil of white.

Jake, chained to the mule, was engulfed in the great wave of snow and disappeared along with Sam, Sam's horse, and the pack mule. Bouncing, frothing, roaring, the snowy maelstrom hurled men, animals, rocks, and trees down the slope.

When the echoes died away and the cloud of snow crystals settled to the ground, only Joshua and his black gelding stood unscathed on the trail at the edge of the timber.

"Hallooooo!…Halloooo!" he called. His call was smothered in the snowy vastness.

Then, "Here! Down here! I'm down here!" It was Sam. He had kind of washed up into a fir thicket along the edge of the avalanche path. Face up on top of several small fir trees, his lower body was twisted around and covered with snow. He'd lost one of his gloves, but his hat was still tied under his chin. "I'm stuck in the snow down here!"

Joshua was able to pick his way back across the slide to where the trail was still intact. The avalanche had wiped the open slope clean of snow drifts and most of the trail, too. The rangy fellow then swung down from his animal, tied it, and worked his way down the mountainside a hundred yards or so to where Sam lay bogged down in the snow.

"Are you okay, Sam?"

"Well, no. Not too good. I think my legs are broke." His face was contorted with pain as he spoke, and it was like he was biting the words off.

His legs were broken. Both of them. One at the ankle, the right one below the knee. "Lordy, Lordy," he groaned when he tried to pull himself free of the pile of snow that covered his lower body. "They hurt like hell when I move!"

"You just sorta straighten out your body and I'll try to pull you free," directed Joshua.

It was a tough job. Sam was a big man, and the deep snow complicated things. Finally Joshua hauled him free of the slide and up against the trunk of a tree which grew at the lower edge of the fir thicket. Sam was a bit more comfortable now with his back against the tree and his legs sprawled out in a big *V*.

"Joshua, what about Jake?" he inquired. "Did you see what happened to him?"

"No, I didn't see what became of him. But don't worry yourself. He isn't likely to get away, chained to the mule that way," he said, dryly.

"We gotta try to find him. He may be alive," urged the constable, always the thoughtful one.

"You're not going to do much looking for a while, and I've got my hands full with you."

"Well, I can holler." So he did, "Jaaake, oh Jake," several times. There was no reply.

"Sam, I'm going to splint your legs, then rig up a travois. We'll see if we can get you to the doc in Etna by nightfall," decided Joshua. He set about it, using his heavy belt knife to cut the lengths of wood. He finished splinting the legs rather quickly, the big storekeeper groaning with pain as his legs were straightened out.

Then Joshua said, "I'm goin' up to get my horse. We'll be on our way shortly."

"Joshua," spoke Sam, looking up at partner. "What if Luther is back there and catches up with us? What do we do then?"

"Oh, I wouldn't worry about that. We'll just tell him we decided to let his brother go," said Joshua, with a slight smile. "Besides, there's not been enough time for him to get all the way up here from the Forks," he said, easily, too easily.

"I kinda think he could catch up," disagreed Sam.

"Maybe so," mused Joshua. "We can talk about that after a bit. I'm going up to get my horse." He disappeared behind the fir thicket and backtracked up the hill.

Sam was shivering uncontrollably. He felt chilled clear to his insides, and he was a little nauseated. Yet his forehead and armpits were moist and clammy with sweat. To make things worse, his head cold was filling up his nose, and it began to run so he had to wipe it with his jacket sleeve.

How long is this going to take? Ridin' a travois on that trail's going to be rough. And the legs. How bad are they? Can they be set straight? Joshua's splinted 'em, but that's not the same as a proper set.

Then as disturbing a thought as any, *What if that Luther is up there on the trail? Joshua is kiddin' himself, if he thinks Luther couldn't travel that far. He oughtta be more wary than he sounded. That kind of figurin' will get us both shot. Or Luther could circle around and lay an ambuscade, if he sees us ahead of him, and get us without half tryin'. Joshua Mitchel may seem coolheaded 'cause he's just plain dumb. Oh, Lord! I sure could use your help.*

A voice rang out up near the trail, but Sam couldn't hear what was said. He lifted the flaps of his cap so he could hear better.

Then, "Crack! Pow!" Two shots. Two different guns, both firing at almost the same time.

Sam thought to yell but checked himself. It was Luther. He was sure. Luther had seen the horse and waited for the rider to return. What had happened? He twisted around and tried to see up the hill. It was useless. He couldn't see five feet. The hairy growth of fir cut off his view completely.

Many minutes passed. It was like an eternity. For a slow thinking man, Sam covered a lot of ground mentally. With Joshua down, or dead, how would he get out of there? Maybe he ought to yell anyway. Even Luther might be a better chance than freezing to death with two broken legs.

Then he heard the sound of a horse easing its way down the hill toward his hideaway. It jingled and clinked as it went. It wasn't the sound of Joshua's horse!

The battered constable pawed under his overcoat looking for his pistol. He found it, fumbled with the holster flap, and finally fished it out. He held it in his lap with both hands, one thumb on the hammer ready to cock it but not wanting to risk the sound of the click just yet.

The jingling horse and its rider were only fifteen feet away and hidden from view behind the firs. They stopped and stood motionless.

Sam's nose was developing an almighty sneeze. He strained. He clenched his teeth. He jammed his left foreknuckle under his nose. It would not abate.

"Dzzzzt!" Even with his mouth tightly closed, it exploded so hard his hat fell off.

"*Gesundheit!*" retorted Joshua Mitchel as he stepped the horse into view. "How you feelin'?"

"Where'd you get that horse?" shouted Sam. "I thought that was Luther's horse acoming down the hill!"

"It is Luther's. Or was. I figure we'll have to use his 'cause that son-of-a-bitch grazed my horse in the foreleg when he and I let go at one another," said Joshua, by way of explanation. "You know, if it hadn't been for the jingle bells on his rig, I might not even have known he was waitin' for me up there," he said, pausing to dismount. "Now how do you suppose he got here so fast all the way from the Forks?" he pondered, then walked over to Sam who was now nearly beside himself.

"Say, what's the matter with you, Sam? You gettin' light headed? You're sittin' there grinnin' like a fox eatin' yellowjackets."

Big Sam chuckled, then snickered, then giggled hysterically as his tension burst into a convulsion of laughter. It was a full minute before he could stop laughing long enough to put his pistol away. Even Joshua, though he didn't quite succumb to open laughter, had to wipe tears from his eyes.

Many months later, Joshua Mitchel came up to Sam's store, riding his black horse and leading a pack animal. Sam, recovered now from his injuries, but with a slight limp, stepped off the porch to greet him.

"Joshua! What are you up to?"

"It's time for me to be moving on, Sam," he said, casting his gaze about at the surroundings, bright with the colors of spring, the green of the meadow grass dotted with flowers, and the fresh new leaves on the hardwoods. "There's some things I want you to do for me," he said, as he dismounted. "But first I want to buy some grub."

After Sam and Amy had filled out his list, Sam helped him carry the provisions out to his animals. Joshua unlashed his load, removed the heavy, canvas-covered rolls used to top off the load, and set them on the ground. Then he went about loading the supplies into one of the leather panniers on the packhorse. Sam stood nearby, leaning on the saddle of Joshua's black gelding, expectantly waiting for what else it was that Joshua wanted him to do.

After a while, the sturdy miner, still concentrating on his packing, said, "Sam, I want you to have my claim to help pay for the raisin' of Charley Houston. I've got a transfer of claim all made out. You can have it worked or sell it. It's all right either way."

Sam's response, in his slow and measured way was, "We've been takin' care of Charley since his ma's burial, as you know. But to tell the truth we've been trying to locate some kinfolk of his to see if they'd rather have him with them. If none show up, we'll gladly raise him. No need for you to have to do this."

Joshua finished packing the food, then crouched down to pick up one of the canvas-covered rolls, heaving it up on top. He reached down for the other, lifting it into position also.

" 'Course if you got your mind made up on it, I'll do whatever you want," added the big storekeeper.

"Let me finish lashin' this down, then we'll talk about it

some more," said Joshua.

After covering the entire load with a canvas tarpaulin and throwing a diamond hitch on it to secure it, he turned toward Sam. "You're a good man. I've known that a long time," he said. "I'm goin' to tell you somethin' that'll be just between you and me.

"A long time ago I had a wife. We lived in San Bernardino, and I had a small freight haulin' business. Used to go back and forth to Santa Fe. The first year I was gone a long time on a trip; had some trouble with injuns. When I got back, my wife had died. She was havin' a baby, and she just...died. Folks in San Bernardino had heard I was killed by the injuns, so they gave the baby to some folks passing through who'd just lost a newborn. When I got back I tried to track 'em down, but they just kinda disappeared. Probably for the best, you see, 'cause I didn't know nothin' about babies.

"Anyway, Mrs. Houston sorta reminded me of my wife, same shiny black hair, same fine nose, same kinda smile; and I figure this is one chance I have to help take care of her child, since I didn't do anything to take care of my own."

Sam's reaction to this was just to nod silently.

"Will you do that for me?" asked Joshua.

Again the nod from Sam.

The rugged miner, former freighter and fighter of bandits, reached into his saddle bag and pulled out a paper and a leather poke of gold dust. "Here then," he said, and placed them in the big man's hands. "So long. Take care." He untied the reins of his horse and swung aboard.

"Wait, Joshua, don't you want to talk to Charley and tell him what you're doing?"

"No, you do that for me. I've got to get movin'," replied Joshua.

"Where you goin'?"

"Far north. I hear there's gold in Alaska. It's gettin' too civilized for me in California. No more grizzlies, rivers all tore to shreds, and railroads all over the place. Railroads are what put me out of the freight business a couple years ago, you know. That's why I came up here. To start over. Now my feet are itchin' again. So long." He rode off toward the river road.

As he approached a big oak beside the road, he saw two boys up in the limbs, trying to hide from him. He rode along, looking away as if he hadn't seen them. They began to giggle. The more they tried to be still, the funnier it got.

When he was right next to the tree, he stopped and looked up, forcing a straight face. It was Charley Houston and Sam's boy, Howard. Howard kept giggling, but Charley's grin began to falter.

No, thought Joshua, *Don't give up that smile so easy.*

He immediately let go the smile he had within himself. It was a nice smile, the hazel eyes sparkling in appreciation of the joys of youth, the even teeth white against his tanned face. Charley laughed a little but stopped as Joshua's smile slowly faded, disappearing unconsciously as Joshua studied the boy: A black-haired boy with hazel eyes and even teeth white against his tanned face.

"Adios, Charley," he said to the lad and rode away.

"Adios, Mr. Mitchel," said Charley.

6
Hogan's Crossing

The biggest complaint lately in the town of Beckville was the condition of the bridge crossing the Yuba River, north of town some five miles. It was at a place called Hogan's Crossing. One abutment had rotted away, causing the deck to tilt to one side and making it impossible to drive a wagon or automobile over it. A person could walk over it; but a horse, at least most horses, wouldn't set foot on it. The townsfolk and the miners who lived or worked on the other side of the river were afraid that come winter, when the river would be too high to ford, there would be no way to get to Beckville from that side except to go all the way around on the Allegheny Road and through North San Juan. That would be a trip of over forty miles.

Beckville, in the heavily timbered northern Sierra Nevada mountains, had been a thriving town fifty years ago, shortly after gold had been first discovered there by a hardbitten prospector named Walter Beck. Now it was much smaller, with only fifteen houses, a garage-blacksmith shop, a boarding house-restaurant combination, and a general store. But it was still a town to the inhabitants. They had a town council whose main duties were to see that the town spring was kept clean and in good operation as well as to travel to the county seat once in a while to demand better maintenance of the main road serving the town and the few mines still operating in the area. The county road maintenance superintendent for the area was actually the county supervisor for the district within which Beckville was located. Since his was an elected position, he was heedful of the demands of the town council, but less so as the population levels in other areas in the district increased relative to Beckville.

Charley Houston, the stalwart young proprietor of the general store and one of the town council, was delegated to go to the county seat, which was Nevada City, and talk to Nate Perkins, their supervisor. When he finally found Nate, who was delivering a load of lumber from his sawmill to a new home under construction on the edge of town, he learned there was a new complication in the bridge repair project.

It seems as though the folks in Sierra County didn't want to help pay for the work. Since the bridge crossed from Nevada County to Sierra County, Nate felt the job shouldn't come entirely from his budget.

"Nate," said Charley, "if that bridge repair doesn't get started soon, it won't get done at all this year. If that happens, several people on the other side will have it real rough this winter."

"Well," responded Nate, "they're all residents of Sierra County. Tell 'em to talk to their Board of Supervisors."

"It ain't that simple. I depend on them for part of my business. I'm having a rough time of it as it is. If I lose much more business, I'll have to close up. Then the town will probably dry up, too."

"Tell you what, Charley, you tell those folks to lean on their Board, and I'll write 'em another letter. Better yet, I'll send Dick Alcott, the road foreman, over to their next Board meeting with a special request. They meet a week from Tuesday, so you better get busy with those folks across the river."

Charley returned to Beckville with the news.

"Gladys, you and Tommy watch over the store now. I'm going to visit the people across the river," called Charley to his wife. Gladys would have been a lovely woman, if she had known about makeup and hairdos. As it was, to people who didn't know her well, her strongest attribute appeared to be that she would do anything her husband asked of her and never complain. It was true, she did feel fortunate to have such a good-looking man as her husband and was attentive to his needs. However, beneath her plain exterior was an iron constitution and a very bright mind.

"How long do you expect to be gone?" she asked.

"Most of the day, but I'll be back for supper. Tell Tommy to be sure to clean out the barn today. The manure's piling up in the stalls," said the young storekeeper.

Tommy, age six, was a happy child who had a great imagination. He was a favorite among the other kids, because he would do almost anything on a dare. The interesting thing was he never seemed to get hurt doing them. Like most boys his age, he needed to be reminded to do the unpleasant chores.

The Houstons didn't have an automobile yet. Though Charley was intrigued by them, it was a matter of expense. Besides, when it rained in these mountains, the roads got too slick for the automobiles and only horses could get around. The Houstons had two horses. Charley had saddled up a stout and reliable sorrel named Jasper and now set off through town on the road north to visit the people on the other side of Hogan's Crossing. When he arrived at the river, a rocky but slow and lazy stream this time of year, it was easily forded.

His first stops were the Clarks, the Whitcombs, and the Smiths. They all resided on gold mining claims from which they eked out a living. He told the head of the household in each instance about the need to pressure the Sierra County Board of Supervisors to help pay for the bridge repair.

Likewise he told the foremen of the Frazer and Pig Iron Mines. They agreed to appear before the Board at the next meeting to support the project. He made a few more stops, riding up sometimes steep, rocky, narrow roads to find mines tucked away in ravines or carved out of wooded hillsides. Most people gave him a friendly reception. Some wanted him to stay and visit awhile.

By midafternoon, on his way back, he stopped in at the Clayton place. Old Man Clayton and his son had a claim with a couple of active adits, or tunnel openings, from which they derived some gold. Just how rich a diggings they had no one knew, because they were particularly closed mouth about that and anything else about themselves. Bearded, almost always dirty, and frequently drunk, they were not the most reputable citizens of the county. Then there was the talk about the mystery surrounding their inheriting the mine from Woodrow Piggot, who had worked the claim before he died in a mine cave-in.

Charley at first thought of avoiding the Claytons, but figured they might be upset to think they were not contacted. Besides, they'd benefit just as much as anyone else and had a responsibility to help, same as the others. So he rode up the long, rutty road that led to the Clayton place. The diggings were around the bend and uphill from the house which sat— more accurately, leaned—in the middle of a grassy flat near the Yuba River and upstream about a mile from Hogan's Crossing. There was a small garden behind the house, which surprised Charley because he didn't think the Claytons had a talent for anything like gardening. Most of the surrounding area was barren, the trees having been cut for mine timbers or for firewood. There were various articles of broken or abandoned equipment scattered around the premises, a not uncommon sight around old mines.

Charley dismounted and tied Jasper to the stump of a small tree. He wondered if anyone would be in the house or if he'd have to go up to the mine. He knocked on the weathered wooden door. There were sounds of someone moving around inside, but no one came to the door.

"Anyone home?" called Charley. "It's Charley Houston from Beckville." There was no reply from inside.

"I say! Is anyone home? I've got some important county business to talk to you about." No reply.

Charley stepped off the stoop and turned to go. After a couple of strides, he heard the door scuff open. Turning again, he saw someone peeking out the door which was open just a few inches. "Can I talk to you?" said Charley.

"What do you want?" It was a woman's voice.

"I need to talk to one of the Claytons. Is either one home?" he asked.

"They're up to the mine," came the reply, somewhat hesitantly:

"Look. I'm not going to bother you any. I'm on the city council up in Beckville, and I'm here on official business.

Can you deliver a message to the Claytons for me?" asked Charley.

The door opened wider and the woman stood in the doorway, with the afternoon sunshine full on her young face. Charley realized he was standing so the sun was at his back, and she had to look into the sun's glare to see him.

"Oh, let me move over so you don't have to look into the sun," said the storekeeper thoughtfully, and moved to his right a few paces.

She stepped down from the stoop to face him. He saw a slender young woman, very shapely appearing, even under the loose-fitting dress she wore. Her legs, though scratched and slightly fuzzy with light-colored hair, were particularly long and straight. She had on a pair of brogans and no stockings. He noticed her face last. She had made an attempt to comb her long thick brown hair, but there was a dark bruise on her left cheek which she stroked self-consciously with her fingertips when she saw him staring. Her fine features were flawed only by the bruise and a look of extreme timidity.

"Who...ahem...Who are you?" asked Charley, amazed at this beautiful creature.

"I'm Esther. I...I'm staying here," she replied, softly.

"Where..." Charley was interrupted by a loud call from fifty yards away, toward the mine.

"Hey! Who the hell are you?" came the coarse query.

"Is that you, Clayton? It's me, Charley Houston, from Beckville," he answered.

"Whatd'ya want?" growled Old Man Clayton, striding across the garden. "Whatd'ya want?" he said again when he got close enough to see Charley's face. Then, without waiting for an answer, he turned to the woman and said, "You go on back in the house." She did so without comment.

Charley explained the reason for the visit in measured terms. Clayton stood a half a head taller than he, but the young storekeeper was not intimidated by him or his bluster one bit. Clayton was noncommittal after he had heard the situation, saying he'd think about it, but had a lot of work to do in the next few weeks.

"Who's the girl?" asked Charley. "She a relative?"

"No. She's the housekeeper," answered the burly old man, looking askance at the visitor. He offered no more information about the enigmatic young woman.

Having completed his task, Charley mounted his horse and rode home, arriving before suppertime.

"You know, Gladys, that sure is a strange situation there at the Claytons. That girl sure looks out of place there. Can't figure how anybody in their right mind would go to work for the Claytons as a housekeeper, 'specially a good-looking young woman like that. And she looked as though she'd been whacked across the face," said the storekeeper. "Do you suppose anyone around here knows who she is?"

"Well, I can ask around. Do you know how long she's been

there?" replied Gladys.

"No, I sure don't, but if she's responsible for there being a garden, she must have been there several weeks."

"When is the last time the Claytons came to the store?" asked Gladys.

"About two weeks ago, as I remember. I didn't notice anything unusual about their supply order," said Charley, his eyes narrowing with the effort of recollection.

"Hmmm."

They turned their attention to Tommy, his father asking what he had done that day.

"I cleaned out the stables and put in fresh straw and hay in the feed bin," he said proudly. "Say, Dad, do you suppose the Claytons kidnapped that girl?" he asked, his healthy imagination taking flight. "Maybe we'll have to rescue her."

"No, no, Tommy. I doubt that's the case," said Gladys. "Besides, rescuing damsels in distress is the sheriff's job."

"Is that right, Dad? About the sheriff?"

"I suppose so, Son," he replied, but his mind was somewhere else. He was considering Tommy's disconcerting comment about kidnapping. They talked no more about it that evening.

The lobbying at the Sierra County Board of Supervisors meeting paid off. An agreement was reached with Nevada County and work began shortly after. It didn't take so long after all. The road crew hauled in some timbers, built some temporary scaffolding, jacked the bridge up and rebuilt the abutment. In fact they rebuilt both abutments because both of them were rotting.

Business picked up from the north side of the river since both trucks and wagons could now cross over the still tranquil stream. One day during an early fall heat wave the Claytons arrived with their wagon. The woman was with them.

Charley was on the porch of the store when they arrived. They went first to the blacksmith, leaving the woman in the wagon, in the middle of the seat.

The blacksmith's shop was right next door to the store, so

Charley could see her plainly. Her hair was done up nicely, and there was no sign of bruises on her face. He caught her eye and waved, friendly like. She first turned to look at the blacksmith's shop. Seeing no one outside, she turned and gave a tentative wave in return.

"Hello, Esther," called Charley. She turned away as though she hadn't heard. Charley knew she had heard him, but he shrugged his shoulders and went inside the store.

A while later Old Man Clayton came into the store with the girl in tow. "Need some stuff," he said to Charley, disdaining any preliminaries. "And she wants to talk to the missus," he continued, nodding in the direction of Gladys who stood behind the counter.

"Yes?" said Gladys, acknowledging the request, and smiling at Esther.

"Come on over here," said Clayton to Charley, indicating his intentions by walking over to the far corner of the store. He pulled out a list and began to refer to it as he placed his order with the storekeeper.

In the midst of this, the younger Clayton, a big-chested fellow in worn pants and suspenders, came up the steps and stood in the doorway. He had a dark beard which failed to cover the perpetual sneer that curled one corner of his mouth. He watched the girl closely as she conversed in a low voice with Gladys.

The two storekeepers collected the various items ordered by the Claytons and piled them on the counter and on the floor in front of the counter. After adding up the total and showing it to Old Man Clayton, Gladys began packaging the goods. Clayton paid the bill with banknotes, and he and his son loaded the packages into the wagon. The girl had been steered out the door to the wagon in which she sat without engaging in conversation. The two miners and their silent ward then rode the wagon back down the road.

"Wasn't that strange?" said Charley to his wife.

"Yes, it was. You know, I think that girl wanted to tell me something else before that big ape came into the store."

"What *did* she talk to you about?" inquired Charley.

"She wanted some feminine napkins and some salve. She sure seemed scared of those two," added Gladys.

"Somebody ought to talk to her some more. She may be in a situation she can't get out of," ventured Charley.

"Why not invite her to come up here for a quilting bee?" suggested Gladys, regretting having said so almost immediately.

That's how Charley Houston came to visit the Claytons' place the following week. The younger Clayton was in the yard splitting wood. Junior was his name.

"Hello," greeted Charley, from the seat of his wagon. "How's it going?"

"Fine. What d'ya want?" answered Junior.

"Want to talk to Esther. The wife wants to invite her to a quilting bee."

"She's too busy here."

"No offense, but why don't I ask her about that." Charley could see her standing back from the doorway, listening.

"She works for us. We tell her when she can get time off to play," said Junior, holding the ax in one hand with the other arm akimbo.

"Well, she must get *some* time off. I'll bet she'd like to have some female company once in a while." He could see her plainly in the doorway now. She was nodding vigorously.

"How 'bout it, Esther? Would you like to join in a quilting bee on Sunday afternoon?" he called to the pretty woman.

Junior turned around, surprised to see Esther in the doorway. "You don't want to go to no quilting party, do you, Esther."

She shook her head and said, "No," in a small voice.

"See? What'd I say?" challenged Junior, turning back to Charley.

"Okay," said Charley. "So long."

"So long, Esther," he added and turned his team back to the entrance road. He looked back to see Junior hurrying to the house.

• • •

Charley and Gladys had a long talk about the situation at the Claytons. Mr. and Mrs. Turner were included in the conversation. He was also one of the town council as well as the blacksmith.

"There's definitely something wrong about that girl's situation and something needs to be done about it," concluded Charley after explaining the outcome of his recent trip to the Claytons.

Mr. Turner said, "That's a job for the authorities in Sierra County. I agree it needs lookin' into, but it oughtta be the sheriff that does it."

"I suppose you're right, but it's a long way from here to Downieville to the sheriff's office," answered Charley.

"Why don't you just call 'im on the telephone," suggested Mrs. Turner.

So they did. Charley was able to talk directly to the Sierra County sheriff, who was very interested in the story. He promised to look into it.

It was a week later when the telephone in the store rang three longs and two shorts, meaning it was for the store, not one of the three others on the party line. It was the sheriff for Charley.

"Please get off the line," asked Charley of the others on the line, knowing some were listening in. "This is a confidential matter we're talking about." There were a couple of clicks indicating the others had hung up.

"Mr. Houston, I sent two of my deputies up to the Clayton place to talk to the girl. They had to insist on talking to the girl alone, but she told them she was there voluntarily and didn't have any complaints. She said she came from Reno and didn't have any kin anymore. I don't see what else we can do, under the circumstances; however, I have to tell you the deputies still think something's wrong there. Let me know if you learn anything different, will you? By the way, the Claytons are mad as hornets at you. They figure you put us up to it. You best steer clear of 'em for a while."

The report was a disappointment to Charley. He had to tell himself it was only that he was being a good neighbor that he was so interested in the girl's welfare, not the fact that her slender form and pretty face had been sticking in his mind these last few weeks.

Charley told Gladys about the call from the sheriff.

"Well, that's that," she said, with a tone of finality.

"No, we shouldn't just drop it," retorted Charley. He was beginning to get wound up. "When a person's in trouble, somebody has to step forward and help."

"But it's not any of our business, anymore. Besides, those Claytons scare me. You don't know what they'd do."

Those were really not the issues. Gladys knew Charley had a strong sense of duty, the kind of person who could always be counted on. She had known that ever since they met in Nevada City nine years ago. She also knew he was not one to back away from a challenge. He could take care of himself. Those were some of the reasons she had married him, and she was pleased to see those same characteristics in her son.

Her real problem was that she felt there was something personal about her husband's interest in that woman with the Claytons.

"I'm going back there again," said Charley.

The rain had been unusually long and heavy for early October. The roads were very muddy, and it was good the bridge had been repaired, because the river would be difficult to ford now. Charley was aboard Jasper, his steady gelding, and was going down the road toward Hogan's Crossing. There had been no rain that morning, and the sun was trying to poke through the gray clouds. The oak trees were losing their leaves and had sprinkled the road with wet brown flakes. Jasper was collecting gobs of mud mixed with leaves on his hooves.

Charley reached a point where a deer trail dived off to the right of the road and headed toward the river. He urged Jasper down the deer trail. It was actually more than a deer trail. It was used by fishermen as a shortcut to the river, and it paralleled the river for quite a distance. The trail was fairly wide and didn't have too many low hanging branches to duck. Taking this route was slower than using the road to where he was heading, but he didn't want to be seen approaching from the road.

When he reached the river, roaring from runoff of the recent storm, he followed the trail upstream till he was opposite the Clayton place. There was smoke coming from the chimney. There were no horses tied near the house, a good sign. The Claytons were probably up working the mine. He continued upstream a bit furthur till he was completely screened from the house by trees along the river banks. He tied Jasper to a sapling, and slid down the river bank, a distance of about ten feet. The river had widened out at this point, the water was much shallower and less turbulent than downstream. Charley waded across to the other side. The water was no higher than his knees, but it was still difficult because of the current and the slippery rocks.

Charley worked his way back through the trees to a spot from which he could get a good view of the house and the garden. He crouched down behind a stump and waited.

He didn't wait long. The back door opened, and Esther came out, carrying a basket. She walked across the open yard to the garden and began to pick some squash.

It was chancy, but Charley stood and walked toward the girl, who was bent over, facing away from him. She heard him coming and turned, startled.

"Don't be afraid. It's me, Charley Houston," he said reassuringly.

"What do you want? If they catch you here, you'll be in a lot of trouble." She was very frightened.

"Don't worry about that. I've come to find out if you need help. Are you being held here against your will?" said Charley reaching for her hand.

She dropped her basket and surrendered her hand. She had a look of despair mixed with relief, and broke out crying. She nodded, "Yes…They…they kidnapped me in Reno. I can't get away. I've tried. They beat me and tie me up at night like…like…a horse."

"Where are they now?"

"Up at the mine."

"Let's go! Now!" commanded the gutty storekeeper. He pulled her toward him by the arm.

"Where're you going?" she said, hanging back and looking for signs of her captors in the direction of the mine, her face pale with fright.

"Across the river. I've got a horse there. Then we'll go to town." They stopped momentarily as she searched his face for the strength she needed to make the decision to flee. She found it. They ran hand in hand into the trees and to the river.

When they reached the edge of the river, Charley turned his back to her and said, "Quick. Get up. I'll carry you across." She leaped up, and they entered the swirling waters. They almost fell a couple of times, and Charley stepped into one hole that was up to his crotch, but they struggled across. The river bank was the next obstacle, and they slipped and slid repeatedly till Charley pulled himself up by a hanging tree root. He reached down and pulled Esther up with him. They were both winded, but much relieved to be safely across the river. Esther, still frightened, kept searching the opposite side of the river for the Claytons.

After a minute, Charley untied Jasper and swung up into the saddle. "Come on. Climb up behind me." he said calmly, reaching down toward her. She did so with surprising agility. Charley headed Jasper down the trail at a fast walk.

Old Man Clayton and Junior, hidden by some trees along the road to the mine, knew right away what had happened when they saw the two riding double on the other side of the river.

Jasper came trotting up the road into Beckville about suppertime. He was wet and his reins dragged along in the mud. He came right into the stable where Tommy had just finished tossing fresh hay into the bins.

"Hey, Jasper. Where's Dad?" said Tommy cheerfully.

Jasper bent his head down so Tommy could pull off his bridle. The lad hung the bridle by a spike in a post and then loosened the cinch, pulling the heavy saddle off to the floor. He struggled to hoist the wet saddle onto a pile of strawbales, retrieved the saddle blanket from the floor, and hung it over a rail.

"Dad! Hey, Dad!" he called running out of the stable. He went to the store, but saw it was closed, so went into the house. "Hey, Dad!"

Gladys was standing by the stove, stirring a stew. "Is your dad here?" she asked of Tommy.

"Jasper came in the stable all wet, but I don't know where Dad went."

There was a pause. "Oh, God," she said.

An hour before dark the Claytons and their wagon came up the road to stop in front of Houston's Store. Turner, the blacksmith, saw them from his shop and hurried over, knowing Charley was last known to have been going to the Claytons, before he ended up missing.

"Oh, oh," he said to himself, when he looked into the wagon.

"You folks looking for Houston?" said Old Man Clayton roughly. "He's back there," he continued, jerking his thumb over his shoulder. Junior said nothing, squinting sideways at Turner through one swollen and blackened eye.

"What happened?" asked Turner.

"Donno for sure. Found the two of 'em in the river near the bridge. Looks like they got bucked off crossing the bridge or fordin' the river someplace. I donno. 'Pears they was traveling together, though. Can't figure why." He spat in the mud next to the wagon.

"What'ya gonna do with 'em?" asked Turner.

"I brung 'em here. What you gonna do with 'em?" was the reply.

"Give me some help. We'll put 'em in my shop for the time being," said the blacksmith, his insides churning with grief over the sight of the young storekeeper and the woman, dead, soaked, mud and leaves plastering their bodies, and bloody wounds on their heads and arms.

The two taciturn Claytons and Turner carried the bodies into the blacksmith shop and laid them side by side on the floor. The blacksmith kept looking over at the Houston house, fearing one of them would come out and see the awful sight.

Just as the Claytons climbed into their wagon in front of the blacksmith shop, Tommy came flying out of the house, the screen door crashing behind him. "Hey! You see my father anyplace?" he called.

Old Man Clayton just nodded his head in the direction of the door of the blacksmith's shop and slapped the reins to the team to get them going.

"Tommy, don't come in here!" said Turner, trying to head off Tommy at the door, but he was too late.

Tommy, stood gasping, alternately staring at his father with the woman next to him and looking up at Turner who was relating the story told him by the Claytons.

"No! No! That's not true. Jasper wouldn't do that! They killed him! They killed him!" Tommy bolted out the door and down the road after the Claytons. "You killed him! You killed him! You dirty…You dirty…" He picked up some rocks and closed on the wagon ahead.

As the little boy pitched his rocks futilely at the two men, Old Man Clayton slapped the reins harder and the wagon pulled away toward Hogan's Crossing.

7
The Legacy

"Click click, click click, click click," the sound of the heavy steel wheels as they passed over the joints in the rails marked the progress of the nondescript passenger train on its long journey from California to Illinois. After a day and a night in the stiff-backed seats of a coach in the middle of the train, Gladys and Tommy weren't so much weary as numb. They had watched the glow of evening settle on the sagebrush covered valleys and mountains of Nevada and endured sleepless hours through the cold, empty desert before arriving in Salt Lake City. After a layover there, and breakfast in the dining car, they had continued on their way behind the puffing steam locomotive.

The sun was rising in the east, ahead of them. In about ten

hours it would set behind them, in the west. So far as Tommy was concerned, the sun had set several days ago in a graveyard in Nevada City and would never rise again. Gladys bereft by Charley's death, nevertheless had pulled herself together and, with the help of friends, buried her husband, sold the grocery store, and made arrangements for her and Tommy to live with her parents.

Thirty years ago Gladys's parents had moved to California to seek prosperity in the Golden Land. Some business reversals knocked the pins out from under them and they moved back to Dekalb, Illinois, from whence they came, leaving their oldest daughter, Gladys, married to a storekeeper. When they heard of Charley's tragic death, they implored their daughter and grandson to leave the rough West and join them in the gentle farmlands of Illinois. And so the railroad was carrying the young widow and her son east across the rugged mountains and vast plains.

Tommy stared out the window at the passing scenery. The horizon stretched out forever, unmarred by buildings, windmills, or fences. Once he saw an antelope, but said nothing. A northwest wind pushed the smoke from the engine to his side of the train, but not so fast that the speeding brace of cars didn't catch up with the oily fumes. Except for the train's smoke, Gladys would have opened the window in spite of the cold November breeze, because the air of the coach was becoming stale. The other passengers of the half-full car didn't complain, possibly because they were mostly men and were mainly responsible for the problem, having been puffing on after-breakfast cigars for some time.

Gladys was having trouble with her hat. She wasn't used to wearing one, but to be proper had worn one when boarding the train and again at breakfast. The rest of the time it was just in the way. It rested on the facing seat in front of Tommy and her, where she would have very much liked to put her feet. Finally she judged to do so would be very unladylike, and dismissed the thought from her mind. She turned to Tommy, wondering when he would regain his sunny nature.

"How are you doing, Tommy?" she said.

"Okay, I guess."

"Would you like to try to sleep again?"

"No. I got enough sleep."

"What are you seeing out the window?" Gladys could see the broad expanse of the treeless plain with gently rolling hills and rough gashes of occasional gullies cutting down the slopes toward the railroad grade. She had never seen Illinois, but understood it was much prettier than this, even in the winter.

"Nothing," answered Tommy.

"Talk to me, Tommy. Momma's getting lonesome for some conversation."

The little boy turned to his mother, black circles under his eyes, the corners of his lips turned down. "Momma, why'd we leave Daddy back there?"

Gladys reached over and pulled her son to her side. "He's not really back there Tommy. What we buried was only a shell he lived in. He's not in it. Part of him is in heaven, and part of him is in you. His hair, his eyes, his stout heart are all in you. He is in you, and I am in you, and Grandma and Grandpa, and Daddy's momma and daddy. They, we, are all in you. As long as you're alive, Daddy and all of them will be alive. And when you grow up and have children, Daddy will be alive in them, too."

Tommy said nothing, then closed his eyes and tried to remember how it had been. Flashes of his father's face ran through his mind. Sounds of Charley's whooping laughter when he and Tommy played tag. His sly wink when Tommy dropped his piece of liver for the dog to eat while Gladys was away from the dinner table for a moment. His urgent shushing when a big trout slowly approached Tommy's offered worm in a pool of the Yuba River. Even his stern warning when Tommy once sassed his mother. Maybe she was right. Maybe his dad was within him.

Gladys rested her cheek upon Tommy's head.

The train rolled on. "Click click, click click, click click."

8
October '43

The hot, humid air stank of the sour odor of decaying vegetation, and the screech of the night birds in the surrounding jungle penetrated even the corrugated steel of the quonset hut where Tom Houston sat writing a letter to his family in Illinois, nearly eight thousand miles away. He had tuned out the constant hum of the distant generator days ago, but the nightly racket of the jungle birds still bothered him. They carried warnings of danger. Alarms. False or true, who could tell?

Also outside, in the darkness beside the airfield, beyond the twin-boomed P-38 fighter-bombers that crouched silently under their camouflage netting, were things one didn't hear, the spiders, the leeches, the scorpions, and the centipedes.

And the lizards and snakes. Yet it had been much worse for the infantrymen who had landed here over two months ago to secure this important stepping stone in the Solomon Islands, part of MacArthur's island-hopping campaign to the Philippines. They had to contend with all the creatures of the jungle plus a fanatic force of Japanese defenders. And the rain. The incessant rain that turned foxholes into frog ponds and combat boots into sponges. The rain that dripped off steel helmets into cookkits, turning hardtack into mush and dried eggs into rubber. The rain that filled the swamps where lived the crocodiles and created the puddles where bred the malaria-carrying mosquitoes. Yes, the grunts who had come to take the island had it much worse.

Fortunately it hadn't taken long to clear out the Japanese. There hadn't been any seen on the island for weeks. Though there was an occasional night air raid from Bougainville or Rabual, the sons of Nippon were gone from Tom's island, or so it was said. Still, the island was good sized, about twenty-five by twenty-five miles, a blob of jungle and swamp with plenty of places to hide. That knowledge weighed on the minds of all the base personnel, especially at night.

Until recently, it had been a twenty-four hour a day show, even after the Japanese had been driven off. Now the hustle and bustle of construction as the Seabees built the airfield was over. The growl of bulldozers and the racket of the rock crushers was over. Acres of pierced-plank landing mat had been placed; quonset huts and tents had been erected; water supply systems had been provided; docks for unloading supplies had been installed; even a PX and a movie theater had materialized, all in less than six weeks. Houston was amazed at how fast American ingenuity could be brought to bear on a problem such as civilizing a remote jungle island.

Now the nights were devoted to waiting for the dawn. The daytimes were still busy though. The P-38s still were flying protective cover for some ship movements in the area, and lately there had been a major buildup of supplies and ordnance for the planes. Stacks of cases of .50 caliber machine gun bullets and 20 millimeter cannon shells were stuffed into the jungle next to the airfield, and containers and racks of bombs were stacked off one end of the runway.

And the radio traffic, encoded as always, had picked up noticeably the past few days. Something big was about to break. Scuttlebutt had it that it was a landing on Bougainville. But for now, at 2:00 A.M. on an October night, it was quiet. Except for the screech of the jungle birds and the generator that droned away in the distance.

Major Thomas Houston was taking his turn as night duty officer for the entire airfield. He sat before a desk made from packing cases, in a quonset hut with blacked-out windows, a bare light bulb suspended from the ceiling, and a field phone at his elbow. He was writing a letter, a V-mail letter, one that someone somewhere would censor, and someone else would copy on microfilm for shipment home. He wondered if the essence of how he felt could ever be transmitted back home under those circumstances.

He had not seen his family for over a year. Called up in the summer of 1941, before the U.S. had gotten into the war, he had been part of a National Guard artillery unit. Shortly after his activation, he had been separated from his unit and sent to quartermaster school. That made sense. He was nearly forty and had managed a trucking company before his being called up. He had a knack for organizing things. Sometimes he thought his reassignment was the only thing that had made sense in the entire two years he'd been in the Army.

He had a towel wrapped around his wrist to keep the sweat from running down his hand onto the paper and smearing the ink from his fountain pen. The heat was nearly unbearable, especially with all the windows covered up.

Dear Helen (and kids),

Here I am again. Everything is fine here. I get plenty to eat (I wouldn't be much of a supply officer if I didn't see to it there was plenty of food).

It was true. He was a good supply officer. He had developed a network with some of his fellow quartermaster school-mates up the line on Guadalcanal; Wellington, New Zealand; and Brisbane to direct more than the bare essentials to his relatively small base near the scene of the action. He also had another buddy in Guadalcanal who made up special orders of fruits and vegetables grown right there on the 'Canal and slipped them onto planes carrying mail and fresh pilots.

His mind wandered. He was thinking of how it must be back in Illinois about this time: cornstalks, pumpkins, apples, burning leaves, and cool crisp nights, especially cool crisp nights.

God, it was hot in the quonset. He tried to picture himself back home, sitting on the backyard lawn, in the cool of the evening, watching the stars with his wife, Helen. He could remember once when he'd ambled over to the grape arbor and picked a bunch of ripe grapes for them to share as they sat searching the sky for constellations.

I sure would like some of those luscious grapes and fresh apples from the yard, though. I bet they're ripened to perfection right about now. By the time you get this letter, I expect Halloween will be over. I hope you picked the fruit this time, before Halloween, so the neighbor kids didn't clean us out that night. I remember a couple of years ago when that happened. Then again, I also remember our kids bringing home a suspiciously large quantity of produce that night, too. How 'bout it kids? Did you behave yourselves this time? No piles of cornstalks set on fire in the street? No eggs thrown against Mr. Deppler's house?

He really didn't think his nine-year-old son or two young daughters would get into serious mischief. Sure, they might filch a few grapes or apples. Kids get hungry running around Halloween night, right?

The business of the cornstalks and eggs was a family joke. A couple of years before, Old Man Deppler, the neighborhood crank, had come to the house Halloween night and confronted

Tom, saying his children were responsible for those acts. Fortunately, all three were attending a church party at the time. Deppler was unconvinced, but Tom was so indignant that Deppler never complained to him again.

Have you looked in on Mother lately? The last time she wrote she sounded depressed.

He worried about his mom. Not only had she lost one husband, Tom's dad, over thirty years ago, but her second husband, Frederick, had died of a heart attack six months ago. Houston put down his pen and reached for a pack of Camels on the corner of the desk. Removing one, he rolled it between his fingers, wondering if he really wanted it. He decided to have one more. It was going to be a long night. He fished out his big shiny Zippo from a pants pocket and lit up.

There was a rap on the door.

"It's Sergeant Fisk, Major. Can I come in?"

"Just a second." Tom rose from the chair, stepped over to the door, and flicked off the light switch. "Okay, come on in."

Fisk entered the darkened hut and closed the door. Tom switched the light back on. "How's everything out there, Sergeant?"

"Spooky out there, Major." The slender, pugnosed, noncom tipped back his steel helmet with the long multicelled flashlight he held in his left hand. Over his right shoulder was slung a Thompson submachine gun. He never went anywhere at night without both items. Sweat beaded his forehead and his damp fatigue shirt stuck to his chest. His eyes looked hollow. They always seemed to get that way after dark.

"Is the moon out yet, or is it still cloudy?" asked Tom, as he offered his pack of Camels to the uneasy sergeant.

"Thanks. Yeah, there's a quarter moon. Just came up about fifteen minutes ago. Didn't help much, but it's better than the rain." He paused to light the cigarette and sucked in a lungful of smoke. It leaked out as he spoke again. "God, I hate night duty. Time drags. Critters come out."

Tom responded with a puff on his own cigarette, "Yeah, I know."

"I was just in the ready room with the night-fighter pilots," Fisk continued. "They're kinda jumpy. Only fifty hours before the big action, they say. I tell 'em it could be worse. They could be waitin' in an LCI. I know. I done that once."

Fisk was remembering the time he and the 43rd were waiting on the landing craft, infantry, before attacking New Georgia. The beachhead hadn't been hard to take that day. The hard stuff came at night. That's when the Japanese infiltrated their lines, calling out in English to get the inexperienced soldiers to reveal their positions, rolling grenades into their foxholes, and firing here and there to create confusion. Their tactics had worked. The panicky GIs fired wildly in return, throwing grenades themselves, sometimes into the holes of fellow Americans. Some had even gotten into hand-to-hand combat with one another, their knives unable to tell friend from foe. After several nights of that, hundreds suffered what was called "war neurosis" and had to be relieved. Fisk was one of those. After he had been given a rest, he was assigned to a base defense detachment. He had never really recovered from his experience. He both hated and feared the Japanese. The fear had come first.

Houston knew about Fisk's problem. He wondered if he, himself, could have taken it. Fisk was a young fellow, only in his twenties, with no prior combat experience. Still, others managed to tough out that first taste of battle without cracking up. Maybe the 43rd had needed better leadership. Tom wondered if he would have been a good combat commander. By now they had all heard of the tactics of the Japanese jungle fighters, how they harassed the dug-in Allies at night, using various tricks to get the soldiers to give away their positions. Things like tying a captive out in the thick of the jungle, then torturing him to scream for help. Or crawling into the American lines and calling "Medic!" or "Corpsman!" At Guadalcanal, the Japanese had massed forces to attack what they believed to be the weakest part of the American lines and had been mowed down by the hundreds. But they kept coming. The Japs were both tricky and fanatic. Formidable enemies. Yeah, Tom could understand why Fisk didn't like being out in the night in this part of the world.

"Are all your men awake?" said the major, a serious question asked seriously.

"Yeah, they're all kinda jumpy, too. Henderson said—"

"Crack! Crack! Crack!" A carbine barked a couple hundred feet away.

"What's that?" gasped Fisk.

Tom was already at the door, snapping off the lights, and snuffing his cigarette. He jerked the door open and stared into the darkness.

"Sergeant-of-the-guard! Japs! Three of 'em!" came a shout from down the line, near the mess hall.

Tom thought he heard feet scrambling across a hard surface, coming from that direction. He stepped outside. Fisk slid out the door to stand beside him. The panicky sergeant switched on his big flashlight and pointed toward the running feet. Three small figures carrying rifles were dashing past them toward the airplane parking area. Fisk pulled up his tommy gun. He struggled to hold it and the light at the same time.

"Dudadudadudadudadudadudaduda," went the gun, in the direction of the fleeing men.

"Stop it! You'll hit the planes!" shouted Houston.

He grabbed Fisk's light and sprinted after the three fugitives. With each pump of his arms the beam of the light would flash across the backs of the three men. They had a herky jerky gait, and Tom was gaining on them rapidly. They had turned from the hardstands where the menacing fighter planes crouched and were heading directly down the runway.

Tom was less than thirty feet from the hindmost one, shouting, "Halt! Halt or I'll shoot!"

He had a Colt automatic in his holster, but he had forgotten all about it. All he was aware of was the flashlight in his right hand. And his quarry, directly ahead.

In a chance motion of the beam of light, Tom could see that they were Japanese soldiers. "Halt!" he shouted again.

The rearmost man looked over his shoulder. As he ran, he pointed his rifle backward toward the oncoming American and pulled the trigger.

"Ka Pow!" The blast of the rifle blew past Tom's ear.

Why, you son-of-a-bitch! thought Tom, filling with fury.

He accelerated and overtook the intruder. He hooked his right arm, with the flashlight in it, around the man's neck and they both went down. They hit the hard steel of the landing mat and rolled over a couple of times. The flashlight went bouncing away. Tom fought to control the smaller man and found himself on top, with both hands on the other's rifle. The other two Japanese disappeared into the gloom.

The desperate soldier, on his back, struggled furiously to get free. He kicked and writhed, grunting from the effort, as he tried to wrench the rifle from Tom's grasp.

Tom, sitting astride the other man, forced down on the rifle till the receiver, near the bolt handle, pressed against the man's throat. Choking and gagging, the Japanese thrashed and twisted. He clawed at Tom's hands, ripping the skin from the knuckles. He kicked. He bucked. Tom pressed harder. They fought on for several seconds.

Finally the pinned soldier stopped fighting and went limp. Tom held the rifle against the man's throat for a few more seconds, then let up. There was no more life in the Japanese warrior. Tom continued to sit astride the lifeless form while he watched an oncoming group of GIs, flashlights in hand, weapons at the ready.

Fisk was with them. "Where're the others?" he asked.

"That way," indicated Tom. "Two of 'em."

Several of the Americans took off running in the direction of the escaping Japanese, flashlight beams probing the darkness of the runway.

A couple of floodlights came on back at the quonset huts, and one near the parked aircraft illuminated the stark deadly noses of the fighterplanes. The extra light shown also on Tom

Houston and his adversary. The man had a wispy black beard. There was dirt caked in his hair and the tip of his tongue protruded from his bloody lips. His eyes stared fixedly at the dark sky. Tom studied the vacant face of the dead soldier. He had an eerie sense of déjà vu.

"You got 'im, Major! You got 'im!" exulted Fisk.

"He didn't put up that much of a fight. I expected...more of a fight," said Tom. He was beginning to feel shaky, but he stood up anyway. He willed himself to be steady.

Fisk shown his light on the body. The Japanese soldier's tunic was filled with objects. Tom bent down and pulled out two boxes, two olive drab boxes marked, "Powdered Eggs."

Tom looked around at Fisk, but couldn't see his face. Tom was glad the sergeant couldn't see his face either.

"Get him off the runway, Sergeant. The planes are due to roll at dawn. And wake up the ground crew chiefs. Tell them to check the planes for sabotage. I'll go report to the old man."

He didn't really expect they'd find any sabotage.

Major Tom Houston walked off carrying the heavy Ariska rifle in one hand and a box of dried eggs in the other.

9
Two for the Show

It was ten minutes before school let out when the patrol boys burst out of the tall brick school building, the big glass doors slamming shut behind them. They split apart and hurried to their posts, buckling their white patrol belts as they went. A wiry, dark-haired sixth grader named Skip reached his post at the streetcorner by the playground just as a brand new 1946 Ford rolled by and down the block past the school, slowing up for the stop at the next corner.

Skip smiled as it pulled to a halt in front of his buddy Johnny, knowing it would evoke some reaction from the other patrol boy. His smile erupted into laughter when Johnny, recognizing the make of the car, waved in Skip's direction while holding his nose in mock disgust.

"Two hundred thirty-one," said Skip to himself. That was the number of Fords he had counted this week. He and Johnny had made a bet Monday, no property wagered, on whether there were more Chevrolets than Fords in their small Illinois town. Skip seemed to be winning, as it was Friday and the counting was to end today.

Skip looked about him and inhaled deliberately, filling his lungs with the clean, fresh air. He was aware of a warm glow inside and a feeling of strength and raw energy.

There comes a day every year when it is clear beyond a doubt that spring has arrived. The exact date depends on the particular year, the locality, and to a large extent on the individual; for, after all, some people are slow to notice the changing of the seasons. Such a day it was for Skip. He'd heard a cardinal while eating breakfast that morning, and the weather was sunny and warm, warm enough to go to school without wearing a jacket. Even his mother realized that. It was Friday, too. Every Friday is kind of special for a schoolboy. Also, this was his last Friday as an eleven-year-old. Next Wednesday was his birthday. Today marked spring for sure. A special day and a special spring.

This spring was his last in grade school. (You're not a little kid anymore when you get out of grade school, you know.) Then, too, turning twelve meant he could join the Boy Scouts and go to camp in the summer. That's something to look forward to, also. And, in a couple of weeks, the grade school baseball league would start and after that the grade school track meet. Skip was eager for that to come. Last year he ran the quarter mile but was beaten by a couple of older boys. This year there wouldn't be any older boys. He secretly dreamed of winning that race. He loved to run.

All these things ran through Skip's mind as he stood on the corner waiting for the other kids to come out. He grew nervous as he heard the bell in the school signaling the end of the school day. If all other considerations were ignored, this would still be a very special day for Skip. Today he was going to make his first date. He was going to ask Nancy Foster to go to the show with him that night. There was a good movie on about a dog. There were women and girls in it, too. He knew she would like it.

Friday was a little late to ask, he realized, but he had been planning to ask her all week. It seemed every time he saw her after school or at recess she was with her girlfriends. He didn't want to ask her in front of them. He couldn't write a note to her in the classroom for fear the teacher would intercept it and read it to the class. Just the thought of that made him blush. So, he had put off asking her till suddenly it was Friday.

During the afternoon recess he had wandered over next to the girl's side of the playground and stood around trying to catch her eye. She was over on the far side of the girls' area, jumping rope with some friends. She was nearly the same height as Skip and her long flowing hair was just as dark.

She was quiet, and her slim body moved gracefully and daintily like a young doe. Her eyes were deep brown and had the same shy and soulful look one finds in such a wild creature as the deer.

He had failed to catch her eye, though, and when the bell rang, he stopped Lois, a friend of Nancy's, as she was running by.

"Say, Lois," he said, as nonchalantly as he could. "Would you do me a favor? I'm supposed to tell Nancy something; so tell her to stop at my corner on the way home from school, eh?"

Nancy usually rode home with Lois and some other girls, with Lois's mother, because Lois and Nancy lived so far from school.

The kids were spilling out the school doors now, and Skip hoped that Nancy would wait till the rush was over so he wouldn't have to ask her in front of all the kids.

Finally the last of the groups of chattering children had crossed the street, Skip allowing them to move when the traffic was clear. All the while he was keeping one eye on the street and the other on the school behind him. At last Nancy and Lois and the others came out of the building and stood on the walk, waiting for their ride. Lois held Nancy's arm, whispering something in her ear, then urged her down the sidewalk in Skip's direction. Nancy glanced at Skip but seemed reluctant to leave her group, while Skip avoided looking directly at her. Instead he watched for traffic, as if his attention was still required. After a bit more urging, she wandered up the sidewalk, calling over her shoulder to her friends that this had better not be a joke. The three girls smiled and giggled and waved her on.

"Hello, Skip. Lois says you wanted to tell me something."

"Well, ah, I was wondering," he stammered, "…you know that movie that's on tonight?"

"It's an animal picture, isn't it?" answered the girl.

"Yeah…yeah. Well, I was wondering if you'd like to go. With me, I mean. I could come to your house, and we could walk down together, and then we could ride back on the bus," he blurted.

"Oh, I can't go, Skip. Penny's having a birthday party tonight, and we girls are going, and after the party we're going to the show."

"Oh." The bubble had burst. They saw Lois's mother pull up to a stop down the street where her daughter stood.

"I guess I have to go," said Nancy, turning away.

"Well, good-bye," he managed, forcing a smile. "Say, what show are you going to, seven or nine?"

She was already skipping hurriedly down the block, but she turned, skipping backwards, and held up seven fingers. Then she turned again, broke into a run, and jumped into the car.

Skip was angry with himself for not asking sooner, then for not asking her at least to stay and walk home from school with him. Then he was angry at Lois's mother for coming before he could ask Nancy to walk home. Finally, he was angry at himself for asking her at all. Now everyone would know he asked her for a date, and he had failed. Big deal. Big dope.

He scanned the area about him for stragglers, then returned to the school to hang up his patrol belt.

Johnny joined him at the school steps. "What were you and Nancy talking about?" he asked. Nancy was the prettiest girl in school, and Johnny knew it.

"Oh, nothing. She was telling me about the movie she's going to tonight for Penny's birthday," he lied.

"Why'd she tell you?" said Johnny.

"Well, we had talked about the movie coming last week. She said she wanted to see it."

"Why didn't you ask her to go with you?" joked his buddy.

"Well, if it hadn't been for her going to the birthday party, I would have," answered Skip, annoyed.

"Sure, sure," kidded the other boy. He'd never seen Skip take an interest in girls before and was skeptical.

"Well, I would have," bristled Skip.

"Okay, okay. I believe it. I believe it," said his friend, in mock fright.

They headed home, talking of baseball.

"There's a Chevy!" yelled Johnny. "That's two hundred eighteen!" Skip held his nose, and they both laughed.

Skip's family had finished supper, and Skip was wiping the dishes along with his little sister, Donna. His mother, Helen, a brusk, efficient woman, was washing. An older sister, Janet, wiped the table and put away the food.

"You can wipe faster than that, Skippy," admonished his mother.

He didn't like being called Skippy. Most of his friends called him Skip. Nancy did, too. Only in a special way. He liked to hear her say it.

"My name isn't Skippy," replied Skip, still touchy from his failure to get a date.

"My, my, little fellow," injected the teenage Janet. "Just what is your name?"

"My friends call me Skip. You can call me Mr. Houston," he retorted.

"Just what do the girls call you? Darling Darrell?" returned Janet with a saccharine smile.

"Boy, you're going to get a lump, big mouth," spat Skip.

"You two be quiet," declared the mother, in command of the situation. All talk ceased, the only sound being that of the rattling dishes and silverware. Janet continued to smile sweetly.

Later Skip's mother asked, "Are you going out tonight?"

"I told you before, I was going to the movie," answered Skip, a bit sassily.

She let it pass. "Are you going with Johnny?"

"No," he said more civilly. "He's going to his aunt's this weekend."

"Well, who are you going with?" she said.

"I'm going to meet Pete and Don at the show." It wasn't really a lie. He knew Pete and Don were going, but he hadn't made any plans to meet them.

"Well, you'd better hurry," urged his mother. "It's nearly seven now."

"It is? Then I'm going now. I'll see you." He headed for the door.

"Wait a minute," called his mother. "Do you have enough money? You'd better get your jacket, too. And you didn't feed the cat."

"I've got money, and it's warm out," he said as he shot out the door. "And I fed Roger before supper. Good-bye."

When he entered the theater, it was nearly seven-thirty. Even though he had walked quickly, it was a half hour from his home. The movie had, of course, been on for some time, since the feature started about seven-fifteen, following the news.

He stood at the head of the aisle letting his eyes become accustomed to the darkness. Finally, when a bright outdoor shot appeared on the screen, he went down the aisle a little way, searching the rows of people. There were Pete and Don on the left, slouched down in the seats with their knees braced against the backs of the seats in front. There was an empty seat next to them. In the center section sat the girls from the birthday party. Nancy sat on the left end. There was an empty seat behind her. He halted part way down the aisle, considering the two empty seats.

"Hey, Skip." Pete had seen him. "Come here."

Skip hurried over to him and sat down.

"Hey, Skip, I didn't know you were coming," whispered Pete loudly. "You missed a lot already."

Don uttered a "Shhh, shhh," and Pete quieted down. He gave a whispered rundown on what had taken place so far. Then the two turned their attention to the picture.

Skip watched the girls ahead and on his right. None of them had looked back. Then, ever so slightly, Nancy turned her head till she could see Skip from the corner of her eye. She carefully raised her left hand and waved her fingers gently. Skip's blood ran a little faster. He blushed there in the darkness but returned her greeting with a stiff gesture of his hand. Nancy turned back to the picture, a small and secret smile on her lips.

The movie ended, and most of the crowd got up to leave. Nancy and the other girls didn't. Skip didn't. Pete and Don, however, had to leave. Pete's father wanted him home early.

"I want to see the first part. You two go along. I'll see you later," said Skip, when they asked of his plans. The two boys left, and a new crowd entered.

Skip thought about moving down behind Nancy, but that would look too stupid and mushy, so he held his place.

The movie hadn't been showing long when there was some movement among the row of girls. They were getting ready to leave. They apparently hadn't missed much. Nancy's leaving bothered Skip. He had felt a pleasant but kind of sad sensation at sitting there in the movie, realizing that Nancy was just a few rows away.

The girls rose and approached him as he sat on an aisle seat. Nancy was first. As she passed, she whispered, "Hi, Skip," but not so anyone else would notice.

Skip stared intently at the screen as the rest passed, so they wouldn't catch his eye. That pleasant sadness left him and followed his girl up the aisle. His girl. Skip was aware of that phrase for the first time. She was his girl. He was sure. She had never smiled or waved at any of the other boys in school in the six months since she moved to town from faraway Colorado. If she had, they would have made a point to tell all the rest.

I bet I could kiss her, he thought, a bit egotistically. Abruptly an idea sprang into full bloom, almost as if it had been there all the time. Indeed, the seed had been lingering in the back of his mind for sometime.

They must have ridden with Penny's folks. They would be returning home in the same car. A couple of the girls lived in the east part of town; Penny lived two streets down from Nancy. Nancy would be the last to be taken home. It should take them twenty minutes to get to Nancy's street. That was about a half mile past Skip's house. He could run there, he felt, by the time they took to drive her home.

He rose, hurried up the aisle and went out to the street. The girls were just climbing into Penny's dad's car down the street a way. Skip turned up the street and commenced to trot. He ran very well for a boy of nearly twelve.

In no time at all he was out of the downtown area and running up the sidewalk of the long, long street which went past his home. He ran with the smooth effortless stride of a trained runner, which he wasn't. But all boys are used to running, and Skip liked to run better than most. He breathed in time with his leg motion. The rhythmic pat, pat of footfalls blended with his breathing. Left, right, left, right. Inhale left, exhale right. Left, right, left, right.

Perspiration broke out on his face, his chest, and his back. His legs felt strong and springy; his chest was light and flexible. He had gone a mile now, and his mouth was a little dry. Remembering the two lemon drops he had been carrying around in his pocket for the last two days, he slowed to a walk. He poked his hand in his pocket and extracted a piece of the yellow candy, covered with pocket fuzz, and stuck it in his mouth.

After a second or two to regain his normal breath, he changed from a walk into his rhythmic lope. The lemon drop tasted sweet and juicy. His mouth was no longer dry.

Now he was running along the stretch where the grave stones in the cemetery rose pale and stark from behind the chainlink fence. He quickened his pace, slowing again as he reached the next block with its row of neat, substantial houses, their porches dark, the inhabitants ensconced within.

A few more blocks and he was nearing his home, so he turned off at a vacant lot, down an alley, and cut across another lot. Only a half mile to go. He slowed to a walk again to catch his breath and to dig the other lemon drop from his pocket, then off he went again.

At the next street he turned left, crossing the street kittycorner and passing under the low-hung street light.

He loped on. *I wonder how many street lights I've passed? I wonder how many a mile? I should have counted them.*

Only two blocks to Nancy's street now. She lived at the end of the street in a small two-story white house on the left.

He stopped momentarily. He wasn't sure what he intended to do, but he didn't bother to ask himself the question. Perhaps he expected to wait till she arrived, then walk her that last block. Before he could figure out something, he saw a car far ahead turn onto the street he was traveling now. It might be Penny's dad's car. He broke into a run again. The car turned up Nancy's street a block ahead of him. He ran faster, trying to get a glimpse of her. He reached the end of her street just as the car backed out of Nancy's driveway and came back down the street. Skip jumped behind a hedge and peered out through the budding branches at the approaching car. He hoped it was some other car, maybe someone to see her folks or something. The car turned the corner and sailed down the street, its taillights marking its course. To Skip, it was a ship of dispair. It was Penny's dad's car, and he had missed Nancy.

He leaped over the hedge and walked softly up the block toward Nancy's house and stopped a few houses away. He watched a light go on in Nancy's house, upstairs, then another. The second went out, then the first. He turned and headed home, a void within him. It was the strangest feeling. What could be the reason for such a feeling? He didn't know and didn't try to figure it out. First love is not easily recognized.

Saturday was a beautiful, fresh-smelling, sunlit day. Skip knew that, only he didn't come right out and say it to himself. Small boys don't think in phrases. They don't feel a need to express an awareness in words. When they have a feeling inside, they show it by actions and expressions.

Skip bounced across the yard and danced down the street, arms aswinging, toward the park. He was finished doing "the work around the house," as his mother called it. Lunch was over and he had the afternoon to himself. Roger, his cat, scurried alongside, darting out from a hedge occasionally to attack his flashing heels.

Roger was strange, even for a cat. Sometimes he was more like a dog. Most cats wouldn't follow along with their master, playing games and engaging in footraces when out of doors. They generally moved slowly and cautiously, always alert, and aloof. Maybe Roger was different because he was so big. A big and tawny sixteen-pounder and not fat either.

Skip's mother didn't like dogs. She said they ate too much and spoiled the lawn. She didn't like Roger much after they had him a while, either. He didn't spoil the lawn, but he ate a lot and nothing but fresh meat. Roger was particular. He'd hunt his own food before he'd touch a can of cat food.

Since Johnny was gone for the weekend, Skip was adventuring alone, or rather he and Roger were adventuring alone. He knew there would be a ball game going on at the ball diamond, if it were dry enough, but the kids playing were all junior-high age and older. He didn't feel like tagging along after them. He was going to do some exploring.

In ten minutes they reached the park and slipped through the split rail fence. The park was a large and sprawling place, impressive for such a moderately sized town. There were even a couple of larger parks in town. This one had ball diamonds and swimming pools and picnic grounds and basketball courts and tennis courts and fish ponds and woods and everything. It even had a special motorcycle policeman. He policed all the parks, in season, watching that the cars driving along the miles of winding road kept the speed down, saw to it that people stayed out of the flower beds, protected the ducks that lived year round at one of the parks, reminded the children to head home at supper time, kept the neckers moving, and locked the gates in the parks at closing time. At least old Mr. Eastman did last year. Skip had heard that the old retired city policeman had decided to retire from the park job, too. He must have been getting too old to buzz around on the motorcycle. The city didn't have a new one yet this year, as far as Skip knew.

When Skip and Roger reached the stream that flowed through the park, they followed it and crossed over on a road bridge. The road came from a wooded area upstream, and, after crossing the stream, looped back upstream toward a picnic area about a quarter mile away. Once on the other side, the overgrown kitten bounded off the road and up into the woods. He wanted to play "jungle hunter." That was a game of theirs. They would take turns stalking one another. Skip would hunt down Roger, stalking through the woods till he found the cat lying in wait in the bushes. The tawny animal would charge, and Skip would run one way and the cat the other. Then Roger would turn and hunt him down. It was great fun. Time would whirl by as the woods were transformed into a jungle and Skip into Frank Buck or Tarzan.

This time he would be Tarzan, and Tarzan had to have a spear. The eleven-year-old, almost twelve, found a long straight branch and cut it off with his jackknife. Then he trimmed off the twigs except for a couple of stabilizers at the end. He sharpened a point and slipped off through the jungle.

He saw a flash of tawny partway up the gentle hillside, so he climbed higher to get above his fearsome quarry. After a while he crept downward toward the spot where he expected to find his lion. Sure enough, out charged Roger, and Skip fled back up the hillside, laughing to himself. Skip found some evergreen bushes to hide in and waited for Roger, who had turned and scurried down the hill to the road to take up the stalk.

Skip heard the motorcycle coming down the road from the picnic area. So did Roger, and he ducked into the bushes, which didn't offer much cover since the leaves hadn't come out yet. Skip peered intently down the hill to see who it was but kept hidden. He didn't want to get caught with a freshly cut branch. You weren't allowed to cut down any plants in the parks.

The rider was in the uniform of the park policeman, but Skip had never seen the man before. He was a husky, red-faced man, maybe forty, with heavy eyebrows, a crew cut under the visored uniform cap, and a pearl handled automatic at his side. He was going slow, looking all around, when he spotted the tawny cat crouched by the side of the road. He pulled up, shut off the engine, dropped his kickstand, and strolled over to Roger.

Roger flattened his ears.

"C'mere, kitty, kitty. Here, kitty, kitty," coaxed the man with his arm outstretched. "Here, kitty. Nice kitty."

Roger was too much like a dog. He trotted out to sniff the extended hand.

Skip watched silently from his vantage point up the hill while the park cop picked up the animal and stroked its fur. He continued stroking the big housecat as he turned about, searching the visible park area. There was not another soul in sight. He turned his back toward Skip and fumbled in his jacket pocket. Skip couldn't see what the man was doing, but he was getting uneasy.

After a few seconds, the man walked over to his motor-cycle and swung his leg over. Then he put the cat down on the road.

Skip was numbed. His pet had one end of a long cord fastened about its neck, and the other end was gripped in the big paw of the park cop.

Roger tried to run away but could only go a few feet. The red-faced man laughed harshly, kick-started his bike, and moved off slowly to Skip's left.

What was the man doing? Skip stood up from his hiding

place, confused, unable to think of what to do.

At first the cat set its feet but was forced into a fast trot when the cord pulled at its head. The motorcycle picked up speed. The cat had to run faster. The machine, rider, and unwilling prisoner turned and crossed over the bridge to the other side of the stream.

The motorcycle picked up more speed on the straightaway on the opposite side of the stream from Skip. Roger fairly flew now, tearing along like a rabbit. The rider held the cord in his left hand, observing Roger's furious effort.

Suddenly he made a sliding reversal and shot back down the road as fast as he could accelerate. The hard running cat turned just as quickly but made the mistake of trying to pull free. The tawny pet was jerked off its feet. It landed with a thud, skidding along the pavement on its side. The cyclist wore a sickening grin as he rounded the turn over the bridge and sped back up the road below Skip.

Skip ran yelling down the hillside, clutching his spear. Fear, anger, and pain fused into a rage he'd never experienced. He came flying, tearing, smashing down through the woods toward the road. He screamed threats, commands, and a stream of invective one wouldn't believe could issue from a boy. The roar of the machine kept the beefy park cop from hearing, and, since he was looking over his left shoulder, he didn't see the enraged boy either.

The motorcycle barreled up the road, leaving a trail of noise, fumes, fur, and blood. Skip hit the road running full tilt as the machine approached.

"You bastard!" he screamed and hurled the spear blindly at the passing biker. The wooden shaft was off its mark and stabbed through the spokes of the front wheel.

The rider floated aloft, it seemed for many seconds, his arms and legs spread-eagled as he tumbled through the air. He slammed heavily into a tree trunk at the left edge of the road and crumpled to a heap at its base. The roaring machine slithered crazily like a thing alive, spun into the stream, and stalled.

The sudden silence was the voice of death.

Skip stood rooted to the pavement. His pet lay near the tree with the park cop. The boy moved closer to the bodies, tears streaming down his face. The cord about the cat's neck was still wrapped around the man's hand. Skip looked down at the policeman. The man didn't look burly and powerful now. He just looked...fat. Blood welled from the man's ears and nose. His eyes stared skyward, blank, unfocused.

Skip stood there, his chest shaking as he breathed. There was still not another person in sight. A mourning dove called eerily from the woods.

Skip bent down and gingerly unwound the cord from the man's lifeless hand. He picked up his bloody pet, sobbing for it to open its eyes, and held it in his arms. The eyes opened, it mewed very faintly, and died.

There stood the boy, choking and crying, for some time. Then he laid his cat back down and wiped his eyes. Somewhere deep in his brain, a thought process began. He trotted over to where the motorcycle had slid into the water. The front wheel was tangled in some bushes. His spear had fallen loose on the bank. Skip grabbed it in one hand and picked up a large rock in the other. He hurried over to the point on the road where the machine had first flipped and placed the rock on the pavement. It lay as if it had just rolled down the hillside and somehow ended up on the road. Then he went back, lifted his Roger from the ground, looked around to see if anyone had seen him, and headed off.

He was going to bury his cat. As he stumbled along, he still sobbed, reluctant to hold the bloody bundle of bones and flesh, yet not willing to put it down. He climbed the hill to the top and plunged into the thickets there. With his spear and bloody hands he dug a grave and lay his tawny pet in it. Covering the hole, he patted it firm and walked away. He tossed his spear into some juniper bushes as he circled far away from the stream and the tree and the dead man. He went home sick at heart and frightened to the core.

What does a boy do when such a thing happens? If he

breaks something at home, he gets a bawling out. If he hits his sister, he gets a stern lecture from his mother. Sometimes he gets a smack on the rear for only being a little sassy, if his father, Tom, is in a bad mood. If he whispers in school, his teacher raps his knuckles with a ruler. Police put you in jail for stealing candy. What happens to a boy if he has killed a man? Skip was terrified of being found out.

No one in his family recognized his fear, however. They assumed it to be little-boy grief over losing a pet, because he had explained his bloody arms and shirt and the absence of the cat by saying that Roger had been hit by a car and killed. They were all properly sympathetic but had other things on their minds and didn't dwell on the matter. Except for his little sister, Donna. She cried as Skip told his invented story and cried a little after, too.

Skip went to bed early but couldn't sleep well. He tossed and turned far into the night, scenes of the smashup flashing through his head. Eventually he came to a conclusion. The man had been evil. He deserved to die, even though Skip hadn't meant to kill him. But it was too much to keep a complete secret. He had to share his feelings with someone. His parents? No. His sisters? Definitely not! His buddy Johnny? No, not Johnny either. Johnny acted a little childish sometimes. He'd tell his folks or somebody.

How about Nancy?

She may be the one. If she really cared for him, if she was the way Skip thought her to be, then she would be the one. She would understand. It would be a secret they could share, just for the two of them. Skip thought of how he would find a chance to tell her, but fell asleep without a plan in mind.

Sunday morning he awoke to see a gray, rainy sky through his bedroom window. His mother was trying to get his father out of bed to go to church.

Skip got through church all right. He didn't remember a thing that was said during the service. He sat in the living room after dinner thinking about wandering over to Nancy's house later in the afternoon. He tried not to think about yesterday's event.

Skip's father came down the stairs after changing his clothes, and, remembering something, strode out the front door. He returned, bearing the morning paper. He threw the funnies on the floor next to Skip, without comment, and pulled out the sports section. His big sister, Janet, picked up the rest. Skip reached for the funnies.

"Mother! Mother! Look here!" exclaimed Janet. "The new park policeman was killed yesterday. It says they found him late in the afternoon, and he apparently hit a rock and lost control of his motorcycle and hit a tree. It says some people in the park heard his motorcycle earlier in the day and that it sounded like he was going awful fast. I thought he'd do that. I saw him last week going real fast, and I said to myself, 'He's going to have an accident, going fast like that,' and sure enough he did."

Skip buried his nose in the funnies.

"Well, isn't that something," said his mother. His father said nothing. He was engrossed in the baseball scores and had not heard Janet.

Janet murmured to herself as she skimmed the rest of the story.

"Skippy, isn't Nancy Foster in your class?"

What in the world was this, now? "Yes, why?"

"George Foster is her father, that's why. He was the new park policeman. It says the whole family is taking his body back to Colorado to be buried and then they're going to stay and live with relatives there."

Skip Houston didn't want to grow up anymore. He didn't want to face fear, worry, and heartbreak yet. There was nothing he could do about it, though. He knew. A boy just grows up. When he has man-sized secrets of love and death, he isn't a boy anymore. He had his secrets and no one else could know now. They were locked away inside him. He would never tell anyone.

10
A Game of Hearts

A cloudy November sky looked down on the passenger train as it rolled southwest through central Illinois. In the tailend car Darrell Houston was trying to sleep, without much success. He'd been up late the night before saying good-bye to his friends, such friends as were still around town. Most of his men friends were in the military, same as he was, or in college, postponing the draft till after graduation. The best girls were either in college or tied up with some older guys, thoughts of wedding bells cluttering their minds. He'd had too much to drink. He had a hangover.

Since leaving Chicago, he had either dozed or read the *Reader's Digest* his mother had given him. The coach car was only about two-thirds full, and no one was sitting next to him.

Those he could see ahead of him didn't seem too interesting. He had seen about all the cutover corn fields he could stand in a lifetime, so watching the scenery out the windows was unrewarding. It was going to be a long ride to Fort Smith, Arkansas.

Darrell perked up some when the train crossed the Mississippi in the afternoon. *How do those barges maneuver around down there*, he said to himself as he looked down from the multispan railroad bridge high above the dirty brown flow. *Hey, we crossed the Mississippi. We're in the west now, pardner.*

Shortly after, the train stopped in St. Louis. *Bus stations and train stations create a feeling all their own,* he thought. *Like a mild case of the flu.* The industrial odor, the shuffling sounds of people moving but seemingly not going anywhere, the gray drabness of the surroundings, all competed with that glimmer of hopeful expectation that rose in the western fringes of his mind when he learned he was being transferred to California from Camp Chaffee, Arkansas. In less than a year, he'd be out of the Army, and, if things worked out, he planned to go to college in California. The train was taking him in the right direction.

He should have been in a better frame of mind, but he couldn't pull himself out of the doldrums. *Must be the hangover*, he thought. But actually it was because he had not been able to convince himself he was seeking new horizons and not just escaping from something in his past, and that bothered him.

In St. Louis he changed trains. He had an hour's layover before the next one left, so got a sandwich and a cup of coffee at a dreary snack bar in the depot. When boarding time came he toted his barracks bag up the train steps and took it up the aisle between the seats. The bag weighed fifty pounds, but he had no difficulty tossing it up into an overhead rack. He was a sturdy young man. There weren't many people in the car, so he picked out a seat by himself six rows from the front.

A group of young black soldiers boarded through the door

at the opposite end and worked their way down toward the front of the car, near where Darrell sat. They were laughing and joking with one another. They sat in a group, with four seated in a set of bench seats that faced one another on the left side, opposite and two rows ahead of Darrell. One, with a coal black complexion, caught Darrell's eye and, recognizing a fellow GI in uniform, smiled, waving a friendly hello. Darrell smiled and waved a hand in reply.

The train got up and going, slowly and jerkily at first, then more smoothly as the powerful diesel engines wound up.

The black soldiers apparently hadn't all known one another when they first boarded the train, so were getting acquainted. In the spirit of camaraderie, one turned to Darrell and asked, "Where you headed, Corporal?"

"Camp Chaffee. From there I'm gettin' transferred to Fort Ord. Where you goin'?"

"Camp Chaffee, too. But it 'pears most of these fellas are goin' to Fort Sill 'fore shippin' out for Korea. C'mon, join us. We're goin' to play hearts to pass the time."

So he joined them. "Corporal, my name's Freddie Walker. What's yours?"

"Houston. Darr Houston."

"Darr?"

"Yes, Darr."

Darr met the others and pulled down his barracks bag to sit on. The ones going to Korea wanted to know if Darr had been there. Even though a truce had been signed several months before, they were still concerned about the danger. Darr had not been to Korea, though he had tried unsuccessfully for an overseas assignment. They all talked and played hearts for several hours.

Evening came and the card playing continued. Finally one fellow said, "I'm hungry. I'm going to have me a sandwich." He took down a small gym bag from the overhead rack and found a sandwich. That sort of broke up the card game for a while. All of them, including Darr, had been hungry, but apparently unwilling to pay the expense of a meal in the dining car and embarrassed to eat a sandwich from home in front of the others. And they all had sandwiches from home.

There was a fair amount of joshing about the choice of sandwiches and miscellaneous goodies in their respective lunch bags. A couple had slim rations, so there was some sharing that went on. After a while, the game of hearts resumed. Darrell offered his pack of smokes and saw the rest of his Luckies disappear. He laughed and crumpled the empty foil and cellophane package. The train made a few stops, there was some getting on and getting off, but the game continued. They were all having fun.

Night had come. The interior lights had been on for some time. The lights from cars and houses being passed flashed by the windows. The group of soldiers were preoccupied with the play of the cards. The queen was about to fall when a large, spectacled conductor entered the car from the rear door. He stopped and talked to some people behind the cardplayers. There was some murmuring and shuffling. The conductor next stopped beside Darr who was seated in the aisle.

"You boys'll have to go to the back of the car. We've crossed the state line." All looked up from the game.

"What?" said Darr.

"These boys have to move to the back of the train."

Darr looked around at his companions. The smiles were gone. In their places were expressions of hurt, resignation, sadness, disappointment. None of the black soldiers questioned the order. Wordlessly they gathered up the cards and their other belongings and slipped past Darr to the back of the coach. He had missed them when he boarded the train, but there were two metal frames with canvas stretched across them that separated five or six rows in the back from the rest of the seats. The black soldiers began to take up seats behind the barrier.

"What's that all about?" Darr asked of the coal black PFC who had first smiled at him.

"State law. We got to sit in the back of the train," he said with a blank face.

Darr finally understood. "Hell, I'll just join you back there and we'll finish the game anyway." Darr was beginning to get annoyed. He dragged his bag up the aisle after the other soldiers.

The conductor, who had continued down the aisle, turned and saw Darr move toward the rear. "Hold on there, fella!" he said. The chunky man was excited and almost ran back up the aisle. "You can't sit back there. You have to sit on this side of the screen."

Some internal switch was tripped in Darr's brain. "I'll sit where I goddamn please!" he said, glaring at the conductor. The man turned apoplectic, fear and anger churning behind his glasses.

Before the man could say anything, the black PFC tugged at Darr's sleeve. "Don't make no trouble. We don't need no trouble," he pleaded.

Darr saw the worry in his friend's face. He glanced at the other black soldiers. A couple occupied themselves with placing their belongings in the racks or under the seats. The others sat, their eyes averted.

"Okay," said the young white corporal. He stood for a while, letting it all sink in. Then he hoisted his barracks bag onto his shoulder, turned, and strode angrily to the front of the car. The crappy mood he'd brought with him in the morning returned, surrounding him like a cloud of gnats.

More stops were made along the line. At one, a trim young blonde WAC boarded and sat opposite Darr. He glanced up, noticing her good looks were tempered somewhat by an appearance of toughness. She gave him an uninterested glance and settled into her seat. She removed a pack of Pall Malls from her purse and lit up with a shiny Ronson lighter.

Darr returned to his unfinished *Reader's Digest.*

The night dragged on, the coach rocking over the sometimes uneven rails, wheels clicking over the joints. People, including the WAC, visited the toilets before attempting to sleep. The overhead lights were dimmed. Darr, alone in his seat, strained in the poor light to read the final story in the magazine. Conversation in the train quieted and stopped altogether.

Darr reached into the breast pocket of his shirt for his fresh pack of Luckies, tore a match from a book of safety matches, and lit a cigarette. He drew a deep breath and exhaled a cloud of smoke which drifted up to the ceiling.

"Excuse me. Could you give me a light?" said someone with a soft southern drawl. It was the blonde WAC. She was leaning across the aisle with a Pall Mall between her fingers. She had her tunic off and the top two buttons of her blouse were undone.

Darr, still glum, studied her for a moment. *Shit. She's trying to pick me up*, he thought. *That damn woman is trying to pick me up.*

"Here." He tossed her his pack of matches. "You can keep 'em." He paid no more attention to her as he finished his smoke.

The WAC held a match to her own cigarette and watched Darr. She decided he was a lost cause. When she finished her own smoke, she put her tunic back on and buttoned up her blouse. It was going to be a long cool ride to Fort Smith, Arkansas.

"Click click, click click, click click."

11
A Distant Tinkling

Darrell James Houston swung his station wagon around next to the sign that marked the road's end, pulled up to a dogwood that was just beginning to turn a delicate red, and set the parking brake. He climbed out from behind the wheel and stretched, arching his back to relieve the stiffness of his long journey from The City, San Francisco. A fresh breeze fluttered the leaves of the quaking aspens making them seem like balconies full of applauding hands. They applauded the beauty of an early autumn day in the Sierras with its freshness following a recent thunderstorm and its sighing and hushing, empty of the noise of the many summertime campers and hikers now returned to schools and jobs.

Darr, as he was now called, ran his fingers through his

shaggy graying hair. Noticing the signs posted on a nearby Forest Service signboard, he strolled over to check them out. The instructions explained the rules of use for the area beyond the sign. No motor vehicles, pack out trash, fire permits required, etc. Except that the list was longer, nothing much had changed since he last had gone hiking in the National Forest nine years ago.

Was it really that long ago? he thought. Yes, it was. The last time had been with a troop of boys, the first year his son had been in the Scouts. He'd been awarded custody of their only child on alternate weekends five years before that. He and his wife split up after a long period of arguing over drinking (hers), not making enough progress on the job (his), and lack of interest in sex (theirs). The fact was that Darr had turned out to be a very private person, never able to connect with his wife on either an intellectual or emotional basis, and neither could live with the consequences. That and the girl.

Darr returned to his wagon, dropped the tailgate, pulled his pack and fishing rod out, and leaned them against the fender. The pack was an expensive, well-built, Himalyan-type frame, like new. He'd bought it while in the process of divorce, determined to return once again to be the outdoor kind of person he once had been in his youth. It hadn't received much use. First one thing then another kept cropping up. A change of companies, a period on night assignments at the computer center, responsibilities at the church to which he felt too obligated to avoid, a wood-carving hobby, all seemed to come before planned trips of backpacking in the wilderness.

Finally he had stirred himself, maybe it was the book he'd read or the TV movie, or the last time a taxi had honked raucously at him when he was slow to clear the crosswalk, or looking in a full-length mirror, or all those things that woke up a younger mind and urged him to get with it and live life more fully.

Once when only twenty and on leave from the Army, he had spent two full weeks in this area, alone, in the early autumn. He'd experienced such a tremendous feeling of being alive, a part of the wilderness surroundings, that there seemed to have been a recording in his brain, a non-erasable command to return. "Return to the majestic mountains, return to the crystal lakes, return to starlit skies, hear the call of the coyote, laugh at the jays, whistle with the marmots. Come back to the mountains where your ancestors roamed, where your father was born. Come home."

He secured the rod case to his pack frame and hoisted the frame to his back. It rested comfortably on his still muscular shoulders. His boots were on, the car was locked, his map was in his shirt pocket. He was ready to go. With legs full of a youthful vigor, he strode on up the trail toward a particular lake, the special lake he'd remembered from thirty-six years ago. It was named April Lake.

April the lake, April the woman. The words caused a surge of nostalgia to well up within him as he trod along the trail.

He was high in elevation and starting to breathe hard now. His hands, forehead, and arms sweat in the midmorning sun. It felt good. His legs were still fine, his pack not heavy.

A lizard skittered from a bush beside the trail, startling him once, and he chuckled to himself. He kicked a couple of pine cones along the trail ahead of himself for a few moments. A jay dove down the slope from a fir tree overhead, scolding him as it went, a noisy, boisterous busybody of the forest. He shouted at the jay, "Hey! It's me! Darr Houston! I'm back again!" surprising himself a little. His shout was quickly swallowed by the green forest and everything was silent...still. Darr cocked his head and listened hard. He thought he heard a distant tinkling...but then no more.

He went on. A view of the rugged stream canyons topped by stark and rocky ridges and peaks unfolded to the east. Pockets of pine and fir broke up otherwise bare slopes. Grassy glades and clumps of aspen, yellowing now, accented the beauty of the evergreens. Higher up and to the southwest lay his April Lake.

As the sun drifted beyond the zenith and the trail grew

steeper, his breathing came harder, his heaving chest pressing against the pack straps. His shirt was soaked with sweat and his legs were growing heavy. He stopped for a blow more often and drank thirstily from two springs he passed.

By midafternoon he was walking with difficulty. Beer and peanuts and fifty-six years had padded his middle with extra pounds. He was light headed and his bloodpump pounded to keep energy supplied to his tired legs. He had left the trail now and was traveling cross country. Then, without fanfare, appeared his lake, below the ridge he'd just ascended. He glimpsed it through the fir and pines, sparkling like several mirrors half hidden in the trees. It was a fairly easy descent now down the rocky slope to the glacier-carved niche where water gathered from the melted snows of winter. At the far end of this modest-sized body of water, no bigger than a football field, was a small stream which gurgled down from a timbered mountainside. To his right was the outlet, a gentle flow through reeds and sandy flats which disappeared downslope into a valley hidden from view and unknown to him. Directly ahead was a low peninsula with grass-covered soil around smooth granite knobs and boulders scattered randomly about like misplaced furniture. A number of gnarled white pines grew in clusters, inviting him to sprawl below them and rest awhile. It was a fine idea. In a while he would set up his camp and fish till dusk, but first the well-earned reward for years of remembering and hours of hard hiking.

He pulled off his pack and leaned it against a rock under the pines to use as a back rest. He sat for a few minutes savoring the moment, then unlaced his boots to ease his sore feet. He sure was tired. He leaned back and closed his eyes.

April Lake. April. His thoughts drifted back in time. Though over fifteen years ago, the face and voice and words were fresh in his memory. They were fresh because he'd renewed them by constant recollection. When he shaved, he thought of how she liked to watch him stroke away the lathery whiskers with his razor. Each time he came upon the ocean with waves pounding on the shore, he recalled how she had whispered, "Remember, I love you," as he left her on the beach, and how her whisper carried, even over the roaring surf; every glowing fireplace he shared with her.

He'd met her during one of those catastrophic occurrences that happen periodically in California. He was on a business trip headed for Santa Barbara by way of the slower Coast Route because he enjoyed the coastline drive and he wasn't expected until the next afternoon. A heavy rain had been predicted, but he hadn't expected it till the next day. It came on suddenly, with a hurricane-like fury when he was south of Big Sur. Torrential rains carried rocks and mud slides down to the road from fire denuded slopes above with surprising swiftness and drove him to take refuge at a little cafe overlooking the shore but high above the violent sea. There was no other establishment or residence for miles in either direction. His clothes were drenched before he could dodge into the entrance of the place. He was drenched again when he went back to his car for luggage after the young couple who were proprietors invited him to stay over till the highways were clear. They lived in a little apartment below the cafe and had their own water and electrical systems and plenty of food. Since there was apparently no one else besides Darr, they felt he could sleep in the dining room on a huge old couch that stretched along one wall, opposite the fireplace.

Darr had changed clothes and was chatting with the Weisfelds (that was their name), while hanging his wet clothes on a drying rack set up near the crackling fireplace. A little lime green car of foreign manufacture wheeled up to the entrance, a door popped open and delivered up a girl with flowing blonde hair, jeans, a turquoise jersey pullover, and a tiny bell hung from a necklace that tinkled when she walked. She was also drenched by the time she entered the door that opened for her as the Weisfelds ushered her into the cafe. The wet clothes clung to her body, smooth and rounded, unhindered by underclothing; she moved with feline grace. On her face was a tentative smile. "Hello," she said. "I'm April. Can I spend the night? The highway's closed in both directions."

So she spent the night and the next and the next, with Darr Houston, in the dining room by the fireplace.

The first evening she wore a shirt of Darr's and jeans from Mrs. Weisfeld, Rebecca, as her own dried. She had no luggage, no coat, no purse, only a comb. She sat smiling on the floor by the fire as the four of them sang songs together. With the bearded Harry Weisfeld chording his guitar, Rebecca's rich contralto, Darr's scratchy baritone, and April's sweet soprano, they blended together surprisingly well. Both Darr and Harry could recall the words to a broad variety of songs. Each came to tell a short tale of when the song had been most memorable. As the evening developed, they all became mellow from the friendship shared and the red wine furnished by the hosts.

Later, Darr found himself holding April's hand in his, as if it were the natural thing to do. Eventually the glasses were empty and the Weisfelds rose to retire. April was urged to curl up on the couch where she could benefit from the warmth that radiated from the fireplace. Darr stretched out off by the side on a thick rug with a blanket to cover himself.

During the night he rose a few times to place more wood on the fire. Each time he awoke he was aware of April's presence, strong, constant, and appealing. He felt her wakefulness and once noticed the firelight's gleam from her open eyes as she observed him in the semidarkness, though neither spoke.

The next day, stormy like the first, was spent mostly inside, all four being busy with cleaning, cooking, doing odd jobs, or reading. There was some opportunity for light conversation, and Harry, with his easygoing manner, helped maintain the light-hearted fellowship established the night before. After dinner the Weisfelds retired early because Harry was coming down with a cold. April and Darr sat relaxed again before the fireplace, side by side, legs sprawled across the floor and backs against the cushioned couch. They sipped from a common wine glass. They talked of things that felt good to them, like light snow against the face on a downhill ski run, or warm wet sand under bare feet, or a sleeping cat purring on one's lap.

Then with deliberateness and purpose not usual for him, he turned slowly and kissed her. Her hands fluttered briefly at his shoulders then held him close as she responded hungrily. The night was filled with their lovemaking. In the morning, before the Weisfelds arose, late in their understanding way, she stood by with her quiet smile and watched him shave.

The two of them walked together, hand in hand, along the debris-strewn beach. They sat for hours on driftwood logs, close together, like two children listening to ghost stories. Gulls and terns roamed the shoreline, squabbling over tidbits cast up by the waves. Word came over the radio up in the cafe that roads would be open by the next morning.

They both came to realize that theirs was no casual encounter. Darr had never even so much as made a pass at a girl since his marriage, and he was shaken by it. Inevitably, just as surely as the sun had to slip beyond the far horizon of the ocean, they had to face tomorrow. It seemed obvious to Darr. Reality was a wife and a growing boy, a job demanding steadiness and reliability, and a clean image at the church. He explained as best he could his awakening responsibilities. April grew somber, conveying by her wet eyes and unfinished questions the depth of her feelings. She and Darr spent the night quietly, clinging to one another as if to hold onto the darkness forever. In the morning before breakfast, unable to eat, he had walked away from her as she stood by the sea.

Darr realized a week later that she had become more important than anyone else in the world to him. He couldn't call or write her; she'd never said where she lived. He didn't even know her last name. He called the Weisfelds. He searched the streets of towns and cities up and down the Coast Highway for her or her car. He placed personal advertisements in several California newspapers, all to no avail. A score of times he pursued little lime green cars or slender blonde-haired girls to find it was not her. For weeks after that, he strove mightily to think of ways to find her. There was no way. Needless to say, these efforts took their toll on his marriage. He could no longer take his wife's liquor-fueled tirades, the accusations, the cold body in the bed next to him, the tension at mealtime. He wanted peace of mind. The hard part was leaving his son, Jason. He had wanted Jason to know about loving relationships.

Darr Houston was nearly asleep as he lay against his pack when he heard a lilting melody, just a few notes, floating on the quiet air. He raised his head, tilting it first one way then the other. Again the sound and then a soft rustling of branches, then a faint tinkling. From out of the forest near the reeds along the outlet appeared a lithe figure, leaping agilely over logs and rocks to the lake's edge. It was a girl with tawny hair glistening in the afternoon sun. She was clad in white jeans with a sky blue shirt that clung tightly to her body. She stepped into the water before pulling off her shirt and casting it to the grassy shore. She waded into the shallow water, her tan contrasting with the white of her jeans, then went all the way to her waist before climbing up onto a large boulder that jutted from the clear cool water. She rose to her feet and then, bending down, slowly peeled the wet jeans from her body. Darr had had difficulty seeing her clearly because of the sun's reflection on the water, but, when she stood erect, naked, he could see that she had to be April. The tiny waist, the upturned breasts, the rounded behind, the flowing blonde tresses, the bell pendant, they all belonged to April.

She stood scanning the surrounding shoreline, then, with a radiant smile, stretched out her arms toward him, calling "Darr! Darr!"

As he quickly shed his own shirt and trousers, he felt the years disappearing. Power surged to his shoulders and legs, his belly was flat and hard, his jaw lean and strong again. He dove into the cool lake waters and swam with powerful strokes toward April's rock. She was in the water now, too, gliding swiftly and surely toward him. They met and embraced, falling below the surface, crying, laughing, surfacing again and then splashing like playful otters toward the shore. They stood on the soft mud at the edge near the outlet and kissed for a long, long time.

She pulled away gently, and taking his hand, drew him by the arm to follow the path from whence she had come. Darr followed eagerly and never looked back.

Nevermind when or how they missed Darr Houston; they did and had been searching for a day and a night in the wilderness when Jason, his son, arrived to join the search.

"Is there an April Lake around?" he asked of the deputy sheriff in charge.

"Let's ask a ranger," was the reply.

Yes, there was, about three hours walk from where they stood, was the ranger's answer.

"My father spoke of it often," said Jason evenly. "I think he was headed for that lake." So they set off and arrived by noon.

They all gathered around the cluster of pines and rock and pack frame against which Darr Houston's body sat cold and lifeless and fully clothed. His boots were unlaced but still on his feet.

People don't say much at such times. There was silence for a while, then the ranger walked off to talk to someone over his handheld radio.

The deputy sheriff, who was also acting coroner, turned to Jason after making his examination. "Looks like he just walked up here, sat down, and passed away. But he died happy, son," he said, placing a comforting hand on Jason's shoulder. "He has a smile on his lips."

Jason walked away to be by himself for a time. He sat on a log near the stream outlet and stared vacantly downward. It was some time before he noticed the paw prints in the mud. Though a couple of days old, they were clear and distinct, a set of large pug marks, without the characteristic toenail marks of the canine family. These were cat tracks, the spoor of a mountain lion, the lithe phantom of the mountains. They had come from the water's edge, and from here they disappeared in the duff that covered the path leading to the secluded valley below. Jason looked down upon the dense forest, untouched by man, eerily silent in the midday sun. For the first time he felt he really understood the faraway look that used to be in his father's eyes.

"Good-bye, Pop," he murmured. Then he turned back to await the litter that would return Darrel Houston's body to the ordinary world down the mountain.

12
It's All in the Genes

Jason Houston, twenty-four, bachelor's in biology, master's in organic chemistry, was working on his Ph.D. During '94, the previous year, he was engaged in research at the University of California at Berkeley to find the precise place in the brain in which instinct resides. He knew generally where in the brain this function took place (others before him had discovered that), but he wanted to know exactly what group of cells were responsible. He worked on mice.

In the early stages of his work, he zapped various parts of adult mice brains with a laser and checked to learn if their offspring would still possess the instinct to suckle their mothers. Of course they did. But he had to do that to eliminate one possible set of outcomes.

Later he took newborn mice, zapped one or another part of their brains and found that some lost the instinct. However, that occurred in mice with one part of the brain damaged as well as mice with a different part impaired. Clearly the instinctive action was involving more than one part of the brain.

In another experiment he discovered a strain of mice that recoiled when struck at by a snake on the other side of a clear screen. He discovered that they did not jump if he zapped one particular part of the brain he had targeted in his suckling experiments. He couldn't state any definite conclusions.

Then his grant money ran out. He was on the street, out of a job, and running out of cash. Either he found another research project or he went back to bartending, a job that had gotten him through graduate school. And, if he wanted a doctorate, he would need to switch the subject of his dissertation to something for which there was money.

He decided to try the DNA (deoxyribonucleic acid) mapping program at Stanford. Everybody knew about the program and everybody, it seemed, working on a doctorate wanted to get into it. He lucked out. Because of his expertise with a certain strain of mice, he was offered a chance to work with a group mapping mice DNA. Jason was happy about that because of his curiosity about how instinct is passed on to the next generation. He thought it had to be by the DNA of certain as yet unidentified genes.

He'd also pondered the question, how did the DNA get encoded with the information that told the cells in a fertilized egg to grow a collection of brain cells that, functioning together with others, told a mouse to suckle, or to jump, or to mate. The difficulty of figuring that out was captured in a cartoon that was pinned to the bulletin board in the coffee room of his wing. A psychiatrist was saying to a distraught woman who lay on the couch:

"Every human has 100 trillion body cells. Every cell, except red blood cells, has a nucleus. Every nucleus contains 46 chromosomes. Every chromosome contains genes. There are over 100,000 genes, all made up of DNA segments, telling the cells to do this or that. There are 3 billion code letters in a string of DNA. With that level of complexity in the human body, what makes you think you should have an orgasm every time?"

To the program director, he proposed, as the subject of his dissertation, to identify the specific gene or genes responsible for instinct, then the segment of DNA of that gene in which the code was located. His proposal was accepted. He had a lab to work in and money for the project's expenses, including a small salary for himself. He had a mentor, Dr. Richard LaPointe, the program director. He had an office. He had a computer. He had his own coffee cup. Life couldn't have been better. Well, not much better anyway.

Jason was on the same floor as a woman, Valerie Henricks, single, thirty-two, Ph.D. in human genetics. She worked on the Human Genome Mapping project and was under the direction of Dr. LaPointe, too. She was cool, very intelligent, hardworking, and meticulous in her work. LaPointe hired her because she was tall, slender, and beautiful. LaPointe was fourteen years older than she, and was married, with two children. LaPointe had managed to get in solid with those in government and academia who had the money and the author-ity to pick and chose project directors. Though he'd won no Nobel prizes, he had written several brilliant papers on genetic research. He was dictatorial, arbitrary, and abrupt, except with those he liked. He liked mostly beautiful women.

One fall day Jason was in a closet off the file room, looking for the chemical analysis for a mouse feed when he overheard a conversation between Henricks and LaPointe who had stepped into the supply room from the adjacent hallway, thinking the little used room was empty. They said too much before Jason realized they were arguing about their relation-ship and decided it was too late to let them know he was there. He stayed hunched over a file drawer and tried to ignore the two of them.

"Why can't you accept it? It's over, that's all." The woman

was trying to be calm, but her voice was strained.

"You haven't given me good reason. I want to know why. I want a rational explanation," insisted LaPointe.

"Why do I have to explain? You had no reason to believe this would go on indefinitely," answered Valerie, becoming exasperated.

"Because we were very close. You know we were very close, Valerie. I've risked a lot for the two of us. How do you expect us to work together if you can't provide a rational explanation?" There was an edge to the way he said that last remark.

She paused to take a deep breath. Jason couldn't see her face, but he sensed her gathering herself to respond.

"Oh, all right, Richard. If you must know. I've had a chance to review your entire profile. Bio, psychological, family history, IQ, medical—"

"DNA diagnosis, too, I suppose," said LaPointe. Jason envisioned the sneer with which he interrupted her.

"Yes, that, too. I've analyzed our two profiles and concluded that we couldn't be compatible in the long run." She could have said more. She could have said that her review of his genetic workup, especially a DNA pattern on one specific gene, had revealed a potential for criminal behavior. She had no evidence of any wrongdoing on his part, but the rest of his profile showed that he was definitely lacking in scruples.

"Well. That certainly is a rational explanation," said LaPointe, his retort buttered with sarcasm. He continued on, more in an admonishing tone, "I had hoped you had more feelings than that. I mean when you were in bed with—"

She interrupted. "Okay! Okay! So I'm not cut out to be the other woman! Is that good enough?"

LaPointe didn't answer. There was a pause. Jason wished he had made his presence known right away. This was more than embarrassing. This was ugly.

"Can I go now, Dr. LaPointe?" said Valerie.

"Yes, Dr. Henricks. You may go," answered LaPointe in a flat voice. They both went out the door and closed it behind them.

When Jason was sure they'd both left the room, he headed back to his office. Without the mouse feed formula.

The tape of the conversation ran repeatedly through his brain and kept catching at one point, the point where he learned that Henricks had access to LaPointe's entire profile. He assumed there was a profile on everyone, including the director. Jason had been required to submit a sample of his hair and some of his saliva to a lab technician, and to undergo a battery of written tests and questionnaires when he had reported for employment, but he understood that all that material would be kept confidential in his personnel file. After all, there were laws protecting the confidentiality of such information including genetic information.

"DNA diagnosis, too, I suppose," LaPointe had said.

Jason wondered if anyone was investigating his own genetic makeup. He was upset to think that someone might do so without his permission. And then have it reviewed by someone who presumably had no business doing so?

Hey, that's an invasion of privacy! thought Jason. *Sure, recording the DNA patterns of individuals is a routine practice. The military was the first to do it in a big way. It makes sense. What better way to identify a part of a body than to do a DNA comparison with the records of missing individuals? That sure beats the heck out of relying on dog tags. But diagnosing someone's genetic makeup without permission? The more he thought of it, the more upset he became. He decided to confront Dr. Henricks.*

He caught up with her just as she arrived at the large glass door of the foyer on her way out of the sandy-colored, four-storied building. He reached around her and shoved the crash bar, opening the door for her.

"Oh, thanks," she said, not really noticing who had done her the favor. Ordinarily she would have. Men didn't bother to open doors for women anymore.

"Dr. Henricks. Valerie. Could I speak to you for a moment?" said Jason, hurrying to get alongside her.

"What about?" she said, still walking ahead.

"Well, it's hard to explain," he said, taking her by the arm and leading her off to one side of the broad walkway, next to the trunk of a large live oak tree.

"Look," he said, avoiding her questioning gaze. "Look," he began again, this time looking her square in the eyes.

"I'm sorry, but I couldn't help overhearing your conversation with LaPointe in the supply room this afternoon."

"Oh?" She glanced away, embarrassed.

"You talked about a DNA diagnosis. What I want to know is, can anybody have access to another person's personal profile in this place? And has there been a DNA diagnosis on everybody that works here?"

"Why do you ask?" she said, defensively. Then, "Do you want to review somebody's?"

"No. I was told, when I came to work here, that kind of information was confidential. And nobody said anything about running a diagnostic on my genes. I just figured someone would have to ask my permission to do it."

"Oh," she said.

"Well?" he persisted.

"No. Your records are kept confidential. And there are no diagnoses done without proper authorization. The only reason I had access to Dr. LaPointe's is because he volunteered to have his profile included with the other volunteers who are involved in my project. I'm trying to correlate various human characteristics with DNA mapping information."

She turned to go. "Oh, damn," she said, looking around with an irritated look on her face. She was already upset to have the subject of her earlier argument come up again, and had just realized she didn't have a way home. She had ridden in with LaPointe, but he'd left without her.

"What's the matter?" asked Jason.

"Oh, nothing. I just don't have a ride home. That's all." She ran her fingers nervously through her long blonde hair, mentally listing the transportation options.

"I'll give you a ride," said Jason. He said it as if it was a decided fact.

"No. I'll find a way home."

"No. I insist. Besides, I owe you one, for eavesdropping."
She turned to look at him. He had a tentative smile on his
strong young face. It was an open face, without guile, and she
was bemused to notice how good looking he was, in a boyish
way.

"Okay," she said finally.

On the way to the parking lot where Jason had his pickup
truck, he could sense she was still distressed. They didn't say
much except when she asked how he liked working there. He
said fine, and explained he was making good progress on his
project. She was interested in his work and calmed down
somewhat as he explained it.

Traffic was heavy as they pulled out of the parking lot.
Valerie gave him directions to her apartment which was some
distance away, in San Carlos. After they struggled through the
traffic in Palo Alto for a while, they turned onto the offramp
to the freeway and headed north. In a few minutes they turned
off into San Carlos.

"Look, it's still early. Why don't I buy you a glass of wine
or something?" said Jason.

Valerie looked at Jason's friendly smile and said, "Why
not?"

They found a small restaurant/bar, parked the pickup, and
went inside. Halfway through a large glass of French
Colombard, Valerie was noticeably more relaxed. They talked
about their work. She was fascinated with the explanation of
his project to determine the code for instincts in mice. She
began to wonder if anyone was working on the genes wherein
human instinct resides.

While they talked, bent toward one another to be heard
over the background music, a hefty middle-aged man approached their booth. He wore a wrinkled sport jacket and a
loose flowered tie around the part of his anatomy where his
neck should have been. He swayed slightly and his voice was
thick as he leaned over their table and said to Valerie, "It's nice
to see two young people having a nice conversahtion, conver-

sation. People don't talk anymore, you know?"

"Yes, thank you," responded Valerie. She turned back to Jason, a quizzical look on her face.

The man picked up a cocktail napkin from their table and wiped his lips. He continued to stare at Valerie. "You two look very nice together. Are you married?"

She shook her head.

"No? Ohhhhh. Why not?" Now he was leaning over more, one pudgy hand flat on the table, the other fingering Valerie's wine glass. She was sliding sideways, toward the wall, the man's whiskey breath assaulting her nostrils.

Jason, sitting on the right of the booth, grasped the man's right wrist with one hand and rose up, a mask of cold anger on his face. "That's enough, buddy," he said as he removed the man's hand from the table with a slow but powerful motion.

Valerie wanted to say something to Jason, but stopped when she saw his look of determination. The drunk noticed it too and felt the surprising strength of his grip.

"Hey, okay. No offense. Sorry." He careened back to the bar and plunked himself down on a stool. He called for another drink.

Valerie and Jason observed as the bartender refused the man and offered to call a taxi to take him home. The disgruntled fellow wandered out the door, muttering to himself.

Valerie stared at Jason. Though his jaw was set, his visage was returning to normal. He gave her a tight smile, but there was no humor in it.

"Should we go?" said Valerie.

"No. We'll stay." He paused. "After all, like the man said, people don't talk enough anymore." The smile this time was genuine.

They stayed and ate dinner and talked more genetics.

In the weeks that followed, they kept in touch on his progress. She wanted him to tell her when he found the DNA chain that coded instinct so she could look for similarities in human DNA maps. They realized the process could take a long time, because Jason had to experiment by snipping out certain segments of DNA and implanting altered genes into mice eggs or sperm to see which alteration destroyed the suckling instincts. But there was more than purely scientific interest involved. They enjoyed one another's company. The two of them were intellectually well matched, in spite of their differences. He appeared to be somewhat easygoing, she was serious, intent. He carried his muscular frame erect; the color of his complexion spoke of his many outdoor interests; and he had a pleasant, though somewhat guarded, smile. She, on the other hand, was a bookworm, a cultured type, a serious scholar, but a good conversationalist. He felt a bit constrained because of her age and status, as compared to his own; she was attracted to his raw masculinity, nevermind his age.

The realization that they were more than just associates with common interests came upon them one spring day. In the South Bay area the arrival of spring meant sunny weather instead of fog and overcast. It meant the chirps and melodies of birds just up from South and Central America and intent on avian romance. It meant the bright green of new growth on the trees and shrubs. It meant the blossoming of sails on the waters north and south of the San Mateo bridge.

Jason and Valerie were eating bag lunches in the warmth of the courtyard of the laboratory building. Valerie noticed Jason had picked up some extra color on his face and arms over the weekend. She thought he looked particularly handsome. His recently bronzed forehead and cheekbones contrasted with the pallor that most of the Caucasian members of the office and laboratory carried through the winter and gave him a somewhat exotic look. He was glowing with vitality.

"You've been out in the sun," she said.

By the way she said it, he knew she approved. "Yeah. I was bike riding with some friends down near Santa Cruz."

"You look good. I didn't realize you were a bicycle rider. Were you with anyone else from the office?" That last question came without forethought, but stemmed from a sudden sense of jealousy that he had been with some girl.

"No, some fellas I went to college with." He didn't pick up on the thread of jealousy. He was just pleased she noticed him in a physical way.

He had always noticed her looks. She didn't attempt particularly to be attractive. She just couldn't help it. She was an eight plus without even trying. That day she wore a sky blue skirt and a white blouse with ruffled front that accentuated her bosom. Her pale eyes were more colorful behind the photo-sensitive glasses she wore, tinted blue now in the bright sun. The blond hair was pulled back in a ponytail, a thing she sometimes did when she hadn't taken time to do her hair properly in the morning. She was the type who can be tanned or pale, no matter, but her cheeks were slightly flushed now, blood rising with some sense of intimacy having been experienced.

"Tell me. What else do you do for recreation?" she asked. Strange as it may seem, after having spent several hours in one another's company, they had talked mainly of their work and their education, never about their personal likes and dislikes.

Jason ticked off a number of activities he enjoyed: mountain bike riding, hunting, fishing, rock climbing, jogging, and reading. He read just about anything in print, even cereal boxes. He elaborated some on his outdoor interests, but understated the degree of interest he had in hunting. Some people didn't appreciate the fact that a person could enjoy stalking and killing game animals.

"A real outdoor person, huh? Tell me more. Are your folks living around here?" she asked.

"Yes and no. My mom lives in Santa Rosa. My dad died a few years ago."

"What was your dad like? Was he like you?" she asked.

There was more to her line of questioning than simple curiosity. She was into genetic research because she had a powerful interest in genetically associated behavior. To her, DNA was the complete blueprint for each person. She seriously believed it would be possible to describe the physical, mental, and emotional makeup of anyone once the DNA codes were fully deciphered. Genetics was her religion. She believed it offered the key to virtually all of humankind's problems. Crime, overpopulation, ignorance, mental health, physical health, social justice, all were manageable if the genes of humans were fully understood and the science of human genetics applied wisely. Sure, genetic engineering of plants to improve food supplies was important, but the future of the world lay in the field of human genetics. The answers to questions were there, and with some imagination, the solutions to age old problems.

"My dad? Well, I guess I'm a lot like he was. He loved the outdoors, but didn't get out as much as I do. Too busy with his work, I guess. But he taught me backpacking and fishing. He was my Scoutmaster for a while when I was in Boy Scouts, so we did a lot of camping and stuff."

"What sort of personality did he have? Was he an ISFP?" she asked.

"A what?" said Jason.

"Oh, never mind. It's a psychology term. Ummm, was he a type A or B?" she pressed, leaning forward toward Jason, eyes alight with keen interest.

"Well, he was a private person, and…ahhh, I suppose he was a type B. If you really want a complete personality profile, I'd have to think about it," he said.

"Oh, I'm sorry, but you know, part of my work is assembling physical and personality profiles to compare with genetic data. I told you that someday I'll be able to determine the personality characteristics of people, before they are born, by interpretation of the DNA of the embryo. Right now I'm ready to do a new group of individuals. Would you like to be one of my subjects? I'd be happy to do a genetic workup on you." She was more animated than Jason had seen her before.

"No, I don't think so. I'd rather remain mysterious." He felt let down. Evidently her interest in him was more professional than he had thought.

She could see the change in his expression and realized her mistake. "Oh, I am sorry. I get carried away sometimes.

Forgive me."

She reached for the hand that rested on his knee and held it momentarily. Her eyes were pleading, her tone sincerely apologetic. "I *would* like to know more about you. But not as a research subject."

"That's okay," he said. "To tell the truth, I'd like to know more about you, too." At that moment she looked vulnerable and appealing. He looked deep into those pale blue eyes. She gazed back, unblinking. They connected.

In the days and evenings that followed, they saw a lot of one another. Casual stops for glasses of good California wines led to dinner dates. Dinner dates led to trips to The City for stageshows. Drives home led to excursions along the ocean shore. Excursions led to picnics on the beach and passionate embraces amongst the sand dunes. One bright Sunday afternoon, on their way home from the beach, they decided to spend the next weekend together at Lake Tahoe.

The following Monday morning, on the third floor where she had her office, Valerie was hurrying down the hallway for a meeting with some important government officials when she saw Jason approaching from the opposite direction.

"Hi, there," she said, as they both stopped in the hallway.

"I was just coming to get you to buy you a cup of coffee in the lounge," said Jason.

"Oh, I'm sorry. I have to get to a meeting right away. Can we get together for lunch?"

"Sure. When?" replied Jason.

"I'll come to your office. It may be a little late, okay?"

"Sure," was the reply. "Are you ready for this weekend?"

"Yes, I am," said Val with a grin. "By the way, don't you think it's time for you to submit to my personality workup before I get into trouble with you?" she said teasingly.

"No. I shall remain a man of mystery," responded Jason, good-naturedly.

Behind a louvered door next to where the two had stopped, stood LaPointe, quietly. As the footsteps of the two young people receded down the hall, he looked out into the hallway to confirm their identities.

About twelve-thirty Jason was bent over his desk trimming his fingernails when he noticed Val standing in his open doorway. "Hi. Ready to go?" he said, rising from his chair.

"Don't let me rush you," said the smiling woman. "Finish your manicure," she said, nodding to the paperclip bowl where Jason had been dropping his nail clippings.

"No. I'm done," he said.

She was staring at the glass bowl, a sober look on her face now. "It's amazing to realize that your entire body is developed according to instructions in your DNA, and that every cell, living or dead, contains that DNA. You are in your fingernails."

Jason put his arm around her and ushered her out the door.

Friday afternoon LaPointe came into Valerie's office. His commanding presence filled the room. "Here's the story on your mystery man," he said, his voice edged with sarcasm. He dropped a report on her desk.

Valerie looked up, her eyebrows drawn together with an unformed question. "What...?" LaPointe turned abruptly and left without furthur comment.

Val didn't want to look, but she couldn't help noticing the name in the identity block, "Jason B. Houston." She picked it up, gazed at the cover page momentarily, and threw it in her wastebasket.

Then she recovered it and looked it over. It was not quite complete, but it had all the usual information gleaned from the employment interview. A mini-genealogy, with grandparents and parents birthdates, living or not, cause of death of those deceased; health history; academic record; employment history; and other matters of record. It also had his personality test and a genetic workup. In spite of herself, she was drawn into studying every detail of the profile.

She was in a quandary. Had Jason volunteered to have a genetic workup or not? If not, should she tell him? There was information in the report that bothered her deeply. By default she came to a decision. She couldn't tell him until she sorted out her feelings about the revelations set forth in the report.

She drove herself home after work. She was thankful that Jason had left early to do some errands. On the way home, her emotions did battle with equally strong feelings about rational pairings of compatible individuals, feelings about family planning, about the future of the human race and her responsibilities as a scientist. Her emotions were losing.

Jason called about seven that evening. "I'm still planning to pick you up at seven-thirty tomorrow morning. Will you be ready?"

She begged off. Female problems. They just came on, in fact she wasn't feeling too well all afternoon.

"Oh," he said. The disappointment was clear even over the telephone. "Do you want to try to go somewhere Sunday?"

Better not plan on it. She'll talk to him Monday.

Monday morning, at eight-thirty when Valerie usually came to work, she walked into her office to find Jason standing by the window, lost in thought. He asked how she was feeling. She was noticeably cool.

"I'm so so. Look, I've got a lot of work to do today. Can we talk tomorrow?" she said.

Jason figured it was PMS, so left her to her work.

For the next four days Jason approached her at coffee break and lunch, and, except for an uneventful sack lunch in the courtyard where the conversation turned to their work, she was essentially unapproachable.

Friday, Jason could not accept this new sense of remoteness any longer. He strode into her office at noon and confronted Valerie. "Val? What's going on?"

"What do you mean?" she said, looking up from her desk.

"You. Me. What's going on?"

Valerie considered the young man who stood before her desk, his hands on his hips, his elbows out to the side, taking up as much space as he could. She had had time to sort out her feelings. She told him. "I've been thinking things over the past few days. I don't believe we should keep seeing one another.

We're not well matched after all."

"What do you mean? We get along fine," demanded Jason.

"You're action oriented. I'm more scholarly, more introspective. You're an outdoor person. I'm an indoor person. There's lots of reasons."

Jason, at a loss for words, just stared at Valerie. He didn't like the expression on her face. It was cold, remote, detached. His hands slipped to his sides, and he turned around to look out the window. All week long he had been plagued with suspicions, wondering what was wrong, but now he was wounded. His stomach churned.

Jason turned again. "There's more to it than that. What is it?"

Valerie was beginning to feel a little sick herself. "Jason, I just don't feel good about our relationship. I should feel good about it, but I don't."

"What have I done?" said Jason, his eyes conveying his distress.

"Nothing."

"What have I said?"

"Nothing. It's just not a good match."

Jason had a cold feeling, a sense of betrayal. He had been put down, dropped like a stale donut. His eyes wandered to her desk, as if there were an answer there, something he could show her to convince her she was mistaken. Instead he saw a report with his name on it. He picked it up. She grabbed for it, but was too late. He stepped back from the desk and opened the cover page. At a glance he could see what it was. He looked up at Valerie. Her face was flushed and her eyes had the look of a guilty child.

"You have my bio! Is that it!" Echoes of an overheard conversation bounded about in his brain.

"Not really. I...," she stammered.

"It is, isn't it?" Jason was angry now.

"Okay. It is. Partly."

"What's in here?" he said, waving the report.

Valerie tried to be calm, dispassionate. She sat up in her desk chair. "Well, for one there's your risk of heart attack. Your father died from that. And most of the men on your father's side died young, too. Your great-grandfather, your great-great-grandfather. You're an INFJ, an introverted, intuitive, feeling, judging type, too. I'm an introverted, sensing, thinking, judging type. Our personalities would clash eventually."

"And? And?" insisted Jason.

"And your genetic workup shows you have a dangerous tendency toward violence."

"What crap!" he fairly shouted.

"See?" said Valerie, recoiling into her chair.

Jason stood still, fuming. Then he cooled enough to say, "You're wrong about me. I don't get into fights. I never even played football in high school. I ran track and cross-country. There's no history of violence in my family. You asked about my dad? He was a quiet, sensitive man. Everybody says I'm just like him. You're wrong."

"Maybe it came from your mother's side. I don't know. All I know is it's in your genes."

Jason considered her for a long moment. "You're the one with the character flaw. You have no feelings. You've got a computer for a heart."

He stomped out of the office. A moment later he came back in. He threw the report onto her desk. "Here. I already know who I am. And another thing. I didn't give anyone permission to do a genetic workup on me. Did you do it?"

"No. I didn't. Someone gave it to me."

"So how do you know for sure it's my genetic analysis?" That was his parting shot. He stomped out again.

Valerie had a bad weekend. She called in sick Monday and Tuesday. She spent those two days cleaning her apartment and doing her laundry. She mopped and scrubbed with a vengeance. She showered both in the mornings and before she went to bed for a night of tossing and turning. She got up

Wednesday feeling as wretched as she had the previous Friday.

She went into work, arriving about ten o'clock. She went down the hall to the diagnostics lab and asked who had done the workup on Jason Houston.

"I did," said Ryan Kirby, one of her fellow researchers. "Why?"

"He tells me he didn't authorize it," replied Valerie.

"Dr. LaPointe authorized it."

Valerie hurried out the door and down the hall to the elevator. After arriving at the top floor, she strode purposefully into the director's office. His secretary was at her desk.

"I want to see Dr. LaPointe."

"He's not here. He's gone to a conference in France and won't be back for three weeks," said the pretty young woman. "Can I help you?"

"No, thank you," said Valerie, and left.

She went down to the floor where Jason's office was located. She stood outside for a few seconds, then opened the door and went inside. He wasn't there. Instead, one of the lab workers was sitting at his desk.

"Where's Jason?" she asked.

"Long gone. Dr. LaPointe told him last Friday afternoon his funding had been withdrawn, so he packed up and left. Some kind of bureaucratic shuffle I guess. LaPointe gave him only two days to tie up the loose ends. We both worked all weekend closing out the files and the lab experiments. I'm trying to digest the memo he left when he went."

"Where'd he go?"

"I don't know. He just said he was going on a lonnnnnng trip. Left yesterday afternoon."

Valerie found herself nervously tapping the desk top with the paperclip bowl and looked down. In it were the fingernail clippings she had seen Jason leave there several days ago. Murmuring a "Thanks," she walked out of the office, taking the bowl with her. When she got to her own office, she put the nail clippings into a container, labeled it "Jason," and put it into her desk drawer.

13
Natidin

The elevator opened into the main lobby of the Embassy East, the largest hotel near the new Denver airport. Some people still called it the new airport even though it had been in use for ten years, since 1995. Jason Houston stepped out of the elevator first, followed by a cluster of people who seemed to be together, but not with him. As he headed toward the main desk, he passed by the entrance to the casino where those trailing him turned in, laughing excitedly. He stopped momentarily and peered inside at the clientele. Most were playing slots or electronic poker machines. Those playing slots were not particularly aware of the novelty of the symbols on some of the flashing images, only the fact that some paid off and some didn't. The symbols were drawings of nudes in various poses instead of the old cherries or oranges. To hit the big jackpots of that crop of machines, one had to line up identical pictures of nudes on all three, or five, wheels. The biggest jackpots matched up pictures of men and women in apparent coitus. For those, the machines gave off a series of groans instead of the usual ringing of bells. The nudes had made their appearance about the same time most states legalized casino gambling. The hotel industry had been successful in Colorado in convincing the electorate that a casino, even a small one, was one of the basic facilities needed to attract the convention crowds. Restricted by state law, this one was tiny in relation to the big ones in Vegas.

Jason wasn't a gambler. He got no particular thrill from winning nor any perverse pleasure from losing. He might invest a few quarters in a slot machine before he left, but not this evening.

The man at the registration desk was a clean-cut young fellow with light brown shirt and a copper and maroon striped tie. "Yes, sir?"

"There's a Valerie Henricks scheduled to speak at the Human Genome Conference. Is she checked in here?" said Jason, pleasantly.

"Just a moment, sir. I'll check." The clerk tapped a few letters into his keyboard and answered, "Yes. Shall I ring her room for you?"

"Yes, please. Put it on the house phone on the end over there," said Jason, pointing toward a bank of phones on the opposite wall. He turned and walked to the phone, dodging passing hotel patrons as he went.

There was no answer in Valerie Henricks' room, so he hung up. Looking at his watch, he decided it was time to eat. The main restaurant was back up the lobby past the casino and the elevators. The waiting line was very short and Jason was seated at a table for two next to the windows that overlooked the interior courtyard. He gave only a glimpse at the elaborate landscaping with the subtly placed lighting in the courtyard. Instead, he scanned the room for a certain blonde head. After a few moments and a couple of close-but-not-quites, he spotted her. She and the three men with her filled all the chairs at a table several tables from his and over his right shoulder. They were engaged in conversation, each of them leaning forward to be heard over the buzz of the room, some occasionally gesturing with a piece of tableware as they ate their dinners.

He watched them for a while until his waitress appeared. He ordered his meal without hesitation. That was characteristic of him. Jason had no problem making decisions. "Chicken cordon-bleu, rice, salad with ranch dressing, and a glass of Chardonnay, please."

The waitress was a slender woman, about his own age, and was pleased to have a customer who didn't require her to go through the usual interrogation process to learn what he would have. Besides, he was good looking, though not as well dressed as some she was serving that evening. Still, in his tweed jacket with elbow patches, he looked more comfortable than the suits. No wedding ring, either. Probably a decent tipper. She gave him a warm smile. "Thank you, sir. I'll bring your wine right away." And she did.

After the wine arrived, Jason thought about what he'd say to Valerie. Earlier he had thought to just say hello, how are you, maybe we can get together sometime during the conference, I plan to sit in on your talk, maybe I'll see you afterwards. That sort of thing. Over the telephone he could be casual, confident. Now she was there in person, and in the company of others. He decided to just play it by ear.

He rose from his chair and turned toward Valerie's table. As he approached her, he thought her hair was a little longer and a bit unkempt. She apparently wore no makeup; not unusual, he recalled, but after ten years it appeared she needed it more than she used to.

He stopped at the corner of her table, between two of the men and said, "Hello." Valerie looked up, surprised, then smiled. Her eyes lit up with the unexpected pleasure of seeing Jason. Over the years she had come to consider the circumstances of their parting as an unfortunate mistake, one for which she still held lingering regrets. In the recesses of her mind, under the file labeled "Jason," she had constructed a scenario in which she and Jason would have a warm reunion, when she explained the nature of the mistake.

"Jason! Jason Houston!" She introduced him around the table and invited him to join them.

Jason could see they were in the middle of their meal. "No, thank you. I don't want to interrupt your dinner and mine will be coming over there in just a few minutes. I just wanted to say hello."

"Don't leave. At least let's get together after you've eaten," pleaded Valerie.

"Okay. How 'bout the lounge, in about an hour?"

"Fine! About seven-thirty. In the lounge," she said. She watched him as he returned to his table, then she went back into the conversation.

Jason sat down with his back toward Valerie's table and sipped his wine. *She's gone a bit to seed*, he thought. *Face looks a little thinner. She's still a good-looking woman, though.* The three men he had hardly noticed, but two were in their late fifties and the third, a straggly haired fellow with a ten o'clock shadow looked like a perpetual grad student. None appeared to have any kind of special relationship with her, he thought. *Hey, why should I care?* he said to himself. His dinner salad arrived and he carefully forked it into his mouth without noticing that it had blue cheese dressing.

At seven-thirty Jason strolled into the darkened lounge and looked around for Valerie. She was sitting in a booth against the right hand wall and was beckoning him to come over. He sat down opposite her and greeted her with a cautious, "Hi." She looked better in the dim light than she had earlier. Jason noticed she had put her hair up in a pony tail, like she used to wear it years before.

"You're looking good. How have you been?" he asked.

"Fine, thank you. You look like you've been taking good care of yourself," said Valerie.

"I noticed your name on the program, so thought I'd look you up. I see you're still at Palo Alto."

"Yes, still with the program. Where are you these days?" she said.

"Michigan State. I'm teaching at the vet school. Animal Behavior. I'm also doing some research. Still trying to find out how animals develop or lose instincts." They were interrupted by the waitress who took their drink orders, a beer for Jason, and a Margarita for Valerie.

Valerie glanced at his left hand and said, "You're not married?"

"No. Not now."

"What happened?" she said, lightly.

"She was killed. Auto accident. Three years ago next January." Jason's shoulders slumped a bit as the recollection of that tragedy popped into his mind.

"Oh, I'm sorry."

"That's okay. I'm over it."

"Any children?" asked Valerie.

"Had one. A girl. Same auto accident."

"Oh, dear," she said, putting a comforting hand on his.

The drinks arrived and they both sipped quietly from their glasses.

"How 'bout you?" said Jason, smiling reassuringly.

"No," she sat up a little straighter as she answered and tried unsuccessfully to sound cheerful. "I decided to be an independent career woman."

"Where's LaPointe these days?" Neither of them was having much luck picking good topics for discussion.

"He's gone. Got into a major hassle with the university over finances. He's teaching somewhere in the East," said Valerie. "The current director is a big, gruff, bear of a man, and he's a jewel to work with. That's Dr. Giannini, one of the fellows I introduced you to in the restaurant."

"Oh, yeah," said Jason.

They talked for a while about others who had been working at the Stanford project ten years before. She asked him about work at Michigan State University. They were careful to keep their conversation safe, impersonal; though Valerie thought once to bring up the subject of their breakup, but changed her mind. When they finished their drinks, Valerie explained that she had to go to her room to make some final preparations for her talk the next day and excused herself. In her room, she opened her notes and stared at them, unseeing, for half an hour. Finally she turned on the TV and lost herself in an old movie. It was *Dr. Zhivago*. She cried at the end.

In his room, Jason watched *Dr. Zhivago*, too, then tossed restlessly in his bed for an hour before he fell asleep.

The following day, on schedule, Valerie gave her presentation in one of the five rooms where talks were being given simultaneously. Except when attending the keynote speech and two others planned for the main meeting room, the six hundred or so attendees had to choose one among the five talks scheduled for each hourly session. The presentations were only given once, so the choices made were often those with the most interesting sounding titles or those given by individuals with big names in the field. The theme of the conference was "Applying Genetic Research: The Answer or the Question?" Valerie's topic was "Emulating the Messages of DNA." The room was about half full, about a hundred people.

Her talk consisted of still pictures displayed electronically on a large screen at the front of the room accompanied by her lengthy and sometimes highly technical comments. She assumed those present knew that the Human Genome Project had been completed for some time, at least the phase in which the order and makeup of the strands of billions of nucleotides, the basic building blocks of DNA that make up genes, were charted. She assumed everyone knew that the building blocks were called bases, and were of four types, adenine, thymine, guanine, and cytosine. Most of her presentation dealt with the recent activities of the research group she headed that was attempting to learn how DNA sent messages to the cells within which it was located. They had concluded that, with the proper stimulation, DNA gave directions for cells to develop into certain forms and to behave in specific ways in response to other stimuli.

Her group was trying to emulate the messages given out by DNA in hopes they could send the correct message to cells that may be malfunctioning due to having faulty DNA strands. To be able to do so opened up a whole new field of biogenetics, one in which human flaws such as schizophrenia, depression, heart disease, and a host of other disorders could be corrected.

She explained they had stimulated DNA segments in various ways, with low levels of electrical currents, with sound waves, magnetic forces, enzymes, heat, chemicals, and other ways, some in combination. She went on to describe how some had reacted in certain consistent ways. The term she used was "they resonated." By selecting genes known previously to be associated with certain genetically influenced diseases, and testing those genes from normal individuals, they had recorded a pattern of resonance which was considered "normal." They then attempted to duplicate that "normal" message, that particular resonance that gave the appropriate cells the "correct" message. So far they had been unsuccessful but were trying a new technique. A computer whiz on the team was trying to digitize the resonance output, figuring they could then cause a computer to spit it back out through some medium to treat defective cells.

At the end of her talk, she took questions from the audience. One wag asked if they had tried to set down the output of the DNA in the form of musical notes, to learn what tunes were being played. Valerie laughed and said they had and when played back on the computer it sounded like *The William Tell Overture*. That got a chuckle. Jason, in the back of the room, laughed along with the rest. After a couple of more questions, her time was up. The moderator announced a coffee break.

Jason intercepted her in the midst of some others who had more questions. Finally he got her aside.

"Let's go have a cup of coffee," he said.

"Okay, that sounds good," said Valerie, and they walked together to the coffee shop, skipping the coffee bar that was laid out for the conference attendees. *Be careful, girl. Be careful,* she said to herself. *Don't blow it.*

"What did you think of my presentation?" asked Valerie after the waitress had poured their coffees.

"Fascinating. Especially the part about computerizing the DNA messages," said Jason. "Just think, someday a computer will be programmed with the perfect human genome. Then just buzz a fertilized egg and out they come, zero defects. Wouldn't GM have loved to have something like that years ago."

Valerie studied him closely to see if he was being sarcastic. Or was he more perceptive than she had expected. Mainly though, she concluded, it was just a joke.

It was. Jason was trying to get this conversation off on a lighter note than the one the night before.

"It won't be that simple. We're having some other problems I didn't tell the audience. Some of these DNA segments we've considered to be "normal" have experienced changes in resonance when subjected to certain other stimuli. We discovered that by accident. We accidentally dropped an adrenaline-like substance into one sample we'd been testing and it resonated differently after that."

"Oh, really? What was that segment associated with?" asked Jason.

Valerie didn't answer at first. Then she said, "I think it's involved in instinct."

"No kidding!"

"Yes. It was the human counterpart to one you had identified in mice back in '95."

"Why did you decide to get into instincts?"

"I thought it was important. What you were doing. I thought it was important. I still do."

Jason measured that response along with her face and body language. She was blushing slightly. He just nodded.

"Something else you'd be interested in. The genetic code

of these altered segments was exactly the same as they were before. They didn't mutate. There was absolutely no difference in the base sequence mapped. They just resonated differently."

"Hmmm," said Jason. "Have you ever considered that the nucleotides, the bases, may not be the code letters but might be coded with some kind of messages themselves? Some kind of tiny, tiny, imprint too small for us to detect?"

"Yes. I have. If that's the case, we've got a long way to go before we unlock the mysteries of life."

"What'd you expect?"

"I don't know."

They sipped their coffees for several long moments, personal feelings displaced by the mysteries of DNA.

Jason spoke first. "Did you say that the substance that caused the change in resonance was like adrenaline?"

"Yes."

"You want to know a wild hypothesis?" said Jason.

"What?"

"Instincts are passed on to the progeny of a pair of parent animals by means of DNA that direct the formation of brain cells. The instincts are someway programmed into the DNA. Right?"

"Yes." Valerie sat up, intent on Jason's every word.

"Some of that DNA can be influenced to modify its resonance, its programs. Right?"

"Apparently," said Valerie.

"Supposing traumatic experiences in the parent can be recorded in its DNA and passed on to the progeny."

"Suppose. Okay."

"Then that would help explain how instincts were developed in animals. The fight or flight response. Maybe if behavior of animals is linked to humans, that could explain why some people behave as they do. They learned it from their parents, or grandparents, before they were born." Jason sat back in his chair, triumphant, his arms folded across his chest.

"That's a stretch."

"Yeah, I know," said Jason.

"You're beginning to sound like you have an explanation for evolution. Or reincarnation. You know, I was the Queen of England in a previous life." Valerie laughed.

"Don't laugh. If one of your ancestors saw the Queen of England get her head chopped off, you may have the memory locked away in your brain." Jason said with mock horror on his face.

"Mmmm. Maybe that's where those crazy dreams come from," said Valerie good-naturedly.

They paused and sipped some more on their coffees.

Finally Jason said, "You know, since you mention dreams, I have a couple of odd recurring dreams."

"What are they?"

"I dream of seeing faces, mustachioed faces usually, threatening me. It's always frightening."

"Many faces?"

"No. One at a time."

Valerie thought of schizophrenia. "Are you one of the mustachioed men?"

"No."

"Do you ever get overcome by these threatening faces; do you ever lose to them?"

"No. I always prevail."

"How?"

"Usually I shoot them. Sometimes I throw things or grapple with them."

"Do you kill them?" Valerie was serious now.

"I don't know. I think so."

The atmosphere thickened perceptibly. They were silent.

They were both thinking of the day at Stanford when she had stung him with the results of his DNA diagnosis.

"Jason, do you remember I once told you your DNA diagnosis showed a tendency toward violence?"

"Yes." His response was flat, unemotional.

"Well, after you left, I did another genetic workup on you. I, we, still had some material to work with. Fingernail clippings, actually. I found your pattern was within normal limits." That wasn't the entire story. Her later analysis had shown him to have a not abnormal, but very real, latent capacity for violence. In spite of herself, for quite a while she had found herself attracted to him, or his image, even more than before. "The results were different than the report I told you about. Someone had doctored the results of that first one." Valerie stopped to get his reaction.

"I see," he said. "Who?"

"LaPointe, I think."

"Hmmph"

"I'm sorry," said Valerie, with obvious concern. "I've been hoping for years to see you so I could tell you that."

"Hey, don't be sorry. That was a long time ago. Forget it." He forced a smile, then looked away.

They raised their cups to their lips and drained the dregs. Valerie tried to read his face, but couldn't.

"Oh, look what time it is," said Valerie. "It's nearly time for the special session in the main conference room. The President speaks in ten minutes."

They each dropped a couple of dollars on the table for the coffee and hurried out the doorway.

The place was nearly full of conventioneers, but Jason and Valerie found two seats together near the back. The room was arumble with shuffling bodies, moving chairs, and the tail ends of unfinished conversations. The lights, at first full on, dimmed perceptibly. The noise level diminished to a low murmur when the chairman at the head table asked the group to be quiet. Then he spoke into a handset. A huge screen behind the head table lit up and on it appeared the presidential seal of the President of the United States.

When the room was as quiet as could be expected, the chairman announced, "Ladies and gentlemen, the President of the United States."

The President's image appeared in perfect clarity. She was seated at her desk in the oval office.

"Thank you Chairman Fitzgerald. Good afternoon ladies and gentlemen. It is a pleasure to address such a distinguished group of scientists. I wish I were there to hear all the latest in the field of applied genetics, but am confident members of my science advisory panel will pass on to me the relevant information.

"My purpose in addressing you today is to emphasize the importance to the scientific community, especially those in the field of genetics, of the historic program being launched in October as a result of the National Health Management Act which I signed into law yesterday.

"As you are all aware, I'm sure, this act was a key plank in the platform on which I ran last year, and which was successfully carried through the Congress after weeks of debate. I and your elected representatives in the Congress heard the need of the people to move forward into the future, in control of our destiny as a leader of the world, to establish an enlightened health system so the women of this country can have the same opportunities to manage their lives as men have been able to do for millenniums past, and to allow society as a whole to avoid the tragedies that sometimes accompany unplanned pregnancies.

"The key to this historic program was the development of the drug, Natidin, which was created by some of you in the applied genetics community. By inoculating all of our female school children by the fifth grade and providing them with positive and infallible protection against unwanted pregnancies, we will make it possible for them to live to their full potential. And again due to the efforts of biogeneticists, by ingesting the drug Biopro, a woman will be able to regain her fertility at such time as she feels she is ready to conceive.

"As you also know, this system has been in use for several years in some other countries successfully, but not considered to be appropriate for use in this country until it had been thoroughly tested and proven to be infallible. Now we are ready to proceed. And due to America's preeminence in the medical and biogenetic fields, we will realize even greater benefits than our friends around the world have so far. Of course we will share with them our successes. For example, there will no longer be any reason for the tragedies of thousands of drug babies, teenage mothers with children they can not care for, babies with cystic fibrosis, Down's syndrome, spina bifida, and many other disabling physical problems.

"Coupled with this program, under the Act, female immigrants to this country will be given the same protection as they would have received if they had been born in this country, if they have not already received such in their place of birth. In time, most, if not all the countries of the world will have similar programs. The United Nations Security Council and the General Assembly have already passed resolutions to extend this program over the entire globe. By this means, not only will all citizens of the world enjoy the same benefits as this country in regards to the creation of new beings, but one of the greatest threats to the earth's environment, overpopulation, will be alleviated.

"With your continued dedication to science and the efforts of other leaders throughout the nation and the world, we will see the end of poverty, most disease, and a host of other afflictions that have plagued humankind since time immemorial. In the months to come, I hope to enjoy your support for this new program, this milestone in human evolution.

"Thank you and good evening."

There was generally polite applause, with some of the audience particularly enthusiastic. Valerie was one of those. She carried on well past the peak of the applause, turning to Jason with a wide smile of pleasure. Jason thought he hadn't seen such radiance since his wife had told him she had just learned she was pregnant. They rose from their seats and walked to the hallway, away from the crowd.

"What do think, Jason. Isn't that wonderful?"

"I don't know." The facts of the program weren't news. The idea had been kicked around for a few years, and the debates during the past elections had shed more light on its chances for becoming reality. There had been a number of feature articles in the news magazines. That Congress was about to make it into law was well known. The President hadn't said that a provision in the law made it possible for parents to decline to have their daughters inoculated. Most people weren't aware of that. Or that the act contained language which penalized states by withholding federal money if the percentage of schoolgirls getting inoculated fell below 95%. The act was also vague about whether children in the higher grades who had already had the contraceptive inserts that provided up to five years protection would be exempted from the "catch up" provisions.

"It's disturbing to me. Scary. There's all kinds of room for abuse," continued Jason.

"Like what?"

"Well, for instance, the next step could be that to get access to Biopro, the neutralizer, people would have to meet some eligibility requirements."

"What's so bad about that?" said Valerie.

"Who's to set the standards?"

"That shouldn't be too hard to do. You're a student of nature. In nature, circumstances separate the fit from the unfit. We humans have removed most of nature's filtering systems. And look at the mess we're in. Overpopulation, serious antisocial behavior, great numbers of unproductive individuals. We humans have reached the point where we have to institute some substitute systems for natural selection."

"Yeah, I've heard that argument before. I still think nature has a way of taking care of things," said Jason.

"So how does nature ensure the right humans get together to have sound genetic stock? What's the mechanism?"

"The mechanism? It used to be called love, I think."

Valerie turned away for a moment, then back again, saying softly, "You may be right. I know you were right about that once before."

Jason met her inquiring gaze. His hazel eyes began to sparkle with unfathomed mysteries.

Valerie saw sand dunes and beaches, waves breaking on

the shore, seagulls, and moonlight. She wanted to get close to him, even closer than bodies can get. She wanted to work her way into his psyche, emotionally rub up against that animal presence she knew existed within him. "Let's go up to my room and talk this over some more," she said, huskily.

Jason just nodded. They rose and walked together to the elevators.

On the way up to the sixth floor, Valerie murmurred into his ear, so the other passengers wouldn't hear, "I got inoculated two years ago with Natidin. I just thought you ought to know." Jason nodded again and squeezed her hand in his.

"Of course, I know how to get my hands on some Biopro, if I needed to," she said, with an impish smile, as she led him by the hand to her room.

14
The Last Voyage of Atlantis

The space shuttle *Atlantis* was fifty-three hours and twenty minutes into its last mission. It alone of the several shuttles built over the years was spaceworthy, having been rebuilt for the final series of missions. This was the last. There was no new generation of spacecraft to take its place. The manned space program was to be put on indefinite hold.

Most of the scientific experiments that would benefit from zero gravity had been completed. What remaining experiments were needed could be conducted in unmanned craft. Communication satellites and other hardware could be put up cheaper by rockets as had been the case most of the time anyway. The reliability of the latest generation of satellites was outstanding. The need to maintain a capability to retrieve or repair satellites in space was not cost effective. There was no compelling need for a space station now. There were enough unmanned craft probing space or orbiting Earth now to provide science with data to analyze for years. The pressing needs for the country in these times was to devote its resources to the problems of environmental degradation, health care, care of the elderly, and the overwhelming need for law and order.

In addition, the nation's worldwide obligations were placing demands on the budget that couldn't be met without cutting back on the non-essential programs. At least that was what some of the testimony before Congress had said.

After much debate, Congress had decided that the space program was low priority. The shuttle program was being phased out. Decades ago the nation had been looking up and outward, to space. There seemed to be enough money to take care of the needs here at home while literally expanding the horizons. But after going out there in space for a while and looking back at that magnificent blue and white orb called Earth, even most of the astronauts began to realize where the needs were. Back there, on the ground and in that thin film of gases known as the atmosphere, the earth was suffering from pollution, overpopulation, overconsumption, and social strife. In the United States, the need for correction of the nation's ills became more and more important. Funds were needed for new alternative energy systems to replace those dependent on the dwindling supplies of oil. And smaller cities and towns needed to be rebuilt to accommodate the resettlement of the unmanageable urban populations, a program that began at the beginning of the twenty-first century. A sizable chunk of the budget went to pay for expanded police forces and prison systems. Not counting the armed forces (navy, army, air force, etc.), one in every two hundred were in law enforcement. "After all," said the majority of the country, "wasn't the first priority of government to provide for the security of its citizens? And health care? And care of the elderly?"

In addition, the U.S., along with the other industrial

nations, had accepted a responsibility for the welfare of the rest of the world several years before. Moral issues aside, it was a matter of enlightened self-interest. If the standard of living of the huge populations of the developing nations were not brought up to some acceptable level, they would ravage their own countries, consuming all the trees for energy or trade products with all the attendant adverse consequences, polluting the atmosphere with inefficient industrial practices, and then many migrating to the wealthier countries, thereby burdening them with increased social costs.

And there *was* a moral issue. The wealthy countries could not countenance starvation in the "have not" nations, or rampant disease, or filthy rivers, not since television had brought those images into the living rooms of the "have" nations. Furthermore, the United Nations had finally risen to the challenge of pacifying the world, putting down civil wars and armed incursions into neighboring countries. To top it all off, one of the sales pitches used to sell the Natidin program to the underdeveloped countries was the promise that the industrial nations would share their wealth with them. The cost to the world of all of this was enormous, but affordable if those countries with the resources put their priorities in order.

The commander of the *Atlantis* was in a somber mood. Colonel James Williamson was the commander of the space shuttle orbiter, an airplanelike craft one hundred twenty-two feet long with a seventy-eight-foot wingspan. He sat in his seat on the flight deck, forward of the relatively small upper crew quarters. That and the similarly small lower crew quarters were forward of the vast cargo bay. Below them all were fuel and storage tanks. A tall vertical stabilizer perched on the rear of the craft, though it had no function now while they were in space.

He was somber because space travel was his profession. He had trained to be a pilot of spacecraft. He had hoped to help build the first really big space station. He had hoped to be one of the first persons to get back to the moon since Cernan and

Schmitt had done it in 1972, and to be the first black man to do so. Instead, after this mission, he would either be desk bound or be retrained to fly military aircraft such as fighter bombers or transports. He thought he was psychologically better equipped to be a fighter pilot, though he was getting old for that. He was thirty-eight.

The others of the crew were not particularly close to Colonel Williamson. Not because he was black, but because he was comfortable being the detached, somewhat haughty, authoritarian military officer that his father had been. In spite of their having trained together for many months, the others kept their distance pretty much, calling him Colonel, and asking his permission to do things the other commanders had delegated readily to their crews in the past.

That is except for Major Fran Katowski, the pilot. She was a blithe spirit, unintimidated by anything, and damn good at operating the orbiter, almost as good as Williamson. She knew what needed to be done and she did it. The commander sometimes feigned a show of irritation at her independence, but privately he was happy to have her backing him up with her competence. It meant he had a little less of a burden to carry. He was acutely aware of the responsibilities of being the commander of a space shuttle mission.

This mission, as had been the case most of the time in the past, had several objectives. One was to launch one large satellite that had been specially designed to fit into the huge cargo bay of the shuttle for launching once the shuttle reached its orbit. Steve Johanson, a civilian mission specialist who was a mechanical genius, was primarily responsible for that task. With the assistance of Ron Baker, another civilian mission specialist, they had accomplished that at MET (Mission Elapsed Time) twenty hours thirty minutes, right on schedule.

Another objective was a targeting task with a new particle beam generator, a classified job that was mostly done automatically with some occasional attention from Johanson.

The other primary objective, the one that was being carried out by the other two members of the crew, was an experiment with fertilized human eggs. Navy Commander Sandra Samuels, who also doubled as the flight surgeon, was in charge of that experiment, aided by Maria Torres, a high-school science teacher from Los Angeles. As far as Williamson was concerned, Torres was along as a PR move, a tactic by NASA officials to keep public pressure on Congress to keep funding the shuttle program. There had been a lot of publicity about her selection in the waning days of the budget battles.

Torres had just finished broadcasting a simple zero-gravity experiment, live, to thousands of high-school science classes. He had to admit she presented a good image. She was bright and articulate and pretty enough to be in the movies. Black hair, sparkling brown eyes, slim, and athletic. Williamson was happily married, though, and made sure their relationship was strictly professional. He had uneasy feelings about her for other reasons. Though he wasn't superstitious, he couldn't help remembering what happened when a previous woman teacher was taken on a mission. It was the *Challenger* and it had blown up shortly after launch.

Samuels was a serious, gawky-looking woman, married, and, at thirty-two, older than Torres by two years. At first Williamson had felt those two women were a bit too young for the responsibilities involved, but after training with them for several months, he felt otherwise. Maria had been particularly resourceful in the survival training phase. The others on the crew were in their thirties, too, but the commander had never had any doubts about them at any time.

The human egg experiment was intriguing to Williamson. Not because of the medical or biogenetic aspects of it, but because of the sociological nature of the matter. Here on the spacecraft were five human eggs from the same individual, fertilized by sperm from another individual, in a semiliquid medium, floating around in five separate chambers, with a bank of instruments monitoring all the relevant environmental factors, and being observed at regular intervals through optical instruments by either Samuels or Torres. The purpose, as explained to the rest of the crew, was to learn what effect, if any, there would be on the eggs due to prolonged weightlessness. The possible effects of particular interest were effects on the genetic makeup of the fertilized eggs, including any possible changes in what was referred to as the "resonance" of certain segments of DNA. At regular intervals Samuels would remove one of the eggs to extract some DNA, and run the DNA tests. There were two undisturbed eggs, actually embryos by now, left.

The reason behind this experiment was to learn whether humans could conceive and develop babies while in prolonged space flight without experiencing genetic transformation in the embryos.

Before the launch, Maria had asked Sandra where the eggs came from, who were the parents.

"That's classified. Even I'm not supposed to know," Sandra had said.

"But you do know."

"Yes."

"If I'm helping to care for some peoples' children, I'd like to know," said Maria with a straight face.

"Are you kidding me? You know they won't be viable after we complete the experiment. Have you been reading those old articles on abortion?"

"No, I'm kidding a bit, but I am curious. Come on, Sandra, tell me."

The two women had grown very close during their period of training together and shared many confidences. Sandra felt better about sharing some secrets than keeping them to herself. "Okay. If I technically don't know who the 'parents' are, I can't tell you, can I?"

"That's right."

"Okay. The eggs are from a friend of mine who is the director of this research project at Stanford. Her name is Henricks. The sperm comes from someone she selected because of the quality of his genes, she said. The man's name is Houston."

Williamson, his lanky frame folded into his cockpit seat, contemplated his crew. *All in all, a pretty good crew*, he thought. "I'd sail around the world with them," he said to himself, smiling at his private joke.

Ron and Steve were on the lower deck, preparing a meal for the entire crew, rehydrating some of the dried food before heating it. Floating next to one another they looked like brothers, both in blue shorts and gray T-shirts, light brown hair, muscular six-footers. The differences were that Ron had a mustache and Steve was wearing mukluks instead of going barefoot.

Samuels was on the upper deck, looking into Katowski's mouth. The pilot was floating upside down, partially curled into a tuck position while the flight surgeon used a small flashlight to peer at the roof of her mouth. Both appeared to have attractive hairdos, their hair all puffed out from their heads in the zero-gravity state.

"Looks okay to me today, Fran," said Samuels.

She called down to the two cooks. "Hey, you guys, don't overheat the food this time. Fran doesn't want to burn her mouth again."

"Okay, Doc," answered Steve. "Maybe she should try the Powerbars. That's what real pilots eat."

Williamson heard that and smiled, in spite of himself. He did like the snack bars the crew had brought along. He had learned to appreciate the flavor and convenience of candy bars on the four previous missions he had made in the shuttles. Actually the entire crew enjoyed them.

"Hey, Maria! Wake up," called Ron. "Lunch time."

Maria, napping in a compartment attached to a bulkhead, opened her eyes and pulled the sleeping sack away from her head. She was groggy and momentarily confused. She had been dreaming that mission control in Houston was calling them to tell them to water the eggs in the five chambers so they wouldn't die. She had dreamt the communicator from Houston was named Houston and he was frantic. The last thing he said was "Maria! Wake up!"

They all picked comfortable locations and ate off the trays of food. The food was nutritious if not particularly tasty. There was no fresh fruit or vegetables because the orbiter had no refrigerator. The trays were attached by Velcro to whatever was convenient, and the crew used knives and forks. It took a bit of getting used to when swallowing in a weightless state, but they managed all right. Fluids they drank from containers with a straw. They had all seen the pictures of previous astronauts sipping from globules of floating liquid, such as orange juice, but Williamson wouldn't allow that in his ship. "I don't want any of that stuff breaking up and floating around to foul up the equipment in here," he had said.

After eating, some read mission-related materials, though Ron was reading a detective novel. Williamson was looking out one of the windows on the top of the crew quarters, which, because the orbiter was inverted now, offered the best view of Earth, technically below them, but like an illusion in a fun house, it appeared to be above. He scrutinized the massive globe, dark since they were now on the opposite side from the sun. He could tell where the land masses were because of the lights of the biggest cities and because of the dim light of the quarter moon above them.

They were in a circular orbit, at an angle to the equator, 300 miles up, and traveling at over Mach twenty-five. As the orbiter shot through space, it appeared the Earth was rotating much faster than it actually was. They were traveling from west to east and would see several sunrises in a twenty-four-hour period, but each one was special to Williamson. They were nearing the "terminator," the edge between the dark side and sunlit side. Williamson looked out ahead to see with whom he was about to share the dawn. There was mostly ocean in view. On this orbit they should be passing over the coastline of Vietnam about now. He figured they would be crossing over the Solomons about dawn, only a few minutes away. Once again he looked forward to the moment when the magnificent blue and white planet would reveal itself in all its glory.

The radio crackled to life. "*Atlantis*, this is Mission Control. Urgent!"

The commander flicked a switch. "This is *Atlantis*."

"*Atlantis*, we have an emergency. An asteroid has been spotted about 3,000 miles, now 2,000 miles, up and headed for impact in your area of view. It's vector will cause it to impact off the east coast of China. You should be able to see it between azimuth 320 and 50 soon."

"How big is it? What's it's velocity?"

"It's…it's about six kilometers in diameter, moving at, what?" There was a barrage of excited voices in the background. The communicator continued, "It's moving at 30 K per second…Oh, my god! This is the big one!"

The crew stared at Williamson. Most knew what that meant. Maria didn't. "What's that all about, Colonel? Are we going to see something?"

Katowski was the first to answer. Her face was blanched. "You bet we are."

Maria looked at Williamson.

"Quiet!" he shouted. "Houston, what's the estimate till impact?"

"About two minutes."

"You better take care of yourselves down there," said Williamson.

"No, you stay on the line. Maybe you can help us down here." There was silence for a few seconds. Then Houston, "Can you see it yet?"

"Negative," said Katowski and Steve, their faces at the windows.

"Negative on the monitors," said Ron.

"Negative," repeated Williamson. Then, "Houston, that's bigger than the one we studied in class, you know."

"We know."

"How long do we stay up here?"

"As long as possible."

There was dead silence in the orbiter cabin.

"Houston? Call our families?" said Williamson, his voice

cracking.

"No time, Skipper."

Long moments passed without comment. Maria looked from one crew member to another, but said nothing. She had never seen such concern in people's faces in her life.

"In case this doesn't all work out, *Atlantis*, good luck," said Mission Control.

"You, too," said Williamson.

They waited.

Like a gigantic shooting star, a flash of brilliant fire shot toward Earth, headed for an area off the coast of China. The burning missile trailed a tremendous tail of bright sparks, lighting up the surface of the land and water below it in the five brief seconds before it smashed into the earth seventy miles off the coast of Taiwan.

Immediately, a blizzard of static filled the airways. "Houston Control! Houston Control!" called Williamson. There was no response. He glanced at the orbiter's chronometers. Unconsciously his mind was composing a report to enter into his log. "At 0330, 5 April 2007, local time; 1930, 6 April, Greenwich time, an asteroid approximately six kilometers in diameter collided with the earth off the coast of Taiwan."

At the instant of impact, a fireball blossomed out in all directions, continuing to grow till it reached the outer limits of the atmosphere, over one hundred miles. With the energy of 175 million megatons of TNT, the explosion caused by the errant asteroid vaporized everything in a ninety-mile radius, including much of the island of Taiwan. Seismic shock waves shot out in all directions, traveling seventy times faster than the speed of sound, rattling every molecule of the earth's crust with force a million times greater than the San Francisco earthquake of 1906. No one heard the roar from the approaching shock wave until it was upon them. The ground bucked and heaved, tossing buildings, cars, and trains into the air like chess pieces fly when a knee hits the table. Power stations fell apart immediately. Japan's several nuclear plants ruptured into hundreds of pieces, spewing radioactivity into the air. A plane landing at Beijing's airport in the predawn lost track of the runway when the lights went out and smashed into the rolling ground of the approach area, killing all eight hundred on board. The office buildings of downtown Manila disappeared in a cloud of dust. Australia's famous Ayer's Rock split completely in two at the same time several hundred vacationers were shaken awake in the nearby campgrounds like they were on a giant oscillator. Singapore's business district collapsed into the heretofore cleanest streets of the world. Hong Kong's thriving urban metropolis crumbled only a few moments before the rickety bamboo and wooden tenements at the fringes fell apart, carrying hundreds of thousands to their deaths. As the shock waves rocketed inland to the hills and mountains, tremendous rock slides and massive rotational earth movements were triggered, some covering entire towns. Cattle, deer, and elephants were knocked off their feet and bounced around like children in a blanket-toss. In the other direction, to the east, coconut trees on low-lying atolls swayed and snapped, coconuts bombarding the sand below; the condos on Maui fell balconies first into the ocean, crushing the sunbathers on the beaches below.

The shock wave hit San Francisco an instant before it hit Los Angeles. All the vaunted designs of the world's most sophisticated structural engineers failed at once. The Golden Gate shuddered under the load of hundreds of automobiles and snapped, the two elegant towers holding the suspension cables falling into the straits below. The famed landmark, the TransAmerica building, disappeared into a pile of rubble like it had been targeted for demolition in an urban renewal project. All the rest of the skyscrapers in LA and The City went at the same time. Auburn and Bullards' Bar Dams in Northern California and dozens of others were shattered, spilling their stored waters into the canyons and valleys below.

The shock waves shot across the North American continent with the same results as in Singapore, Tokyo, Honolulu, San Francisco, and San Jose. Salt Lake City, Las Vegas,

Denver and Dallas disappeared into great clouds of dust. Hoover and Glen Canyon Dams split and the huge reservoirs behind them gushed down the Colorado. Chicago, Toronto, New York, Atlanta, and Washington were shaken apart like collections of dominos. The Sears Towers, Rockefeller Center, the Metropolitan Museum of Art, the Smithsonians, and the Capitol disintegrated. The sounds of the dying were lost in the thunder of the collapsing structures in the cities. Only in the suburbs, where the one- and two-story frame structures housed those who happened to be home that time of day, was the shrieking and screaming of the injured heard, for those buildings fell apart, too.

Central and South America caught the deadly blow of the first shock waves a bit later than North America, but the results were even worse. Construction design and methods were generally of lower quality, especially in the residential areas. And the slides in the mountainous areas caught up to even those out in the open. A village of indigenous people deep in the Amazon country froze in horror as the friendly and protective trees of the jungle fell upon them and their huts. A second series of shock waves hit South America about the same time as the first. These second ones were those from the opposite direction, from the east. After ripping through Asia, Africa, and Europe these crossed under the Atlantic Ocean and smacked Brazil first, then doubled the destruction of those waves coming from the west.

Asia, Africa, and Europe suffered the same as the Americas, except it was evening or night on most of those continents, so most people were home, not in the high-rise office buildings. That only meant they died among family not among coworkers.

All of that in less than fifteen minutes.

On the heels of the shock waves, a gigantic tsunami over three miles high rolled out in all directions, traveling hundreds of miles an hour, inundating Taiwan, Japan, the Korean peninsula, the Philippines, coastal China, Vietnam, and Malaysia, all in the predawn hours. It roared across Laos, Cambodia, and Thailand with a sound like a million typhoons all rolled into one and onto the Bay of Bengal. Then onto southern India, sloshing over the Western Ghats into the Arabian Sea. The cities of Arabia, Ethiopia, the Sudan, and Egypt melted like children's sand models on the seashore.

Toward the north, the monstrous wave ripped through the Yellow Sea, over the Korean peninsula, into Manchuria, taking Shanghai, Nanjing, Tiajin, Beijing, Seoul, Pyongyang, and Shenyang. It raced through the Sea of Japan, over Japan, Sakhalin, and the Kamchatka peninsula to the Bering Sea. It wiped the Aleutian chain clean and smashed into and onto Alaska, whacking up against the mighty mountains of southwestern Alaska, and sloshing over into the Yukon River drainage and over Nunivak Island, Kotzebue, and the Bering Strait into the Arctic Ocean. The massive tsunami, still not spent, continued on across the polar ice pack onto Greenland.

Southeast, the awesome wave swept over the tallest peaks of the Owen Stanleys in New Guinea and smashed into the north coast of Australia, surging across the deserts and emptying into the Great Australian Bight. It rolled over the Great Barrier Reef, wiping out Brisbane and all the coastal cities of eastern Australia, covering the Solomons, New Hebrides, and Fijis. It clobbered New Zealand, covering even the top of Mount Cook.

To the east, the monumental wall of water raced across the Pacific, diminished not a bit by the islands of Micronesia, including Bikini atoll, once equated with man's most outstanding example of destructive force. Not even Hawaii's majestic volcanic peaks of Mauna Loa and Muana Kea were able to surmount the devastating froth of the angry ocean. The wave charged onward, sliding over Baja and the Sea of Cortez, splashing over the Sierra Madres and down into the Rio Grande River drainage. The peaks of Pococatepetl and Orizaba poked up through the turbulence as the wave fell into the Gulf of Mexico and crossed the Gulf to Florida. The immensity rolled over Guatemala, Honduras, and all of Central America to the Caribbean where it widened out and drowned Cuba,

Hispaniola, and Puerto Rico.

Before the wave hit Mexico, it collided with the coast of Oregon and California, inundating the Coastal Ranges, the Willamette, Sacramento, and Central Valleys, storming up the Sierra Nevadas and slopping down into the Great Basin through the passes named after the trailblazers of 150 years before. Los Angeles, already a huge basin of rubble from the shock waves, disappeared as the mammoth breaker roared on, devastating Arizona, New Mexico, and Texas, joining the downwash from the Sierra Madres into the Gulf.

The coastal towns of South America were washed away within minutes of one another, as the prodigious roller smashed the shore and surged up the slopes of the Andes. The great cordillera of the southern hemisphere bowed its back and stopped the onslaught from the Pacific. But the tip, Patagonia, was washed over.

The energy of the tsunami, diminished by its battle with the continents, still was sufficient to cause the wash into the Caribbean to swell out into the Atlantic, raking the east coast of North America all the way to Newfoundland.

It also plunged onward to the west coast of Africa and Europe. The flow onto the coasts coursed inward over the lowlands, joined by the companion wave from over the Arctic Ocean, and pounded Morocco, Portugal, France, Norway, and the British Isles. Paris, London, Amsterdam, Lisbon, Casablanca, and Gibraltar all succumbed to a combination of a terrestrial shakedown and a marine mugging.

The last of the initial wave, only a few hundred feet tall, but still with the power of a thousand sons of Neptune, passed into the Mediterranean, and roared over Sardinia, most of Sicily, and up against the boot of Italy, drowning all before it up to midslope of the Apennines. The north coast of Africa suffered also, being devastated by the right flank of the watery legion. Greece, Albania, and Turkey were pounded and plastered by the frothy seas, as though in a gargantuan agitator.

Though the interiors of the North and South American continents along with the vast interiors of Eurasia and Africa escaped the effects of the immense tsunami, destruction was near absolute due to the initial shock waves and the following aftershocks which reverberated over the globe like the vibrations of a huge gong struck by a giant hammer.

The crew of the *Atlantis* had seen the shock waves that bent the sky below them in concentric rings and they saw the tsunami spread out from the point of impact as they raced it across the Pacific. But what held them frozen in awe as they peered out the windows, heads bunched together like inquisitive apes, was the fireball. The energy of the impact created a mushroom of fire, many times hotter than the sun, that grew larger and larger, billowing up into the atmosphere, as the *Atlantis* sped westward. The fireball expanded much more slowly than the speed of the shock waves, and soon it fell behind the position of the speeding orbiter, such that the crew could see it only in the screens of the television monitors that covered that portion of the viewshed.

The crew backed away from the windows and stared at the monitors until even the great fireball was out of sight over the western horizon. Maria had a bubble of bright red blood on her forehead. In the scramble to see, she had been bumped into some fixed object but hadn't noticed it. Sandra was the first to notice the wound.

"Maria! You're bleeding!"

"Where?"

"On the forehead!" Ron answered for Sandra, stabilizing her with an outstretched arm.

"Hold still," said Sandra. "I'll get a bandage." She pulled herself to the companionway between the upper and lower crew compartments.

Maria reached up to touch her forehead. "No! Don't touch it. You'll have blood floating around in here," said Ron. He found a Kleenex in a container and dabbed at her cut. When he pulled the tissue away, he examined her forehead. "It's not much. Here, hold this on it," he said.

Ron's hand was shaking visibly when he handed the tissue to Maria. Hers, accepting the offered help, was shaking, too.

They were all trembling and pale, except Williamson. He was not his normal coloration, but he was not trembling. And he alone, with the exception of Katowski, knew the full import of what had happened. Those two had more reason than any of the others to be filled with fear.

The commander had already begun to consider their future course of action. To do that he had to have a clear head, had to have his emotions under control. He would not, did not tremble. Not visibly, at least.

"My god! It...What...Geez!" said Katowski.

Steve swallowed hard. He was having trouble talking.

"Colonel?" said Maria. "How does that affect us?"

"It's not so much us, Maria. It's how does it affect them," said Ron, pointing over his head toward the blue and white sphere.

"Colonel?" said Maria again.

"It's them *and* us," answered Williamson. "We covered this kind of thing in a class a couple of years ago. If Houston was correct about the size of that thing, it's the worst catastrophe in sixty-five million years."

"What's happening down there?" said Maria, still holding the tissue against her forehead.

"Wait till Sandra gets back up here, then I'll explain," answered Williamson.

Samuels, the doctor, was already returning to the upper compartment, using one arm to propel herself and holding a first-aid kit in the other. She gently pulled Maria's hand from the wound and began to tend to it. "Go ahead, Jim, I'm listening." The formality of the command structure had disappeared along with part of Taiwan so far as Samuels was concerned. Williamson noticed it and was pleased somehow.

"Scientists believe an asteroid or a comet hit the earth sometime about sixty-five million years ago and caused the extinction of the dinosaurs, and probably other animals and plants as well. One the size of the one back there could do that. The fireball that was building will spread out over the upper level of the atmosphere with tremendous heat, maybe enough to ignite the flammable material below. The material in the fireball along with other material spewed out of newly activated volcanoes and from burning forests will envelope the globe with smoke and other particles and prevent sunlight from reaching the ground. No photosynthesis will occur for several months. Earthquakes will continue for months, maybe years. Tsunamis will be triggered repeatedly from the quakes. That one giant tsunami we saw down there will probably have wiped out everything along the coasts, maybe inland for quite a ways." He paused to let that sink in.

"What about Los Angeles? What will happen to it?" asked Maria, thinking about her home, her school, her parents.

"Probably gone," said Katowski.

"How 'bout Cape Canaveral?" said Maria. She was the only one asking questions. The others were afraid of the answers, if they didn't know already.

Williamson didn't respond at first. Instead he put one big hand over his eyes and massaged his temples with thumb and forefinger. His wife and two children were waiting near the Kennedy Space Center at Cape Canaveral for his return.

He was praying that they were safe, somehow. "I don't know."

"Let's call and find out," said Steve, finding his voice.

"Okay. Fran?"

"Roger, Jim," answered Katowski, pulling herself to her pilot's seat and flicking a switch.

"Kennedy, this is *Atlantis*. Kennedy, this is *Atlantis*." There was some background crackle through the speakers but less than before.

"I hear something, Jim, don't you?" said the pilot.

They all listened for several seconds.

"I don't think that's a transmission. I think it's still the result of the explosion back there," said Ron. Ron knew radio communication very well.

"Try Houston Control again."

"Okay, Jim."

"Houston, Houston. This is *Atlantis*."

Static.

"Houston, Houston. This is *Atlantis*."

They tried White Sands. They tried the tracking station at Canberra. They tried the Goddard Space Flight Center. They tried alternative frequencies. No response.

"We'll try again later," said Williamson. The quakes probably cut their power. Maybe they'll get back on the air with the backup power supplies after a bit. Let's check the monitors forward."

The crew adjusted the television monitors. Some went back to the windows. There was nothing ahead but blue ocean overlain with brush strokes of white clouds. Everything looked normal. Maybe the thing back there wasn't really that serious. Maybe the problem with communications was only due to electromagnetic interference. Maybe the good old Earth could take a licking and keep on ticking.

The orbiter continued on over the Pacific, headed for the west coast of South America. Ron Baker and Katowski kept trying the communications systems. The interchange between the shuttle and selected satellites was okay. They scanned the commercial bands, military and government frequencies. Nothing. The contact with the ground was negative, null, nil, non-existent. The audible signs of life they had unconsciously come to depend upon were absent. Dead. They turned on the high resolution cameras to record the scene below.

After about thirty minutes they were approaching the coast, somewhere near Santiago, Chile. They had outraced the tsunami, but the initial shock wave had preceded them. Where the sky over the land was clear, they could see clouds of dust at ground level. From Santiago there were small black columns of smoke mixed in with the dust.

"What do you suppose those clouds of smoke are from?" said Steve.

"Fires? From the quake effects?" offered Maria.

"Probably," said Williamson.

They were approaching the Andes. The peaks were covered with snow. Puffs of white, like clouds or fog, could be seen below the peaks, avalanches caused by the continuing aftershocks. Over the pampas and on to Buenos Aires. The silence of the spacecraft was marred only by the background hush of the radio speakers. The black smoke columns rising from Buenos Aires were more noticeable.

"What do you think, Jim?" said Sandra, the flight surgeon. "What do you think the injury toll is down there?"

"What do *you* think?" answered Williamson. His mind was racing ahead. They were now floating over the Atlantic, headed toward Africa. In a while they would be in the vicinity of the spreading fireball. Even if they were to pass 200 miles above it, would its heat damage or destroy them? Should he burn more fuel to gain some more altitude? He decided to wait and see.

"Fran, prepare to go manual. Steve, position yourself so you can keep track of the temperature of the skin. In about fifteen minutes were going to pass close to the fireball. I want to be ready to go up higher if we need to escape the heat," ordered the commander.

"Roger."

"Roger."

The stark white orbiter glided silently over the Atlantic and toward the terminator, the edge between day and night. The time over ocean seemed interminable, till the outline of the Dark Continent was revealed in the faint moonlight. They would cross over southern Africa. Normally there would be the glow of city lights, especially along the coast this time of the night, about nine o'clock, but there were no city lights to be seen. Instead there were flickers of dim light, obscured apparently by shifting smoke.

Atlantis slipped by the coast of Mozambique. Above the Indian Ocean and then over a darkened India. Ahead of them and to the right, at azimuth eighty degrees, was a pronounced glow on the horizon. Williamson observed the phenomenon for a few minutes, then said, "Stand down. We're going to miss it." The shuttle passed on through a China night toward a dawn over Manchuria, leaving the growing fireball behind once again.

Over the Kamchatka peninsula, Fran turned to Williamson and said, "Jim, shouldn't we be thinking about landing before that fireball covers the entire globe?"

"I've been thinking about that, too. That wasn't a problem we covered in class, but I was curious enough to give it serious thought when we studied asteroids back then. I believe the greatest danger is being on the ground when the fireball is overhead. We should wait till it cools down. Besides, depending on where we are when we head down, we could end up passing right through the worst of the heat, if we didn't wait for it to cool down."

"Won't we...oh, oh. I was going to say won't we be in big trouble trying to land on a runway in smoke and clouds, but I realize there probably aren't any runways safe enough to land on if it were clear."

"Right."

"So we'll have to bail out?"

"Wrong."

"So it's a water landing?"

"Right."

"Where?"

"Let's discuss it with the rest of the crew," said the commander, unfolding his frame from his cockpit seat.

"Listen up everybody. We've got a few problems to work out. We can't land at Edwards or Kennedy or on any other runway because they'll be broken up due to earthquakes. It's too dangerous to bail out into those conditions down there. We have to make a water landing. We can't land until the fireball dissipates 'cause it might cook us on the ground. We won't have good visibility, maybe none at all, so we have to pick a body of water that's big enough for a long glide path."

"How 'bout the ocean off Canaveral?" said Ron.

"I don't think so," said Williamson. "There'll be huge tsunamis for a long, long time. We'd get creamed in the ocean. Besides, there's another consideration. We have to think about how to survive after we land. There may be nothing there, no food, no fresh water, no people in the vicinity."

"We've got food and water on board, Colonel, ahh, Jim. Won't that do?" said Ron.

"No. I'm talking weeks, months. We need to be somewhere in the interior where there are food supplies that haven't been destroyed. And where there's fresh water."

"We'll need a lot more than that, eventually," offered Samuels. "Why don't we identify all the criteria needed to select a landing location?"

"Good idea," said Katowski.

"Jim," said Steve, "tell us more about what to expect down there before we decide on the criteria."

"Okay. As I said earlier, we can expect a layer of smoke and dust to blanket the globe. It's April. There won't be crops to harvest in the northern hemisphere, except far to the south. What's there now will probably burn anyway. The sun will be blocked for several months, maybe longer. There will be no new crops for at least a year. The livestock will probably be destroyed. Most large wild animals, too. The best source of food in the short term will be stockpiles in granaries or warehouses that survive the fires."

"Supermarkets, too," interrupted Maria.

"Yes, supermarkets, too. We also have to think of water supplies. We can probably filter freshwater from some lakes, but I'm not sure about streams or rivers. Most'll be highly polluted."

"There's another thing from that class that I remember now, Jim," said Katowski. "The heat of the fireball is supposed to be great enough to create acid ions from the atmosphere and from the sulfur in the earth's mantle which is pulled up in the explosion. That'll result in acid rain. Much worse than ever in the past."

"You're right. In fact the weather will be a lot different than we've ever seen. Lightening storms, tornadoes, hurricanes, whatever. We'll have to contend with the whole gamut, probably. Also, the smoke and dust blanket will bring winter back to the entire planet, at least until the stuff settles out."

The spacecraft was approaching northern Alaska. Ron had a glimpse of it in a monitor. He said, "The Eskimos live in the ice and snow. We can, too."

"Sure, if you know how to spear seals," said Katowski, taking a friendly swipe at his head.

"Well, seriously, we're going to have to use all the survival skills we've learned," said Williamson.

"Jim, do you think they'll be many survivors down there?" Samuels looked stricken as she posed the question.

Williamson knew she had a husband down in Houston, a doctor, too. Jim knew him. Ben was a brilliant man, but sort of an absent minded professor type. He was more or less dependent on his wife for the day to day decisions. "I don't know. I suspect there'll be many survivors initially, but when the food supplies run down, I don't know."

Williamson looked around at the others. Katowski, single, but with a steady male friend in Houston. Torres, single, no current romantic attachments. Baker, married, no children, wife in Houston, too. Johanson, married, one child, a son. Wife and son waiting for him to land in Florida. Or they were waiting, once. Like Williamson's family.

Katowski recognized the despair in the faces of her fellow crew members. "There'll be survivors. Who knows for sure what'll happen down there. Maybe the tsunamis won't reach all the coastal areas. People can ride out earthquakes, especially if they're in the open. Besides, there's a number of underground facilities left over from the Cold War. Especially around Washington. Room and food for thousands when they were in a state of readiness. Old missile silos, too. Probably same sort of thing in other developed countries. Heck, even some private companies have safe hideaways."

"But how many of those are still in use? And how many people had time to get to them before the first shock wave hit them?" said Samuels.

"Yes, and how many will hold together under the effects of repeated mega-earthquakes?" added Steve.

Williamson could see morale was breaking down. "Okay, okay. We can't do anything for the people down below right now. But we can look out for one another. There'll be people down there. I guarantee it. Like Fran says, people out in the open could survive the earthquakes. They can get shelter from the fireball. There are crews in submarines. They'll make it, too."

"Yeah," chipped in Katowski. "There's farmers in root cellars and the Mormons in Utah. They're prepared for this sort of thing. At least they have food stored."

That helped some, but Samuels still was downcast. Maria noticed a couple of tiny droplets of liquid in the space between her and Samuels, spherical tear drops hovering before her like lost souls in a bigger universe. They floated away when Samuels waved at them with the back of one hand. Maria placed a comforting arm around her friend's shoulder.

"Okay, everybody," said Williamson. "Back to the immediate problem. Criteria. We need a big body of water without mountains around it so we can establish a long, flat, glide path. It can't be a reservoir because a dam failure will let the water out. It should be away from the coastline so that it will be unaffected by the big tsunami created by the impact. It should be in an English-speaking country, preferably the U.S. The water should be free of pollution if possible. There should be cities or towns nearby so we scrounge for food. It should be in a climate that'll support agriculture once the sky clears up. What else?"

"Jim, shouldn't it be near a major city so we have access to all the equipment and supplies available in a city?" asked Samuels. "There'll be more food to salvage in a city."

Katowski answered first. "I don't agree. We need to think about the social aspects of this. You know how much civil unrest there's been in the cities, even with the beefed up security forces. There might be more food but there'll be more survivors, too. And there won't be any government left. Can you imagine the fighting and killing over food that'll occur in the cities?"

Williamson looked around at the rest. "Maria, what do you think?"

Maria lived in Los Angeles. She rode a bus to school in which sat two armed guards to protect the passengers from one another. There were armed guards in the hallways of her school. After dark, the gangs and the security forces waged war in parts of the city. One reason she applied for the NASA assignment was to get away from Los Angeles. "I agree with Fran," she said.

"Steve? Ron?"

"Why don't we shoot for a place near small towns, with the ability to travel to bigger places after things settle down a bit?" said Steve. "But I don't think we want to head for the wilderness."

"I agree," added Ron.

"Sandra?" Williamson met her eyes and she nodded.

"Okay. Anymore criteria?" No one answered.

"I have a couple more," said Williamson. "Preferably someone on the crew should be familiar with the area. And another thing. The earth's rotation may have been affected by the asteroid. We'll have to use the original coordinates of our landing zone for the automatic systems to bring us down there. We'll get no help from the ground I'm afraid, so we'll depend on satellites to determine our position. If the earth has moved we'll need some leeway to locate the lake. That's why we need a very big lake, one that's oriented with our likely approach."

After a few moments, Katowski said, "Anybody got any objections to landing in Lake Superior?"

"Why there?" asked Ron.

"Because it meets the criteria, and I got my undergraduate degree from Lake Superior State University. I'm familiar with the eastern end, near Sault Ste. Marie."

"I was thinking of Lake Superior, too," said Williamson. "There's another advantage. From there we could travel long distances over water. Even down the Mississippi, with a little effort at the west end, or down the St. Lawrence to the east and eventually to the ocean," added Williamson.

"You're talking major exploration, Jim," said Steve.

"Maybe it won't be us that does the exploration. Maybe it'll be our descendants," responded Williamson.

Maria studied the tall black pilot. She saw him in an entirely different light than ever before. She thought of the two embryos floating in their protective capsules. "Are we talking about starting civilization all over again?"

"Maybe."

15
The Frank W. Dixon

For sixty-six and a half hours the *Atlantis* cruised over Earth. What had once been an extraordinarily beautiful blue planet had gradually changed colors. First the intense glow of the spreading fireball crept out over Eurasia, Australia, the Pacific, and Africa. It appeared to lose some of its energy as it reached halfway around the globe, to the Americas. Then, as the fireball cooled, the Earth was enveloped by a dirty gray cloud. The orbiter crossed over the fiery mantle several times without overheating, so maintained its original altitude.

Before the fireball reached the United States, the ship had passed over the northern edge of the Gulf of Mexico. The cameras recorded the scene below. When Ron played the videodisk back on the monitors, they saw both Houston and

Kennedy awash in water that reflected the sunlight much like the Gulf itself. It was a hard thing to watch. They played the disc over several times trying to detect signs of life till Williamson told them to shut the monitor off. When next they passed over the area, the fireball had blanketed the entire globe. They could see nothing below.

While they floated along, marking time, waiting for the heat energy of the fireball to dissipate, the crew readied themselves for a landing. Katowski had computed the time at which the retrorockets would be fired to slow the ship, allowing it to slip out of orbit and enter the atmosphere. It had to be at a precise time on a specific orbital path so the long glide would bring them to Earth on Lake Superior, at the eastern end. The entire cockpit and crew quarters had been checked to be sure there were no loose articles that might cause trouble when gravity began to take effect. The cargo bay had been secured earlier in the flight, following the launching of the satellite. The crew had donned their G-suits in case the heavier air upon reentry caused them to experience more than the usual three Gs of force. All other usual preparations had been completed. The crew members were buckled into their positions.

"Switch to manual control," directed Williamson.

"Roger," answered Katowski. "On manual."

"Test elevons." Katowski operated some controls and checked instruments. "Elevons are go."

"Adjust roll 180 degrees."

"Roger." By firing the maneuvering rocket engines in brief pulses, the orbiter was rotated until the bottom of the craft faced the surface of the Earth. An interminable time passed as they waited for the countdown to begin.

"Ignition minus 20 minutes," said Katowski.

"Minus 10 minutes."

"Minus 5 minutes."

"Minus 1 minute."

"Minus 30 seconds, 29, 28, 27, 26, 25, 24, 23, 22, 21, 20, 19, 18, 17, 16, 15, 14, 13, 12, 11, 10, 9, 8, 7, 6, 5, 4, 3, 2, 1, ignition." Both engines burned for the prescribed length of time, then went off automatically. The orbiter had been slowed to about 16,000 miles per hour. They had begun their descent. The ship was over Indonesia.

They lost all view of space above them as they entered the atmosphere, the dirty cloud obscuring everything.

Williamson and Katowski scanned the instruments, talking to one another in low, clipped tones.

The descent continued.

Steve tapped his fingers nervously. Others prayed. The effect of gravity began to be felt. They were conscious of their cheeks sagging, their feet beginning to press against the deck. Soon the weight of their bodies forced them deeper into their seats. Deeper. Deeper. Three Gs, three point one, three point two. The counter pressure features of their G-suits were triggered automatically. The G forces peaked at three point five.

Katowski spoke up loudly, so the rest of the crew could hear. "We'll be landing in about twenty minutes. Fasten your seatbelts and bring your seatbacks into the upright position. In the unlikely event of a water landing, your seat cushion is a flotation device."

Williamson looked at her and his lips turned up in a thin smile.

"Jim, we'll be okay," said Katowski.

"I hope so. I've done this a few times in the simulator, but there's nothing like the real thing, Baby," the echo of an old cola commercial popping into his mind as he responded to his fellow pilot.

The orbiter's velocity had slowed considerably, and the G force was well under three. They were at about 100,000 feet but couldn't be sure. The effects of the extra drag caused by the saturated air of the upper atmosphere was difficult to estimate. They couldn't tell how much more than normal the drag had pulled them down. The radar altimeter was giving suspicious readings. The barometric altimeter couldn't be relied upon, either. There wasn't much they could do about it until, or if, they saw the ground, or in this case, the water, hopefully.

The dust and smoke was beginning to take on a different look. With the craft's horizontal attitude, Williamson and Katowski couldn't see much through the windshield. They had to rely on the TV cameras. Like a submarine diving into the ocean, the orbiter was sinking toward utter darkness.

"There's something down there!" shouted Ron.

"What?" said Williamson. He wanted to shout, too, but didn't.

"It's uniform...I think it's...it's water!"

"Speed?" said Williamson, both hands gripping the controls, eye's glued to the windshield.

"220."

"Attitude?"

"Go. Everything go," answered Katowski.

Gradually, slowly, the view below and ahead became more clear. They were over water. A long dark outline sprinkled with flickering lights appeared out of the gloom dead ahead.

"Land at twelve o'clock! Clear water at two o'clock!" called Katowski. She looked desperately at Williamson.

He was already making a right turn, *Like flying a brick*, he thought.

There was more open water ahead now that he had completed his turn. The deck was coming up fast. He should extend the glide path. He started to, then saw a dimly lit shoreline out before him in that direction, too. He quickly flared the nose up to slow their speed, then let the big ship down.

They hit the lake surface at 200 knots, wheels up. The slick skin of the orbiter slid across the water like a giant speed boat. The big spacecraft bounced some and shuddered in the chop of the waves. The speed diminished. The hull mushed down into the embrace of cold, cold Lake Superior, just short of the entrance of the St. Mary's River, the outlet of the big lake.

"Superior!" shouted Ron.

"Thank you," said Williamson. "Katowski, where the hell

are we?"

"White Fish Bay, I think. The St. Mary's River would be just ahead. The wind and current should take us right down into the Soo Locks."

"Is that dangerous?" asked Williamson, his face barely visible in the darkened cockpit.

"Shouldn't be…Although the locks may have been broken open by quakes. If they are, we could be in for a ride. Could also get carried over the rapids. Same thing only bumpier."

"Looks like it'll take a while to float out of this bay. You see any need to abandon ship before we hit the locks? We'd have time, if we need to do that," said Williamson. He looked out the side of the cockpit windows. The shoreline to the right, to the south, was clear, but the land behind it was breathing smoke. The wind was pushing the smoke to the southeast, and the flicker of flames could be seen on the ground. Scanning the visible horizon, he and Katowski could see the entire landscape was on fire. Johanson and Samuels, seated behind them, could see the fires, too.

"I think we're better off to stay with the orbiter, like we planned. We'll drift up to shore someplace ahead, I'm sure. I think it'll be tough enough to make out around here without leaving all the good stuff in this ship behind." said Katowski. "Hey, this thing is floating just fine."

"Yup. Just like they said it would," said Williamson. "Crew, you can stand up for a few minutes. Get your sea legs, but hold on to something. The swells are making it bumpy. We're headed for town, but we won't be there for a while."

Baker and Torres joined the others, the entire crew crowding the cockpit to look out the windows, their faces a mixture of relief and anxiety. It took them all a few minutes to realize that what little light there was to see by was mainly from the fires on the shoreline.

"What time is it?" asked Williamson.

"Mission elapsed time 122 hours 30 minutes."

"What time local time?"

"Ten-thirty, eastern standard time," answered Katowski.

Two hours elapsed before the tall tail fin of the orbiter passed by the wreckage of the bridges that had once connected Sault Ste. Marie, (the Soo), Michigan, with Sault Ste. Marie, Ontario, Canada. Like Jaws, the mythical shark, the spaceship had slipped quietly into the canal upstream of the Soo Locks, the multiple locks that stepped down the twenty-one feet from Lake Superior to the river below and bypassed the Falls of St. Mary, Le Sault de Sainte Marie. If anyone had been watching from shore, they might have seen the silvery white apparition in the flickering firelight of the two cities. But no one was watching.

Gradually the speed of the floating spacecraft had been increasing after it entered the ship canal. Faster and faster it headed downstream, rudderless. The wind pushed against the tail fin and turned it around, nose upstream. There was a thump and a scraping noise as it contacted a concrete seawall along the canal.

"Geez, I don't like this flying backwards business," said Katowski. "We're going pretty fast. Either we're headed for the rapids or the gates of the locks are open."

The metal orbiter scraped the side of the canal again. One wing caught on something and the current swung the ship around again so it pointed downstream. The speed increased. Suddenly the spacecraft entered a lock, the water from the lake above rushing in a roaring torrent through the broken gates. The *Atlantis* sped down the long canal and popped through the lower gates into the turbulence of the lower St. Mary's River. In a few minutes the flow smoothed out. The river was quiet again. The *Atlantis* passed between the twin cities as the river widened out. The crew had given no thought to trying to snag something as they passed through the narrows. For the time being, they were just along for the ride.

Onward, carried by the current, sometimes nose first, sometimes tail first, the spacecraft followed the ship channel. The crew could make out little along the shores on either side. Baker tried scanning the maritime radio frequencies. Once he heard a faint voice saying, "Anyone, Anyone, this is the

George Peacock. This is the *George Peacock.* We're aground off Copper Harbor. Repeat, we're aground off Copper Harbor. Anyone, Anyone."

The *Atlantis* couldn't transmit on that frequency, so they listened as the message grew fainter and fainter.

Williamson told Steve to break out the Powerbars, the first food they had eaten in twelve hours.

About six hours after shooting through the locks, Katowski saw a large object ahead, higher than the land on shore, odd shaped, like a tall blocky house. The nose of the *Atlantis* was pointing just to the left of it.

Easily, gently, but with the great force of the following current, the orbiter slid up against the object, between it and the shore. The nose of the craft was lifted upward. A groaning and grinding noise accompanied the motion. Then the noise ceased.

"We've gone aground," said Katowski.

"What the hell is that next to us?" asked Baker.

"Get out and see," said Williamson.

"Who? Me?" said Baker.

"Yes. This is as far as we're going tonight. Open the hatch and see what it is."

Baker and Johanson went down into the lower crew quarters and opened a hatch on the side opposite the strange object. The two men were immediately surrounded by the pungent odor of wood smoke. A gravelly bank along the shore held up the left side of the spacecraft. Beyond the shoreline, small tongues of fire licked away at the fallen logs and at the bases of still-standing trees. The top of the bank was only a few feet lower than the hatch opening, and with a powerful flashlight, Johanson could see it was close enough to jump to. Both men were in their flight suits, having taken off the G-suits shortly after landing.

Baker jumped cautiously down to the ground. As he landed, almost crumpling to his knees, he stirred up some ashes, but there was no fire under his feet. There was no grass or bushes either, just the crunchy feeling of cooked duff.

Johanson stood in the hatchway with a light while Baker explored the surroundings with another. The air was oppressive and heavy with smoke and they had to fight to keep from coughing. Walking past the nose of the *Atlantis*, he played his light on the strange object next door. It was several times longer than the *Atlantis,* appeared to be made of metal, and the top edge, which was about even with the top of the spacecraft, was surmounted with a railing. It was some kind of ship and it was listed slightly toward the river. He returned to the orbiter and reported his findings.

"It's a freighter, I bet," offered Katowski.

Williamson nodded and said, "Let's go check it out."

"I'll go," said Katowski.

"No. You stay here. Keep the hatch closed and the support systems active. I mean keep the air conditioning system going. The air's not good out there."

"Want to wear a space suit, Jim? It'll provide some protection from the smoke," said Samuels.

"Too bulky, and we don't need 'em," said Baker.

Williamson and Baker went outside and scrambled along the shoreline, dodging the hotspots while inspecting the ship. When they neared the bow, they could see lights above them, coming from the windows of the cabins under the wheelhouse; a long extension ladder was planted in the shallows of the shoreline, its upper end leaning against the railing along the deck. A knocking noise, something like a wooden mallet against steel, came from just behind the wheelhouse.

"Hello the boat!" hollered Williamson. The knocking stopped. "Hello the boat!"

"This ain't no boat! This is a ship! The *Frank W. Dixon*! Who the hell are you?" came a voice from up on deck.

"This is Colonel James Williamson of the space shuttle *Atlantis*!"

"Sure you are! And when I'm not a deckhand on this ship, I'm Sandy Claus!" Williamson and Baker exchanged glances.

"Can we come aboard?" called Williamson.

"Just a minute and I'll get the Captain."

In a few minutes, two heads popped over the side, looking down at the space travelers, who stood transfixed by the spotlights of the two sailors. A different voice asked, "Who did you say you were?"

"I said I'm Colonel Williamson of the space shuttle *Atlantis*."

"The hell you say."

"Look back there near the stern, on your port side," said Baker. "What do think that is?"

"Go look," said the one to the deckhand, who did as he was directed.

After a few minutes, he came back at a trot. "It sure as hell is a space shuttle, or an airplane with little wings. I think it's a space shuttle."

That's how the crew of the *Atlantis* met the crew of the *Frank W. Dixon*, grounded on St. Joseph Island, where the St. Mary's River widens out just south of Neebish Island, in the St. Lawrence—Great Lakes Waterway.

16
Survival 101

The *Frank W. Dixon*, Great Lakes freighter, 730 feet long and 75 feet wide, a self-unloader bound for Montreal, had been stopped well short of its destination. Having been the winner in the annual race to be the first to get up into Lake Superior after the spring breakup, the *Dixon* had arrived in Duluth April 1, taken on a load of wheat grown in America's breadbasket, and steamed east to the Soo Locks.

While the heavily laden ship rested, leviathan like, in the Poe Lock, the devastating shock waves from the asteroid's collision with the Earth passed through without warning. It demolished all the fixed structures in the area, snapping the outlet gates and causing the water backed up behind the gates to gush out into the river below.

The *Dixon* first bounced around like a toy boat in a bathtub, was then shot down the lock, through the gates, and into the St. Mary's. It took agonizing minutes for the giant screws to generate enough speed relative to the water to recover steerage. Just as the huge vessel was lined out properly, a great wave created by the quakes pushed the ship off course. Aftershock after aftershock created new waves. The *Dixon*'s captain struggled for control, finally losing it twenty-five miles downstream and running aground to port on St. Joseph Island, a sparsely settled, wooded island, twelve by twenty miles in size and part of Ontario, Canada. The captain was lucky. Most of the other vessels in the Great Lakes that day were sunk by the battering of the horrendous chop.

Two days later the fireball, spreading in all directions, reached the Sault Ste. Marie area, first baking then igniting the forests and towns in the vicinity. The ship's radio had received a confusing message about the coming holocaust and was advised to take shelter. Several of the crew earlier had either been off ship at the locks or thought to seek safety on dry land after the grounding and had left the stranded ship. The captain, first mate, cook, and eight other crew members remained. The two ship's officers were American, the cook Filipino, four crew members American, two Canadian, and two Portuguese. They rode out the firestorm below decks, spraying water on themselves and the superstructure over them to protect them from the heat.

The ship's paint was blistered and burned, the hatch covers damaged, and several windows broken. The captain and his remaining crew survived, unnerved, but intact. The only casualties were the slightly burned hands of two crewmen.

The generators were operable, with plenty of diesel fuel on board, including that for the engines. They still had lights, water, and most of their equipment, including lifeboats and a motor launch. The men of the *Dixon* were making repairs when the *Atlantis* drifted up beside it.

The crew of the *Atlantis* scrambled up the ladder and aboard the huge freighter, Williamson first and Katowski last, after making sure the orbiter was secured to a long line cast over from the deck of its neighbor. Walking past the 250-foot long, trusslike apparatus used for unloading that extended sternward from the forecastle at the bow, they were ushered into the messroom in the aft superstructure by the ship's captain, who waited until all the visitors were seated before he introduced himself. "I'm Captain Clinton McGrady. This is Arthur Carlson, first mate," he said, indicating a thin, gray-haired fellow standing next to him. Both men had the rough, weather-beaten faces of lifelong sailors. McGrady, younger and stockier than the first mate and with a black, brushy mustache, introduced the others of the crew, all grimy and unshaven, like the ship's officers.

The *Atlantis* crew, in bright blue flight suits, introduced themselves in turn, shaking hands all around.

"How's about telling us how you ended up here in the ship channel?" said McGrady, a quizzical yet friendly look upon his face.

Williamson explained the entire story, interrupted only a few times for questions, and ended with an offer to be of assistance to the crew of the *Dixon*. His manner was matter-of-fact, unemotional, professional, as an astronaut should be.

Carlson snorted at the thought that the *Atlantis* could be of help to the ship's company. "Looks like maybe you're the ones that need help the most."

"I'd say we're all in need of help," said Katowski. "What say we help one another?"

"I think you're right, miss. Let's get comfortable and talk it over. Bring us some coffee," said McGrady to Luis, the cook.

Around the crowded table, the discussion made clear the gravity of the situation. One of the first items deliberated over was food. They learned that the *Dixon* was supplied with food intended to last about thirty days, under normal circum-stances, for the original number of personnel on board. The

Atlantis had only enough food for its crew for twelve more days, including the "contingency pantry." Not much considering they had no prospects of growing more food for several months, maybe a year. Not much indeed. Except that the holds of the *Dixon* carried thousands of tons of wheat.

"We can survive a long time with all that wheat," said Maria. "I can make a half dozen different foods with wheat alone. Luis, I bet you have some sourdough starter in your galley, don't you?"

"Yes. I do," he said with a heavy accent and a warm smile. "I make the best pancakes!"

What once would have been referred to as the daylight hours, was a dim, oppressive condition, the surroundings lit with something like the effects of a quarter moon. By six o'clock it had turned pitch black outside, the only illumination being the shafts of light that shown out the windows, playing on the smoky air surrounding the freighter. Twice during the evening there was a violent aftershock, but the giant ship held its position.

After over an hour of intense conversation, an unspoken understanding was reached. They would join forces. They would face the uncertain future together. There was a lull. Everyone was bone tired, dirty. The mental exhaustion was evident in the eyes of all.

"If I'm not mistaken, the sleeping accommodations in your spaceship aren't much good here on the Earth. Why don't you bring your duffel on board? We have enough empty cabins for each of you, if you don't mind sleeping on a slight list for now," said McGrady.

Upon that invitation, Williamson led his crew back to get their gear. "We'll get some rest for now and scavenge the orbiter for usable equipment and supplies tomorrow," he told them.

There were two vacant officer's cabins with private toilets and showers. To make three, Carlson moved his things and graciously offered his also, so each of the women could have one. They accepted. McGrady offered his to the orbiter commander, but Jim declined.

Katowski encountered Williamson next to a companion-way to the wheelhouse. "Jim, we ought to have a planning session first thing in the morning, don't you think? You know, to develop a strategy for the future."

"Yes, I'm on my way up to talk to McGrady now about doing that very thing. But let's do it after a shower and breakfast. Okay?" He smiled.

McGrady readily agreed, and at Williamson's suggestion, agreed also to include the entire ship's company in the discussions.

The next morning the group gathered together. McGrady began. "Folks, we're facing a situation nobody in the history of mankind has ever faced before. We're the nucleus of a new community. Assuming there are others like us who survived, we are part of what may be a whole new society, maybe a new country, maybe a new civilization. Colonel Williamson and I talked about it last night. We have short-term problems to work out and long-term problems. We need to tackle the short-term problems first. For the time being, we'd like to see us make decisions by consensus. If we run into a snag, Colonel Williamson and I will work out a decision between the two of us. How's that set with you folks?"

There were nods and grunts of assent all around. The Portuguese didn't quite understand it all, but agreed anyway.

"Clint, if you don't mind, I'd like to be referred to as Jim from now on," said Williamson, before taking his turn to address the group.

"Sure, if you'd like."

"We've started a list of subjects to discuss for which we need some plans or understandings," began Williamson, taping up a large sheet of paper to a bulkhead. "I'd like to review and add to it before we dig in to individual topics."

The list read: food, water, clothing, medical, security, exploration, communications, sanitation, environmental monitoring, habitation. The group added some items to the list, then Williamson led the discussion. He was looking for lists of known facts, possibilities, and action items for them to pursue. Later they broke down into smaller groups to develop more information. It became obvious to the crew of the *Dixon* that all the astronauts were impressive people. Baker's knowledge of communications systems was mindboggling, even to the *Dixon*'s electronic technician. And Baker obviously knew a lot about fishing.

Johanson seemed to know all about electrical systems, engines, winches, carpentry and a lot more. He also had considerable experience with sailboats.

Maria had a broad science background and had many ideas of how they could satisfy their nutritional needs. She was very skilled at getting participation from the three foreign members of the crew.

Samuels, being a doctor, obviously had knowledge of medicine. She also was the first to inquire into the availability of books, videotapes and discs, magazines, computer diskettes, CDs, and other items of educational value.

Katowski was the systems specialist. She knew how to organize information and material to the best advantage.

Williamson was an organizer, too, but his ability to forecast, to describe possible outcomes, to think ahead, was superior to all. It was he who addressed the matter of security. "Whether there's a hundred or a hundred thousand people surviving who are within traveling distance of us, there'll be some who recognize no laws, no moral codes, no standards of conduct. They will kill for what they want. We're sitting on a figurative gold mine, a ship full of wheat. We can expect people, good and bad, to come here for food, if for no other reason. And there are other reasons. One is you three women."

Several people started talking at once. "Give the grain to whoever wants it…What weapons do we have around here?…I can take care of myself…How many survivors do you think there are in this area?"

As the first day's discussion drew to a close, a few significant decisions had been made. Some of the group would conduct an inventory of everything on board the two ships.

Baker, Carlson, and two of the *Dixon*'s crew would set out on foot to search the island for survivors and for salvageable supplies. Three crew members would alternate making repairs on the ship and monitoring the radar for passing vessels.

One issue that took a lot of time to clear up was the matter of sharing the food supply with people that may come to them in need. The policy would be that they would load up everyone that came with all the wheat they could carry, but would tell them that the next time they came, they would have to trade for it. Not much would be required, but something of value.

"What if people come who are starving?"

"We won't let anyone starve. We'll feed them wheat till they're healthy."

"What if they don't have anything to trade?"

"If they have two hands, they have something to trade. We'll assign them tasks. We'll have a thousand jobs that'll need to be done."

"What about the elderly, small children?"

"We'll give them something to do. They need to contribute to the well being of all, or at least believe they're contributing."

"Remember, one day the wheat will run out. Everyone will have to be productive, in some way, to survive."

Not everyone agreed with the policy, but Williamson was adamant. McGrady agreed. It was the only time during the day that command authority came into play.

Another decision, one with ominous implications, had to do with security. The officers of the *Dixon* had two pistols, a high-powered hunting rifle, and a semi-automatic military-style rifle.

"That's not enough," said Williamson. "Someday someone is going to come up this river armed with machine guns or rocket launchers and want to take everything we have. We need more protection."

Steve had been sitting quietly during the discussion of security. Finally he spoke up. "I think I can rig up the particle beam generator on the deck someplace." There was silence all around.

"What a particle beam generator?" asked one of the Portuguese.

Steve answered, in his laconic way. "The PBG is a device that fires sub-atomic matter in bursts of high energy that is released when it hits a target. The experimental model we have is capable of sending a burst of energy at the speed of light, as far as you can see, and sufficient to destroy a tank or plane or sink a freighter. The main drawback is it takes several hours to recharge the accumulator with our power supply, so to be practical, we're talking one shot in an encounter. It's aimed with a laser beam. It's extremely accurate. I know. I tested it several times on this last mission."

Steve was assigned to start remounting the PBG the next day with the help of two of the ship's crew.

That evening, after a meal of fresh produce and French toast, food otherwise subject to spoilage, the three women sat in Samuels' small but comfortable cabin and talked.

"Something's been bothering me all day, but I didn't want to bring it up before the entire group."

"What's that, Sandy?" asked Katowski.

"We don't know how many people survived the initial effects of this catastrophe. Let's hope it was a lot. We don't know how many will eventually starve to death or die of disease brought on by unsanitary conditions. We don't know how many of the survivors will be women. In a few decades, there won't be any human race if there aren't enough fertile women to keep it going. Now here's a big, big complication. Seventy or eighty percent of the women of child bearing age, and even younger, in the world and in this country, have been injected with Natidin and can't have babies without having the neutralizer, Biopro, first. We don't have any idea how much Biopro is still left in the world. It doesn't have a long shelf life. It's impossible to manufacture except in a high-tech lab. Do you see the problem? Things are even more desperate than we'd realized."

"So what can we do?" said Maria, her brown eyes dark, her complexion pale.

"It's obvious isn't it?" said Katowski. "We search for Biopro in the Soo. Both Soos. And we search for women who need it."

"How about us?" said Samuels, in measured terms.

Each woman looked at the others, question marks on their faces.

Finally Samuels broke the silence. "I haven't had Natidin. Ben, bless his heart, didn't think it was fair that I had to be the one to be infertile. He didn't agree with those, including the majority of us women, who considered Natidin to be the magic elixir. The magic elixir that freed us from fear of pregnancy, solved the abortion dilemma, and solved the world's problem of overpopulation. He had a vasectomy. I could have children."

Katowski spoke up in a small voice. "I was sick with the flu both times NASA conducted the program. I didn't get the shot. Remember Sandy? You were supposed to make the arrangements for me later."

"I remember. I forgot. On purpose."

"How about you, Maria?" asked Samuels. She reached over and placed her hand on Maria's wrist.

"I got the injection back at my school, before I got connected up with NASA." Maria was forlorn, tears began to form.

"Well, there isn't any immediate hurry, but eventually we need to be thinking about choosing mates, at least you Fran," said Samuels. She would have included herself in that category, except that she wasn't ready to believe her husband, Ben, was dead, just yet.

"I knew you were going to say that," said the erstwhile pilot.

The three of them lapsed into thought, staring at their hands which they wringed unconsciously, as though kneading bread.

Maria raised her head. "What about those two remaining

embryos in the orbiter? Can they be used, somehow?"

Samuels was quick to respond, "Yes. As a matter of fact they could. They still should be viable. They're still in a controlled environment. But I don't know how long they can be protected. For the next couple of days, they could probably be implanted into some woman at estrus."

Katowski posed the obvious question. "Who?"

"I'm on The Pill. I could stop and start a cycle, but it would probably take too long to reach estrus," said Samuels.

"Me, too," said Katowski.

The two turned to Maria.

She sat up straighter, an almost triumphant look about her. "I'm in estrus, now, I think."

Samuels knew that Natidin didn't interfere with the whole process of ovulation. It only rendered the eggs produced resistant to fertilization. The body of a woman prepared each month to receive the sperm of a male and when no egg was fertilized successfully, it started the entire cycle over again, a natural process. Except that with Natidin the eggs would never develop into an embryo, a baby.

"Are you offering to make a baby from one of those embryos?" said Katowski.

"Not one. Both."

17
Fire

What a glorious day! The island, barren and ugly when the coating snow had first melted off, was now brushed with green, the forbs, grasses and brush that had miraculously appeared when spring unfolded two months ago. A soft, warm breeze wafted the scent of life over the land and the broad river, two and half miles across to the mainland. The hum of insects could be heard among the young plants and along the shoreline. Such a wonderful feeling that was to the survivors of the "Big One," as the community centered around the *Frank W. Dixon* referred to the collision with the asteroid.

And the summer solstice had come. Fran and Jim had taken great pains to determine exactly when the sun reached its highest point in the sky compared to the time they would have predicted using solar tables and the chronometers of the *Atlantis*. Jim was curious whether the collision had changed the time of rotation of the earth. They were unable to detect any differences. Fran figured that was cause for celebration.

The little group, swelled to over thirty now, had had no holidays for six months, since Christmas. April 5, the anniversary of the "Big One," was noted but not observed. The first celebration held had been the middle of August. That's when they concluded there was enough sunlight for plants to grow. First, tiny needles of grass poked through the duff, then birch trees and sugar maples began to sprout. Previously the remnants of shrubs and trees had made valiant efforts to grow new shoots, but had failed due to the perpetual gloom caused by the blanket of dust surrounding the Earth and to the acid rain that pelted the ground during the summer that wasn't a summer. But in mid-August plants were definitely growing again. Shirley Tonini, a newcomer who had been crying practically the entire summer, stopped whining. And Fran actually went swimming. The little community had eaten a big breakfast, McGrady offered a prayer of thanksgiving, and they all went to work planting a garden.

The soil, where it hadn't been washed away from the frequent rain and sleet storms, was fertile enough and there was thought to be time to grow lettuce, turnips, spinach, and radishes. Following Maria's directions, the Dixonites, as they called themselves, collected soil from the sediment fans that formed at the mouths of gullies and hauled it to make raised gardens ringed with stones. Excursions in the *Dixon*'s motor launch to the Sault Ste. Maries had located some vegetable seed along with numerous other supplies and implements for gardening.

Those trips had also brought them in contact with other survivors in the area. The first trips were dismal, heartrending experiences. Baker and Carlson and the Canadians had been the vanguard. Carefully picking their way up river in the launch in the gloom, they visited Neebish and Sugar Island, the neighboring islands, occasionally sounding a small handheld air horn, hoping to attract attention. They didn't venture far inland and found no one on the islands on that first trip. Traveling furthur upriver, they came to the American Soo.

In the darkness, they didn't at first appreciate the destruction that had occurred. The fires had nearly burned themselves out, yet the odor of burnt plastic, rubber, and various other substances pervaded the murky air. Carlson was familiar with the town's layout and led the four of them on a search for food. He was able to locate what had been the old post office, which was near the water, and the ruins of what had been a grocery store in the vicinity. There they met a half dozen sooty individuals working with flashlights, searching through the rubble for food and other supplies.

Those people had been at their task for a couple of days and had stockpiled a small amount of goods. Some appeared to be tough, resourceful people, but others had nearly surrendered to despair.

Carlson and Baker questioned them about the situation, told them about the wheat on the *Dixon*, and then continued on their reconnaissance. It was impossible to determine where they were in the near darkness. The streets were jumbles of broken pavement. Buildings had collapsed and burned so they couldn't be identified. Water from ruptured mains and shattered storage tanks had washed down debris that stacked up in what once were gutters. Away from the downtown, the charcoaled remnants of trees lay across streets and the burned-out basements where homes had been.

They learned there were large numbers of burned and injured and much greater numbers of dead in the town. There weren't really enough survivors to tend the injured, though most of the badly burned had died within the first twenty-four hours. And no one had time to bury the dead. The enterprising ones among the survivors had scrounged up food and fashioned shelters for themselves. Small bands had gravitated together, young and old, without regard to their previous station in life. The size of the groups averaged about ten due to some innate sense of efficiency. Most were in wretched condition. Many people didn't understand what had happened, most didn't have any idea how they would feed themselves after the food supplies salvaged from the few stores and warehouses not completely consumed by fire were exhausted, and some were waiting vainly for the second coming of Christ. These latter individuals nevertheless had some peace of mind, at least those who considered themselves worthy of redemption. Fortunately, most of them later changed their minds before they starved to death. They were all relieved somewhat to learn from the crew members of the *Atlantis* and the *Dixon* about what had happened and what to expect in the future. Most importantly, they were informed about the availability of the wheat to tide them over until crops could be grown the next year.

During the ensuing months, the Dixonites made several trips to the American Soo and to the Canadian Soo as well. The town on the Canadian side was considerably larger than its U.S. counterpart, but had suffered as much with identical results. After it was judged safe enough, McGrady took Samuels upriver to the two Soos to administer to some of the injured. While there, she searched for neutralizer for Natidin, but found none.

Sandra worked long and hard in the former towns and was instrumental in persuading the survivors to dispose of the dead for reasons of sanitation. This was done to the extent possible by burning them, many for the second time. Most, buried in debris, were never found. Except by the surviving rat population. And the flies. The stench lingered till the freeze came.

In time the small bands established contact with one another, including those across the river. They worked out arrangements with some who had been able to get a few small boats into operating condition so as to make runs to the *Dixon* for wheat. They bought into the barter system established by the Dixonites, trading everything possible, from pipe to batteries, from containers to vitamin pills, from clothes to books.

Within a month of the catastrophe, a handful of people

from both sides of the river reestablished the Coast Guard, operating the one usable U.S. Coast Guard launch. This group scoured the channels and islands for survivors and useful equipment. They managed to get some radios into service and discovered the existence of the *George Peacock*, the freighter grounded off Copper Harbor. It too was laden with grain and was serving survivors way up in the Copper Country around the Keweenaw Peninsula. By the end of summer, these diligent people had a rudimentary knowledge of conditions up and down the Great Lakes. They estimated the survival rate at one in five hundred. There were about three hundred people left in the vicinity of the two Soos, plus the Dixonites.

The uplifting effects of the resumption of sunshine in August was short-lived. They had harvested a couple of baskets of spinach and lettuce, but most crops failed to mature due to early frosts. Winter came then and was a miserable time. Sleet storms lashed the *Dixon* and the shelters of the survivors in the vicinity. Then came snow, then the freeze up of the lakes and the river. Boats were useless now. Trips to pick up wheat from the *Dixon* had to be made over the ice. A few snowmobiles were in operation, but fuel was scarce so no unnecessary trips were taken. The people in the Soos suffered badly. Those who had first chosen to make it apart from the townspeople were driven to town for subsistence because conditions were generally even worse out in the boondocks. Several people died before the spring breakup allowed boat traffic to resume. It was the coldest winter in memory.

In comparison, the Dixonites did well. A few people from St. Joseph's Island and others previously overlooked from the nearby islands had joined them, doubling up in the vacant cabins and some sharing the ship's lounge. They were relatively comfortable, even though occasional aftershocks still rocked the ship, wakening them from sleep from time to time. From one of the islanders—a part-Indian man named Curtis Saylow, with two young daughters—they learned how to make fish traps, and before ice up, trapped many salmon, northern pike, walleyes, and perch. Some of these they dried and laid up as a supply for the winter. Even in winter, they managed to catch some fish through the ice. Due mainly to Maria and Luis's resourcefulness, the Dixonites ate a varied menu and endured the winter without going hungry. They were mostly occupied with the business of keeping alive and assisting their neighbors in doing the same.

Still, there was some free time; so Katowski, Samuels, and McGrady organized training sessions. It occurred to them that the critical skills and knowledge available in their small group were irreplaceable unless others were taught those skills so as to carry on in the inevitable event of death. That realization led to the same conclusion that Samuels had made the second night after the *Atlantis* nudged up against the *Dixon*. To have a future, they would have to make one. That meant establishing a new generation to succeed them. In August, when a renewal of life seemed possible, Sandra conducted a survey.

"There are thirty-six people at Dixon," she said, standing before the group at a community meeting on the freighter. "Thirteen are female. Of those females, eight could bear children, counting Curtis's two daughters. I don't know what the situation is at the Soos, but suspect about that same ratio, or about twenty to twenty-five percent, can have children. I don't want to press anyone, but sooner or later these women are going to have to match up with a man."

"Does that include you?" said McGrady.

"I'm one of the eight."

"Who are the others?" said Williamson.

"I don't think I should say."

"Sandy, we have to know. If people are going to pair up, both need to know if a family will result. Some men may not want to be fathers, or maybe can't be fathers," persisted Williamson.

"I don't know, Jim. I still don't think I should say. I think the women themselves should be the ones to say."

There was some murmuring among the group.

"I want to say something," said Maria, rising to her feet. She looked at Samuels. Sandy nodded.

"I am pregnant. I'm going to have twins. Next January. But I can't have any more after that. I just thought you all should know," said Maria, scanning the room for a reaction.

There was silence, then smiles, then congratulations, then several people went to Maria, hugged her or shook her hand. Luis smiled broadly and patted her on the back. It took several minutes for the group to settle down again. No one asked the expected question, but some of them glanced from face to face to see who might betray himself as the father.

Samuels spoke first. "The father isn't anyone here. She was pregnant before the space mission began." Maria and Samuels had agreed on that explanation some time ago.

"Now I don't want to overstate the matter," continued Samuels. "But, you need to give this matter of raising families some serious thought."

No one else chose to speak on the subject, so the group went on to other business.

Later that day Samuels had a meeting with all the women, except Curtis's daughters. They were only eleven and ten. There would be time later for them to hear Samuels' speech.

"What I have to say is mostly directed to those of you who can bear children. We're a very small group. The children we have will have awesome responsibilities. In a larger sense, they will have to help rebuild civilization. In a more personal sense, they are the ones who'll have to take care of us when we get old. So far as we know, not one of us women has a husband anymore. The men will be competing with one another for each of you. Maybe they already have. You can and should be selective. Frankly, I think you should be thinking of picking men with the best genes."

"What do we know about the genes of anybody around here," complained Shirley Tonini.

Maria thought about the two babies growing inside her and said nothing.

"Well, I guess we don't know much. What I meant to say was look for the healthiest, the most capable, the most intelligent."

"Gee," said Beverly, a twenty-five-year-old woman from Neebish Island, "I just got divorced before the "Big One." I had five empty years. My husband was cold as a fish. This time I'd like to marry someone who loves me, not just some stud with papers."

Sandy thought of Ben, her gentle surgeon from Houston. "Maybe we can find some who fit both criteria. Let's try."

It was June 24, the day to celebrate the summer solstice. It was three days too late actually. So what? Fran Williamson, nee Katowski, was the organizer. Her countenance glowed with happiness at being alive, and at carrying a child. She was four months along. She and the four other pregnant women were a tight group, including Samuels-McGrady. But Maria was getting most of the attention. Because of her two lively babies, one a girl, Hope Henricks Houston, with feathery blond hair and blue eyes, and the other, Joshua Henricks Houston, with shaggy dark hair and hazel eyes, she had lots of help from her women friends and from Ron Baker, the foster father.

Most of the community had gathered on the deck of the *Dixon* where the view of the wide river was best. Luis was overseeing the meal preparation in the galley. Though much of the spring they had been beset with stormy weather, there were some early vegetable crops to harvest and herbs for flavoring. There were dandelion greens, cattail shoots, and wild watercress. A fresh catch of walleye would provide the protein, with loaves of baked dill bread for carbohydrates.

Steve Johanson came out from the radio room to report on the daily radio traffic. By now they had a network that extended all the way to Buffalo. By chance, several ships had been in or near Buffalo when the "Big One" hit and had survived. There were enough survivors and resources to provide the basis for some kind of maritime organization. Between the Coast Guard bunch at the Soos and the small fleet from Buffalo, a sense of togetherness, of security had been established for those on the St. Lawrence—Great Lakes Waterway.

"What's new?" asked Williamson of Johanson.

"A new unit's joined the network near Cleveland. They have two boats. Some guy at Duluth has two cows and is looking for a bull. The trading vessel from the Soo is coming down here tomorrow morning. And the Bay City boys say a couple of those pirate boats have been reported at the upper end of Lake Huron, near Mackinaw. They're raiding for food and women like they have been all spring. They say to keep an eye out for them. They're in thirty-five-foot launches with shark teeth painted on the bow. They're armed and very dangerous, they say."

Williamson, unconsciously stroking his whiskered chin, glanced at the PBG mounted at the bow, in front of the forecastle, under a canvas cover for protection from the elements. He was about to say something to Steve when Fran interrupted.

"Honey, would you go down and set up the volleyball net? The food won't be ready for an hour and people need something to do while they wait. You're recreation director for the day, you know."

"Sure. Maybe I'll stay down there and play for a while, too," said Jim. He liked volleyball. He was the best player in the community. Crossing the wide deck, he stepped onto the long unloading boom that now served as a footbridge, spanning the space from the freighter to the ground.

A half hour passed. The small group gathered on deck was enjoying the soft summer breeze. Fran was musing, her eyes half closed. Years ago while a student at the Soo, she had enjoyed sitting in the sun, watching the puffy white cumulus clouds sail across the sky, and listening to the screech of the diving and hovering gulls. This was like such a day, she thought, when she had had no cares except the final exams that she was sure to ace; when she had looked forward to the prospect of visiting her parents again before taking a summer job as a lifeguard; when there was a world of opportunity ahead of her.

No, on second thought, it really wasn't like such a day. She had no parents, no job, no finals coming, and there were no seagulls. Not one. But there was a world of opportunity ahead of her, and the person inside her.

"Here comes Curtis and the girls!" called Beverly.

Far across the water, they could see a small open boat with a man pulling at a set of oars, headed toward St. Joseph's Island, where the *Dixon* rested. The little craft was angled upstream to allow for the current and the breeze. In the binoculars, Beverly could see that Curtis had his outboard motor shut off and tilted out of the water, conserving the precious fuel.

"Oh, Beverly! What's that coming up river? It looks like two motor launches," cried Fran.

Beverly swung the glasses to her left, down river from Curtis's boat about a mile. "They're two cabin cruisers. I can't tell who they are."

"Are they Coast Guard?" asked Sandra, straining with her naked eyes to see the two boats.

"No. They seem to have some kind of design on the bows. Looks like a shark's mouth. You know, big teeth."

Steve had been watching, saying nothing, just mildly concerned until he heard Beverly describe the shark mouths.

"Give me the glasses!" He jumped to his feet and grabbed the binoculars from Beverly.

"Geez," she said, as he took them.

Steve knelt down and steadied the glasses on the rail.

In seconds, he stood up and yelled, "Somebody get Jim! Now!"

Fran ran across the deck to get Williamson.

When Jim arrived, breathless, he knew something serious was happening. The eyes of all on deck were peering anxiously at the two cruisers as they motored up the channel. "What's up?"

"It's those two pirate boats we heard about. They're heading up channel. Here, take a look." Steve handed the binoculars to Williamson.

There were several people on deck of each of the boats. They were too far away to tell much about them, but Jim could see what appeared to be a large machine gun mounted on the foredeck of each. "Steve, uncover the PBG! Fran, tell Carlson to start the generator. He's down below in the engine room. We're going to need power to operate the gun."

Steve rushed to the odd looking, space-age weapon and jerked the cover off. Fran ran to the forecastle, climbed up the ladder to the wheelhouse, and got on the intercom to call Carlson. Williamson studied the two raider boats.

"They're going to intercept Curtis," said Beverly, pointing in the direction upstream where Curtis and his two girls, unaware of the danger, made their way toward the *Dixon*, oars dipping, pulling, and swinging.

Jim swung his glasses and focused on Curtis's boat. Then he lowered them abruptly and sprinted to the ladder to the wheelhouse. Seeing Fran on her way out, he yelled, "Get to the ship's foghorn and sound the danger signal!"

Fran turned around and headed back to the wheelhouse. Jim ran to the PBG where Steve stood, waiting for the power to come on. Jim stopped, swinging the binoculars back and forth between the pirates and Curtis, watching the space between them narrow. It was apparent the raiders were intending to intercept Curtis.

The electricity came on, followed by blasts of the ship's foghorn, "Woonk! Woonk! Woonk! Woonk! Woonk!"

Steve was startled at first by the noise, but immediately grasped the controls of the weapon and looked into the eyepiece of the laser sight. A light in the eyepiece told him the accumulator was fully charged.

Fran kept sounding the horn. Curtis stopped rowing and squinted at the *Dixon*, then looked about him on the water. He saw the oncoming raiders, still traveling at half speed. Curtis dropped the oars into the boat and stepped to his outboard motor. With a couple of violent jerks on the starter rope, it roared to life. Curtis pointed his craft at the *Dixon* and revved up to full speed, his two girls clutching the gunwales and urging him on.

The men and women on the ground beside the freighter, hearing the horn, scrambled up the foot bridge to see what was going on. McGrady was first to reach Williamson. "What's wrong?"

"There're two pirate boats. They're after Curtis and his girls!" Williamson was still studying the scene with the binoculars. "Steve, zero in on the lead boat."

"Roger." Steve manipulated the controls to lock on his target.

McGrady ran back toward his cabin while Steve kept tracking the pirate boat. The two raiders cranked up their engines and began to close rapidly on Curtis. They were about half a mile away from the little craft which carried the hard-pressed father.

"Steve, are you on target?" said Williamson.

"Roger. Locked on and holding."

McGrady came hurrying up carrying two rifles. Fran joined him with another more powerful set of binoculars in her hands. She held them to her face and fixed them on the pirate boats. At that instant, the lead boat fired a burst of machine gun fire in front of Curtis. She had a clear view of the men on board the speeding cruisers. They had Mohawk haircuts and red bandannas around their heads. Some carried small arms, others binoculars. They were ignoring the *Dixon*. They were intent on capturing the little boat with the two girls.

"Prepare to fire," ordered Williamson.

Fran, standing next to Jim with her more powerful glasses could make out the faces of the raiders as their boats came abreast of the *Dixon* four hundred yards away.

"Jim! They're black!"

"What?"

"The raiders! They're blacks!"

Williamson seized her glasses and pressed his brows against the eyepieces, leaning forward, trying to get closer to the menacing cruisers. There was a long pause, agonizing, gut wrenching.

Steve tracked the lead boat, his laser beam spotted amidships, waiting for the command.

The lead boat fired another burst toward Curtis.

"Fire!" growled Williamson.

The PBG gave a curious sounding "chug" and the pirate craft exploded into a ball of fire and smoke. The force of the blast tipped the second boat onto its rails.

"WHAP!" The sound of the explosion hit the group on the *Dixon* like a massive hand slap.

The second boat of pirates came about and sped off down river, the echos of the sudden eruption beating on the backs of the terrified men.

The little skiff, with a wide-eyed Curtis Saylow and his daughters aboard, gargled its way toward the *Dixon*.

18
The Adolescents

Hope was thinking about her breasts. She was sprawled out in a recliner in the Sunday afternoon sun, by herself, at the very point of the bow of the *Frank W. Dixon*, clad in shorts and T-shirt, her arms folded across her chest. The huge freighter still rested on the bottom even though its cargo had been nearly completely removed over the past fourteen years. It rested on the bottom because some of the holds had been flooded to prevent it from being floated away in a storm. The ship was still the headquarters of the community of Dixon, although many of the residents lived on shore in small cabins. Hope lived on board with her brother, Joshua, and her father, Ron Baker.

She was thinking about her breasts because her mother,

Maria, had died a month ago of breast cancer. She had heard that breast cancer was hereditary. Dr. Sandy had known Hope's blood mother and told Hope she was just like her.

Hope was tall, just as tall as Joshua, though he was still growing, and she was blond. Very intelligent, too, said Dr. Sandy. But Dr. Sandy hadn't said anything about her blood mother's breasts or whether she had ever had cancer. Hope decided she would ask the good doctor about that.

Breasts are a problem, thought Hope. *They can kill a person. And you have to hold them up with a bra.* At least Maria had thought so. For a while Hope had ignored the need for a bra till Maria talked to her about it. Maria managed to get some bras that fit Hope from the trading vessels that came by Dixon from time to time. It was amazing what was available from those traders, mostly goods that had been salvaged from burned ships, stores, or warehouses, but much that was crafted or grown by the scattered populations of survivors around the Great Lakes country. Hope tried going without a bra a few times even after she first got one, but became uncomfortable by the stares of the men of the community, especially the two Portuguese who had not been able to find wives for themselves.

Breasts are a problem. Why have them when you don't have children to nurse? she thought. She resolved to wear blousy shirts and to stop wrestling with the boys.

Joshua was thinking about breasts, too. He was thinking about the breasts of the Saylow girls. The day before, while he was hoeing in the fields, the two of them were working near him. When they bent over, he could see inside their shirts. Then, at noon break, they both sat down in the shade of some young sugar maples and nursed their babies. Their husbands had joined them after a while, so Joshua was discouraged from staring any longer. It was not that he hadn't seen nursing mothers. It was that he hadn't quite realized before how attractive a young woman's bosom really was. He was fourteen. There were feelings stirring around in him that were troubling.

Joshua was the oldest of the new generation, and other than his sister, Hope, who didn't count in this case, there weren't many women his age or younger who had developed enough to have the appeal that the Saylow girls did. There was Dory, a year younger than him, but not particularly attractive. Sort of chunky. She idolized Joshua and was always finding excuses to talk to him. Joshua was patient and polite, which endeared him to her all the more. She was eager to please him, a quality he suspected would change over time, if she was anything like her mother, Shirley.

Joshua sat on a bench near the short, rock and timber pier, thirty yards down the shore from the freighter, repairing a fishing net. He was supposed to have it ready for use the next day, but was having difficulty concentrating on the task at hand. It was Sunday, supposedly a day of rest, and the sun overhead was especially pleasant. Yesterday had been mostly cloudy, and a slow day, because he had worked all day in the field. This day his energy level was high, too high to work with his fingers. The source of his energy seemed to come from somewhere below his waist. Instead of seeing nylon cord, he kept seeing the Saylow girls. Disgusted with himself, he tossed the net aside and rose to his feet.

"Hope!" he called, shading his eyes with his hand as he looked up toward his sister in her recliner on the bow.

"What?" she answered, not rising to look over the rail.

"I'm going for a run down to the point. If Dad comes looking for me, tell him I'll finish the net before supper."

"Okay!"

Joshua took off at a trot down the worn footpath along the shoreline. The gritty sand of the trail provided good traction for his bare feet, toughened by years of summers of going without shoes. In the winter he wore boots, but in the summer he disregarded even the tire tread sandals that many people wore. They were too hard to run in and Joshua liked to run.

With the sun at his back, he jogged effortlessly along, ducking from time to time to avoid a branch or to miss a cloud of gnats that sometimes appeared in his way. The young growth of birch and sugar maples was lush and sheltered many insects, though this late in the summer there weren't many mosquitoes. Up a slight incline and down the other side he ran, leaving the little community behind. The broad river, on his right, flowed peacefully toward the narrows between Detour on the mainland and Drummond Island. He'd been to Drummond several times on fishing expeditions. Nobody lived there. Beyond that was Lake Huron. The year before he had sailed with Steve Johanson and some others all the way to the Straits of Mackinaw. There was a small settlement at Mackinaw City on the south shore of the straits. There were no kids there his age, however. Raiders had taken all the young women years before.

Joshua's favorite place was a point of rocks that jutted out on the south end of St. Joseph Island, about five miles from Dixon. The rocks were worn smooth from glacial action millenniums ago, looking deceptively hard but comfortable to sit or lie upon, if one fit oneself into the hollows and swells of the gray-colored mass. When the sun shown down on the rock, the radiant heat was soaked up, warming the surface, some-times till it was too hot to walk on in bare feet. Then Joshua would have to splash water on it to cool it down. This day, however, it was just right. When Joshua reached the point, he leaped over a crevice and walked to a couchlike formation with a small shrub growing over one end. He stretched out and recovered his breath.

The run along the shoreline had taken most of that excess energy. The warm, gray granite soaked up the rest, much as it had soaked up energy from the sun. He looked to the east, toward Potagannissing Bay and Drummond Island beyond. He studied the other small islands in the bay. They, like St. Joseph Island, were lush with regrowth, some as high as twenty feet. The blackened fingers of the old tree trunks still standing after the fire were nearly all fallen down or cut and removed for firewood.

Joshua often wondered what it was like before the "Big One." Books he had read told about, and showed in pictures, great forests of tall trees, some that were said to have been two hundred feet tall. And he studied them on videodisks, over and over again. It was hard to believe. And there had been many mammals; some, like moose, weighing as much as eight or ten men. Some animals even bigger on other continents. Now there were no large wild mammals around, only mice, chipmunks, weasels, and feral cats. Once he had heard of bears being seen north of the Soo. *Gee*, he thought, *wouldn't it be great to see a bear?*

There were some domestic livestock in some of the settlements to the south and to the west of the Soo area. He understood they sometimes were eaten, if they were too old for other uses. He had never tasted the flesh of mammals, only fish, shellfish, turtles, and crawfish. He had never tasted bird meat, either. As far as he knew, all the birds were extinct.

Joshua was fascinated with books, tapes, and discs from the old days. He thought it must have been wonderful to have lived in that world. The others, the older folks who had survived the "Big One," told stories of technology and conveniences that boggled the mind. Sometimes they got teary eyed when they talked of those times. Joshua wasn't made sad to hear of the old days. He was just enthralled.

Books and other educational materials kept coming to Dixon on the trading vessels. He liked the books best because he could take them with him when he went for hikes or for boat trips. To understand some of the more sophisticated writings, he had even taken to reading the dictionary sometimes. Maria, before she died, was in charge of the community education program and encouraged Joshua and Hope to study a wide range of subjects. They both helped Maria by coaching the younger children. Joshua missed Maria a lot.

Joshua was lying on his back on the warm stone. He closed his eyes and imagined a world full of people and mechanical things. Then he imagined a world far from that world, one in which he was alone, just himself, maybe with a boat. That was easier to picture than the world of planes and cars and great crowds of people. He saw himself paddling along a rocky shoreline, discovering unexplored inlets and bays. He pictured himself rounding a wooded point and entering a sheltered cove and surprising a half dozen naked girls, like fairies, who, seeing him, ran into the woods, their laughter lingering behind. In his mind he peered into the woods, trying to get a glimpse of them again.

As he lay there, eyes closed, legs crossed at the ankle, his dark hair gently ruffled by the breeze, he thought he heard a woman singing, a silvery windblown song. He rose up abruptly, looking about him. There was no one in sight. He cocked his head and listened. There was no more singing, no woman, no birds, only the waves gently lapping at the rocks.

19
Two Fishermen

One summer day of his sixteenth year, Joshua was daydreaming in the bow of Curtis Saylow's fishing boat as it sailed across the rippling waters of the lower St. Mary's River. In tan shorts, his long, strong legs lay crossed over a mound of fishing nets. His dark hair, ruffled by the slight breeze, hung low over his forehead, an indication he needed a haircut, something his father Ron had been after him about for several days. Curtis was at the tiller, his piercing blue eyes, contrasting with his otherwise dark Indian features, focused on a small island about a quarter-mile ahead. The boat, a twenty-foot dory that had been fitted with a swing keel and a fifteen-foot mast, was the workhorse of the small collection of boats used for fishing by the people of Dixon. Joshua had become a constant fishing companion of the taciturn Curtis and was very comfortable with both the boat and the man. The two of them were searching for a new place to stretch their nets, intent on adding to their already generous catch so far that week.

Curtis was in charge of the fishing operation for the community. That was an increasingly important responsibility as the number of people at Dixon had swelled to over twice the original size, due mainly to the number of children borne by the small group of fertile women. In addition to the children were several temporary residents from other communities, because Dixon had become a training center, a school for higher learning.

There was no established government in that part of the world, only a loose confederation of the communities on the Great Lakes, joined by radio communication and waterborne transportation. Chicago, with nearly 10,000 people, had become a commercial and farming center, Buffalo likewise a commercial center and a key transfer point to the lower St. Lawrence Waterway. Other locations were evolving into functioning towns as well. Dixon with its unusual collection of talent, especially the crew of the *Atlantis*, had taken on the role of a training center. Radio communications, electronics, mechanical engineering, sailing, navigation, and medicine were subjects offered to those in the Great Lakes region. There was a strong feeling among the survivors that the basic knowledge of the past life had to be preserved and passed on to their successors. It was a heavy burden and much was expected of the emerging generation.

"What are you thinking about, Josh?" said Curtis, noticing that Joshua had an expression of concern on his face.

"Oh, nothin' in particular," he said, caught unawares wrestling with a vexing problem.

"Oh?"

"No. Nothin'."

They cruised through the water in silence for a few moments.

"Say, Curtis? Do you think I ought to be an electronics

technician or mechanic or engineer or something like that?" said Joshua, pulling himself upright and leaning aft, toward Curtis.

"Why do you ask?"

"'Cause Dad has been after me to choose a specialty, you know, a profession of some kind. He says everybody has to develop some skills, for the benefit of the rest of humanity, or somethin' like that."

"What skills do you have?"

"Oh, I don't know. But they gave me an aptitude test last spring and it said I can do lots of things, or have the potential anyway."

"I can believe that."

"What do you think, Curtis?"

"Well, you're gonna be full grown pretty soon. You have to be thinking how you're going to earn a living. What do you want to do?"

Joshua thought a few moments, not sure he wanted to put his feelings into words. "I want to be a fisherman, like you. Maybe a sailor, too. You know, explore the lakes."

Curtis grunted.

"What do you think?" asked Joshua again.

"You're a smart fella. You could do a lot more than be a fisherman," answered Curtis.

"Yeah, but that's an important occupation. Feeding people, taking care of people. What could be more important than that? And exploring, finding out about places. That's important, too."

Curtis, didn't answer. Instead he turned his attention to the approaching island, a low, rocky irregularly shaped mound mostly covered with young birches and maples and about four hundred yards long. "Watch out ahead. We don't want to run onto any rocks," he said to Joshua, who, doing as he was directed, swung around and scanned for obstacles ahead.

"Coming about," said Curtis, reaching for the lines to the boom. They were running downwind, but the jib was not up, so there was nothing required of Joshua.

"Okay," said Joshua, still watching for rocks ahead.

Curtis executed a neat port jibe, a left turn downwind, jerking lines loose and reattaching others with one hand while controlling the tiller with the other.

The small boat rounded the end of the island and entered a cove on the lee side, the north side, with the shoreline shaded slightly from the midmorning sun. The calm water in the cove was like a mirror, reflecting the trees and rocks and puffy white clouds overhead. Dragonflies flitted from shore to boat and back again.

"Curtis! There's something swimming out there," said Joshua in a hoarse whisper.

A hundred feet ahead of the boat a dark object was moving through the water, at the point of a V-shaped ripple that spread out over the smooth glassy surface.

Suddenly, "Whap!" With a loud smack on the water, the creature disappeared. It left a gurgling boil that sent out concentric rings that sparkled in the sunlit waters.

"What was that?" shouted Joshua.

"That...that..." came the echo from the shoreline.

"That's a beaver," answered Curtis, his eyes shining with pleasure.

"Wow! A beaver! I thought they were all gone. Extinct." Joshua had his gaze still fixed on the spot where the big rodent had been. "Was that noise from his tail? I read once where they used to slap their tails as a danger signal."

"That's right. They did...and they still do." A smile had formed on Curtis's lips. It stayed there all the rest of the day.

20
Plus 20

"Okay, okay, everybody. Quiet down. The meeting will come to order." Captain McGrady rapped his gavel on the worn wooden surface of the long table behind which he and the four other members of the community council sat. Fortunately he had been selected chairperson for the current year. He exercised good meeting discipline. They were going to need that this day.

Janice Kitchener, an elderly woman who had been a secretary before the "Big One," and who now sat by herself at the right end of the table, commenced to take the official minutes. She wrote with a fountain pen on a tablet. "Special Meeting of the Community Council. Convened at 9:00 A.M., August 1, Plus 20 (2027 A.D.). Present: Chairperson Clinton

McGrady; Francis Williamson; Ralph Rutgers; Marin Johanson; Ordway Futchic."

A cool breeze from off the water fluttered the curtains in the open windows along the west wall of the long, low, concrete block building that served as the meeting hall, dance hall, theater, and church for the community of Dixon. It was nearly filled with the seventy or so people that sat in the rows of benches arrayed in front of the council table. The colorful artwork that lined the walls seemed inappropriate, considering the business at hand. But the acoustics were good. Even the youngsters who sat or stood near the open doors at the rear of the building could hear McGrady clearly.

He continued, "The case of Joshua Houston, charged with homicide, is now underway. Let the record show that Joshua is present," he said, nodding in the direction of Joshua, who sat stiffly in a low-backed chair behind a small table between the audience and the council and to the right of the five grim council members. The tanned face with hazel eyes under tousled, dark hair betrayed no emotion, but not without great effort.

"Because of the obvious conflict of interest, Fran is excused from the balance of the proceedings." The chairman leaned forward and looked down the table to his left at Fran, who, with red-rimmed eyes, rose from her chair and walked, chin up, to a seat on the end of the first row of benches on the opposite side of the room from Joshua.

McGrady unconsciously stroked his heavy gray beard, then picked up his gavel, twirled it in his fingers, and put it down again. "Arthur, you're going to state the case against Joshua?" he said to his former first mate, who sat on the same bench as Fran.

"Yes, I am, Clint." Carlson arose and walked confidently to a small lectern placed a few feet in front of his bench and stood so he could speak to the audience as well as to the council.

Joshua clasped his hands in his lap. His fingers began nervously working, working, as he looked first at Carlson then to those who sat on the bench to his right, about ten feet away. Hope, her blonde hair done up in a ponytail, was watching the council members intently, one of her toes tapping the dusty concrete floor. Both she and Joshua were wearing their best jeans and identical dark blue T-shirts.

Dr. Sandy sat next to Hope, wearing a dark skirt and looking professional with a plain white blouse and a string tie. She smiled reassuringly at Joshua.

Carlson cleared his throat before beginning. "Joshua Houston is charged with homicide in the death of James Williamson, July 27. It is charged that he struck Williamson with a rock in the head, causing injury that resulted in his death later that same day. He has admitted that to several people. He has contended—"

"Hold it, Art," interrupted McGrady. "If you're going to tell us what you think Joshua said, let's hear it from Joshua."

"Okay."

"Joshua, tell us what happened," said McGrady.

"Do I go to the stand over there?" said the young man, starting to rise to his feet.

"No. Just tell us from where you're sitting."

Rutgers, on McGrady's right, turned and murmured in the chairman's ear, "Shouldn't we swear him in first?"

"Not necessary," answered McGrady. Turning to Joshua, he continued. "Tell the truth. Just tell us the truth."

"Well, last Sunday morning I decided to go blueberry picking, so I got a pail and started off. I was walking—"

"What time was that?" asked Rutgers. He was a slender, intense-looking man, about forty with close-cropped hair. He delivered his question like the first blow of a hatchet in the process of falling a sapling.

"Around nine," answered Joshua. He stopped and waited for furthur direction.

"Go on," said McGrady.

"I was walking through the playground area when Rose came running up to me. She wanted to come with me. I said okay and waited for her to go get a pail."

McGrady glanced at Fran. She was looking at the ceiling.

Joshua continued. "We went on up the path to the big berry patch near the old Crockett foundation."

"How long did that take?" asked Rutgers, whacking away.

"Fifteen or twenty minutes, I guess." said Joshua. He squirmed a bit to get a more comfortable position. "Then we started to pick berries, at least I did."

Rutgers interrupted again, "Are you in the habit of going off alone with Rose?"

"What?"

"I said, do you often go off in the woods with Rose, just the two of you? I mean you're nineteen and she's fourteen and she's—"

"Okay, okay, Ralph. We all know Rose," said McGrady. "Go on, Joshua. Answer his question."

"Well, all us kids do things together all the time. Rose right along with the rest of us. She went berry picking, just like everybody else. She'd hang around me sometimes. She's a nice kid. I've taken her berry picking before. Sometimes there was just the two of us, I guess."

"How many times?" asked Rutgers.

"I don't know. Three of four times, maybe," said Joshua.

"What happened next?" said McGrady.

"I was bent over picking when I sensed Rose was right behind me, so I stood up and turned around. She was standing there, stark naked. She—"

"Tell the truth, Joshua! He said to tell the truth!" cried Fran from across the room, her fists clenched on her knees. Murmurs and grumbles broke out among the audience.

"Now just a minute!" said Rutgers, an accusatory finger shaking in Joshua's direction.

"Quiet! Quiet!" said McGrady, his voice rising above the rest. "Stop interrupting! Let him tell his story!" He rapped his gavel and the room quieted down.

Joshua took a deep breath and looked impassively at McGrady.

"Go on," he said to Joshua. In the meantime, seeing

himself serving no useful purpose at the lectern, Carlson returned to his seat.

"She was standing there naked. I said, 'Rose! Put your clothes on!' She wrapped her arms around my waist and wouldn't let go. I had a pail in my hand. I couldn't get her loose. I tripped in the bushes and fell down, on top of her. She was still hanging on."

"Then what?"

"I heard somebody yelling, 'Get off her, you son-of-a bitch!' It was Jim. I managed to get up to my knees when he grabbed me by the arm and jerked me off her. He spun me around, my berries went flying. Then he hit me, hard, across the face."

"With his fist?" said Rutgers.

"With the flat of his hand. I said, 'Hey! Hey! Stop it!' He didn't stop it. He held on to me and just kept hitting me. He was big. You know. He outweighed me by fifty pounds. I couldn't get loose."

Joshua paused, the recollection of the assault by the tall, powerful, Williamson almost real. The anger on the older man's face, the pain of the blows, the utter violence of it all caused a rush of adrenaline in his veins now just as it had the first time. His hands unconsciously curled into fists. His throat went tight. This time no one prompted him.

"So I kneed him, in the groin. He let go and staggered around for a couple of seconds. He yelled at me again, 'You son-of-a-bitch!' Then he tackled me. We went down. I managed to get out from under him and stand up. He rolled over and crouched in the brush. He held up his fist and said, 'I'll kill you, you son-of-a-bitch!' Then he came at me. I hit him. With the rock in my hand. On the side of the head. He went down and didn't get up."

The room was hushed. Fran, her jaw clenched, struggled to keep the tears from flowing. Her oldest son, Jim Jr., sitting on her left, held her hand and looked with wonder at Joshua. He had just heard, firsthand, how his best friend had killed his dad.

"Where'd you get the rock from?" Rutgers broke the silence.

"I don't know. I guess I picked it up when we went down. All I know is it was in my hand when I hit him."

"Did you mean to kill him?" This question came from Ordway Futchic.

"I meant to stop him."

"Why didn't you just run?" This from Steve Johanson's wife, Marin.

"I don't know."

"What happened next?" asked McGrady.

"I looked Jim over to see how bad he was hurt. He was unconscious, but breathing. Some blood was coming out of his nose. A trickle. I shook him to wake him up, but he wouldn't come to. I got Rose out of the bushes and made her get dressed. Then I made her follow me back here for help. I went right to Dr. Sandy."

Joshua turned and looked at Sandy McGrady. She returned the glance and then turned to her husband, as though she was anxious to speak.

"Then?"

"Then you and me, Captain, and Dr. Sandy and Curtis went back to get Jim and bring him back to the infirmary."

"Then we all carried him back here, right?" said McGrady.

"Yes."

"Dr. Sandy will tell us about the injury to Jim in a few minutes," said the chairman. "First let's ask Joshua any remaining questions we have of him," he said, speaking to the other members of the council.

"Why didn't you run from Jim when you got away from him? Everybody knows you're the fastest runner in Dixon. Why didn't you just run away instead of hitting him?" said Mrs. Johanson, leaning across the table toward Joshua.

"It didn't occur to me...He was right there. He was attacking me...I just reacted."

"You say Rose took off her clothes and grabbed you around the waist. Why would she have done that?" Futchic asked that question as much of Fran as of Joshua, as he looked back and forth between them both.

"I don't know," answered Joshua.

"Because he made her do it!" blurted Fran.

"Fran. Fran," said McGrady, holding up his hand for quiet. The people on the benches were stirring around again. Some had their hands up, begging to be recognized.

"Why don't we ask Rose?" said Rutgers.

"That's not a good idea," said the chairman. Fran was shaking her head vigorously. "Arthur interviewed her. Arthur, what did you learn from your talk with Rose?"

Carlson returned to the lectern. "I first asked her to tell me what happened out there. All she would say was, 'He killed my daddy. He killed my daddy.'

"Then I asked her if she had her clothes off. She said, 'Yes.' I asked her what she and Joshua were doing when she had her clothes off. She said they were 'lovin'.'"

All eyes turned to Joshua. He shook his head slowly side to side.

"What else did she say?" asked McGrady.

"That's all she would say," answered Carlson.

Dr. Sandy had her hand in the air.

"What?" said McGrady, acknowledging his wife.

"I talked to Rose when I examined her. Can I speak now?"

"Okay."

Dr. Sandy walked briskly to the lectern as Carlson stepped aside.

"I checked Rose over after we tried to revive Jim. She was uninjured. Just some minor scratches from the bushes. I thought there might be other questions, so I, ahhh, gave her a complete check up. There was no sign of sexual activity. I asked her whether Joshua hurt her in any way. She said, no, they were loving. She's a loving child, hugging people all the time. I think she was just—"

"Not without her clothes on! She doesn't hug people without her clothes on!" challenged Fran, her anger directed at the doctor.

Sandy, composed, turned to Fran. "Did Rose ever see you and Jim making love without your clothes on?"

Fran didn't answer.

"Hey, this is ridiculous. Let's get Rose in here," said Rutgers.

McGrady thought a bit, then turned to Sandy. "You finish telling us about your treatment of Jim, but don't say anything more about what Rose said. After a break, we'll have her come in here."

He looked out at the audience, but avoided Fran's eyes. "We'll have Rose come in and answer a few questions after a break."

Sandy finished explaining how Jim passed away despite her best efforts. He never regained consciousness and was declared dead shortly after midnight. The cause of death was a massive brain hemorrhage due to a fracture of the left temporal bone.

McGrady declared a break of thirty minutes.

The meeting room was filled again. No one had lost interest. All the principals were in their same places, including Carlson, who was at the lectern.

McGrady rapped for order, then nodded at Carlson.

"Jim, will you bring Rose up here," said Carlson to young Jim Williamson, Jr.

A tall handsome fellow of eighteen rose from his bench with his sister holding him by the hand. Young Jim was a light tan, the color of maple sugar, that sweet bounty provided to Dixon by Mother Nature from her rejuvenated woodlands. His sister was the same color, and, some used to say to her, just as sweet. Her hair was done up in braids. She had on a dress of homespun linen, died orangish red by the juices of the wild sumac. Her round face reflected the worry of those of her family. She sensed she was going to have difficulty in this situation. She knew she was different. She even knew the name of the reason, Down's syndrome.

"Rose," said Marin Johanson, the designated interrogator,

in as kindly a voice as she could manage, "Can you tell us what happened the day you and Joshua went picking blueberries?"

Rose heard the question from her place beside her brother. She whispered something to him. He said, "Go ahead, Rose, answer Mrs. Johanson."

She whispered again to young Jim.

"She said, 'He killed my daddy,'" said Jim to the council members.

"Rose, what were you and Joshua doing before your dad came?" asked Marin.

Again she whispered to her brother.

"She said they were picking blueberries."

"No, I mean right before her dad came. Rose did you have your clothes on?"

Rose shook her head, no.

"Rose, who took your clothes off?"

The frightened girl didn't respond. Jim Jr. murmurred in her ear and she whispered back.

"She doesn't want to answer," said Jim Jr.

"Did Joshua take your clothes off? Rose, did Joshua take your clothes off?" broke in Rutgers in a loud voice.

Before she commenced to cry, it appeared she shook her head, no.

"That's enough!" Fran leaped from her seat and wrapped her arms around her daughter.

McGrady watched the three Williamsons and then the entire family as the other three Williamsons, two girls and another boy, all younger than Jim Jr., joined in the tableau at the lectern.

"Okay, Fran. You can all sit down."

After further questioning of Joshua, Dr. Sandy, and Carlson, which provided no additional information, McGrady prepared to adjourn the meeting. He picked up his gavel to do so when Hope, Joshua's sister, sprang to her feet.

"Captain McGrady, I want to say something!"

"Okay, Hope, come to the lectern."

Hope, a striking beauty, a blond female version of Joshua, slimmer, not as tall, but with erect posture, wide shoulders, strong chin and straight nose, addressed the council. "You all know Joshua as well as anyone else in this community. You know he's honest. You know he's a kind person. He, and I, were the firstborn after the 'Big One.' All the kids that came after idolize him. Us kids, we're like one big family. He's been especially good to Rose. He caught her a mouse once for a pet. And a little copper-bellied snake. Right, Mrs. Williamson? Remember how she carried it around till you made her let it go?"

Hope went on for a while, pleading for her brother, till she ran out of words. She walked slowly back to her seat next to Dr. Sandy.

Fran waited till Hope was seated, then, leaving Rose in the care of Jim Jr., went to the lectern. With deep emotion, she addressed the audience and the council. "There were six of us that came to Dixon on the space shuttle, *Atlantis.* There are four of us left. None of us would have made it if it weren't for one man, my husband, Jim Williamson. He never, never, lost his temper. He was the coolest head in this community. Over twenty years as one of the leaders of this place he proved his character time and time again. He would not have fought with Joshua unless he had good cause. And he would never, ever say 'I'll kill you, you son-of-a-bitch.' He was murdered by a boy who was assaulting my daughter." She fixed each council person in turn with a righteous glare then sat down.

The room was silent, the morning breeze had slacked off. Heat was building in the enclosed space from the bodies inside.

Ron Baker, from his place next to Hope, rose to his feet. He waited for the chairman to recognize him, then went to the lectern. "I'm speaking on behalf of my son," he said in a strong voice. "He is not of my blood nor of my wife Maria's, but he is my son. A father knows his son. This father knows his son. Joshua is a fine boy...young man. He is honest, direct, hardworking, and kind. He has a great respect for people and nature. And he admired Jim a lot. He's told me so, many times. Yes, and Fran's right. Jim was an exceptionally cool head. I was one of the *Atlantis* crew, too, I know. I miss Jim. He was my friend. But he could make mistakes. He was human. I think he made a mistake. He evidently thought Joshua was assaulting Rose, and he reached that point where even a father with the greatest self-control would lose it."

Ron paused. He met the gaze of each council member in turn. Then he said, "There was no crime committed here. A tragedy has happened, but not a crime."

He returned to his seat.

After Ron was seated, Rutgers spoke up. "What has happened here is somebody is dead. An important and respected man is dead. He was killed by a young man who even now shows no remorse. Even if Jim did attack him, and who could blame Jim, does that excuse the use of deadly force? Did he have to use a rock? Why didn't he just run off till Jim cooled down? There is something about that young man that scares me. He is a killer. He—"

"Hold it, hold it, Ralph. We'll debate that in closed session. Is there anybody else who wishes to speak?" said McGrady.

From the back of the room, from his seat with his daughters and sons-in-law and grandchildren came Curtis Saylow. His black hair, combed back, brushed his shirt collar. His broad shoulders—slightly sloped with years of labor hauling fishnets, pulling oars, and moving heavy objects for the weaker members of the community—straightened perceptibly as he approached the lectern. He grasped the edges of the stand with two big hands. Joshua watched him, eyes glowing.

"I know Joshua as well as anyone. He and I, we fish together. We talk. I trust him. He's as straight as an arrow. And he has a rare quality. Jim Williamson had that same rare quality. In a crisis he will act. He will not waste time in useless talk or unproductive thought…Flight or fight. You know how our bodies are made to react to crises. The blood rises, the muscles tense. Run or fight. Joshua will not run, he will fight.

So would Jim. We need people like Joshua. He has not committed a crime. He has followed his instinct." Curtis scanned the audience as if to squelch any doubts that might exist out there. He returned up the center aisle.

Joshua pushed his chair back and stood. "Can I say something more?" he said to the council.

"Yes, Joshua, go ahead," said McGrady.

Joshua remained standing behind his table. Taking in the entire room as he spoke, he said in a soft voice, "I'm sorry I killed Jim. I liked him. He taught me lots of things. He was a fine man. I don't know what happened, why Rose had her clothes off, why Jim attacked me. I...I was just defending myself...I'm sorry."

He sat down.

There was no more testimony. McGrady adjourned the meeting and went into closed session to decide the outcome of the case.

Late that afternoon, Carlson rang a ship's bell outside the community hall to signal a resumption of the meeting. People beginning to prepare the evening meal covered the food and set it aside. Youngsters working in the gardens put down their tools. Repair projects on the buildings were suspended. Dr. Sandy's medical students, preparing for a test the next day, closed their textbooks. Steve Johanson's mechanical engineering class, assembling a diesel engine in the freighter, *Dixon*, left the parts lying on the deck of the engine room. Parents called to their children in low voices. Everyone returned to the hall.

McGrady and the other three members of the panel sat again at the head table. McGrady rapped his gavel and called the meeting to order. The secretary began to write. Joshua squared his shoulders and waited, expectantly.

"The council has reached a decision. By a vote of three to one, the council finds Joshua guilty of manslaughter. The prescribed penalty in our rules is banishment.

"Joshua, tomorrow morning at eight o'clock you will be

provided with food and clothing and escorted to the boat dock in the cove on the northeast side of the island. There you will be given a good seaworthy canoe. You will leave the island and never come back. You are not to go to either of the towns at the Soo. They will be notified of our action and will not accept you. The action of the council is final. God be with you."

Far beyond the recreation area, on the fringe of one of the vegetable gardens and concealed in the brush, a stranger lay on the ground, staring through his binoculars at the procession of Dixonites leaving the community hall. He focused on a slender woman with a blonde ponytail and dressed in jeans and a dark blue T-shirt. He had waited all day for one last look at her.

Yes, she was the one. He rose to leave, his Mohawk haircut brushing the low limbs of the trees above him. Tomorrow he would return with his companions and take her, and any other young girls they could capture.

21
Destiny

The sun is well past the zenith. Puffy white clouds float overhead. The surface of the water off in a distance is barely rippled by the soft breeze. The smooth gray rock outcroppings at the head of the open slope are warm and pleasant to the touch. The scent of ripening grass and late summer flowers fills the air. Along the edge of the opening, the shamrock green leaves of the trees flutter gently.

Joshua, crouched behind two boulders at the upper end of the opening, peers intently at a jumble of rocks near the shoreline, well below him and some three hundred yards away. A man's body lies in front of and in the shade cast by Joshua's boulders. All the blood has oozed out onto the sandy slope. Flies buzz, circling, and alight on the sticky ground.

Down below, beside the rocks that Joshua watches, are two more bodies, sprawled grotesquely, close enough together that their body fluids are mingled into a burgundy puddle on the ashen surface of a bare granite bench.

Ironic. That's the word. Ironic. Yesterday I get banished from Dixon for manslaughter. Now here I am, defending the people that kicked me out from those men down below.

Banished. A hell of a word. Me, one of the first of the new generation, experienced sailor and fisherman. Well educated. A valuable member of the community. Banished. Now here I am, saving Dixon. With a hole in my side. And Art Carlson dead.

Do they know what's going on here? I doubt it. I'm on the other side of the island.

They're too far away to hear the shots. If they did hear them, they'd come, wouldn't they? Wouldn't they?

There's no movement down there now. Bet those guys are trying to wait me out. I'm not moving either.

What kind of a person am I? Am I a bad person? I don't think so.

Yet I have those dreams sometimes. I'm fighting, killing. And I hit him. God, I did hit him.

Is killing wrong? Books are full of stories of men who fought and killed. Heroes. Natty Bumppo, Jonathon Zane, Daniel Boone, Davey Crockett. Alvin York and Pappy Boyington. Yeah, and David in the Bible. When is it wrong? I guess I know...You don't kill your friends.

What was that? Are they up to something? That was a leg that stuck out from behind that little ridge for a second. I better pay attention.

They're stupid. At least they started out stupid. They should've waited until we got closer. That way they could've got us both. I've got a scope. They don't. At three hundred meters I've got the advantage.

They got lucky, though. They got Art right through the chest. Hit me, too.

Sure, they have automatic weapons, but they ended up shooting single shots. They must be conserving their ammunition. I don't have a lot, but I've got plenty for the four of 'em that's left. Three shots so far and two of 'em are dead. Gee, I didn't realize this rifle was so deadly. Held the cross hairs on the target, just like I was taught. Squeezed the trigger. Bam! Down they went. Knocked 'em right off their feet! Satisfying.

Why'd they attack us? When we saw 'em, we waved. Friendly waves. They just started shooting. I suppose I know why now. They're raiders. They want our food, or our women. Just like the bunch that came nineteen years ago and Jim blasted out of the water with the PBG. Some got away. Maybe these are the same ones. Or their sons. Their hair's cut Mohawk style and they're wearing red cloths around their heads. But they're not blacks. I understood those other ones were all blacks. Like Jim.

Jim. Damn it all, it's his fault. I didn't touch her. By God, I didn't touch her. I'd never touch her. Nobody would take advantage of somebody like that. A special person. Everybody takes care of her. She was nice. I liked her. I've known her all her life. She followed me around a lot. I wouldn't touch her.

I shouldn't have let her go blueberry picking with me. Sure, she'd gone with me and others before, but she'd been looking at me funny lately. I should've known there was going to be trouble.

And Jim. Why'd he do that? Why'd he hit me?

I suppose I could've run. But I didn't.

There they go again. One's trying to crawl out of that ravine. Probably wants to circle around me. If he gets into the trees, I'm in big trouble.

Okay, I've got him in the cross hairs…There's something familiar about this. Like I've done this before. Not just today.

Sometime in a long ago. The warm touch of the walnut gun stock against my cheek. The perfect heft of the rifle in my arms. The spot way out there where I know the bullet will hit.

BAM!

There's only three left now. They can't get out of there without my getting a shot. It's too open.

'Course I can't get away without exposing myself either. What did they used to call this? A Mexican standoff? I wonder where that phrase came from.

I bet they're scared. More scared than me.

"HEY! YOU GUYS WANT TO SURRENDER? YOU CAN'T GET OUT OF THERE! SURRENDER!"

ZIP! POW! ZIP! POW!

"—uh-you!" What's that they said? I guess they don't want to surrender. I still bet they're scared.

I must not be hit too bad. The bleeding's stopped. And it doesn't hurt too much. I don't feel too good, though.

I didn't explain the situation very well at the council meeting. If I had, they wouldn't have banished me. And Art, there, would be alive. My escort. I didn't need an escort. I would have left the island...Except that my canoe is down there. At the landing down below where those raiders docked their launch.

Good thing I had this rifle. Curtis said I might need it. It was his. He's the one who taught me how to shoot it, long ago. Him and Jim.

Jim was a good man, really. He just misunderstood and lost his temper. A person can get into a lot of trouble losing their temper. I know. I never saw Jim get mad before. He was always so cool, so in control.

Rose was his first daughter. She was special to him, I guess. I'm glad he and Fran had other kids. Jim Jr. will take care of 'em.

Wonder what those three are thinking now? Bet they're waiting till dark. I would if I was them. Then what? Will they come after me or retreat?

I have to wait, too. I have no choice...We'll see.
Suppose they leave when it gets dark?
Then I'll go back. I'll have to explain about Art.
Suppose they come after me?
I could slip away in the dark.
If I stay, will they get me?

No. No, they won't get me and they won't get by me. I have an instinct for this sort of thing. It's my destiny. That's a good word. Destiny.

22
Hope

"Hope, why are you packing that knapsack?"

"I'm going to go away, Dr. Sandy."

"What on earth for?"

"I can't stay here any longer."

"Why do you say that?"

"Because from now on, everyone will treat me differently. They'll look at me and think, 'She's the sister of that killer, Joshua. She's got bad genes.' I can see it in their eyes already."

"No, no, Honey. That just happened. He just left here this morning. It'll blow over. People will accept you for yourself. You'll see. There's nothing wrong with your genes."

"Well, I'm still going, Dr. Sandy. To tell the truth, I don't think Joshua or I would have stayed here much longer, anyway."

"Why?"

"Because there's a big world out there. I want to see it,
experience it. I know who I am, Dr. Sandy. I want to find out
what I am. And I want to find out why I am. Joshua felt the
same way. He told me so."

"Oh, Hope, I wish you wouldn't go. We need you here."

"I'm sorry, but my mind's made up."

"Have you told your dad?"

"Yes."

"What did he say?"

"He didn't want me to go, either."

"It's no wonder. And it can be dangerous out there,
especially for a woman."

"I can take care of myself, Dr. Sandy. Besides, Dad gave
me a pistol. I'll be all right."

"Where will you go?"

"Down to Lake Michigan for now. I hear Grand Haven is
a beautiful place."

"And how will you get there?"

"I'll take the trading vessel from Chicago. It's at the Soo
now. I'm going to catch the Coast Guard boat back to the Soo."

"What will you do in Grand Haven?"

"I'm a teacher, Dr. Sandy. Remember? There are children
there to be educated. I'll earn my way. And there's a seaplane
there, too. Someday I'd like to fly one. I'd like to see the plains
and the mountains. You've seen the plains and the mountains.
You've seen the entire world. You understand, don't you?"

" Yes…I think I do understand…We'll miss you."

"I'm leaving now. The Coast Guard should be at the pier.
Dad's waiting there to see me off. Say good-by to everyone for
me."

"I will…Good-by…Take care…And Hope, if you ever
see Joshua, give him my love."

Epilogue

At the end of the first year following the initial blast and subsequent fires caused by the asteroid, there were approximately 6.5 million people living on Earth, about 1.3 percent of the population that existed in the year 1 A.D.

Of those who had lived in North America, about 400,000 were alive to see the first anniversary of the "Big One," all from the interior of the continent.

Sandra Samuels-McGrady had been wrong in her initial estimate of the percentage of women survivors who were fertile. The Natadin program had been highly effective; in North America only about 42,000 females had the capability to bear children and of those, 31,000 were under eleven years old. Year Plus 1, as it was called by the inhabitants of Dixon, began with 11,000 women available to be mothers in what had been the United States, Canada, and Mexico.

By the year 2027, or Plus 20, the population had grown to 475,000. Still, only 32,000 were fertile females over the age of fifteen, less than 9,000 from the new generation. Few were as beautiful, intelligent, and resourceful as Hope.

There were about 120,000 men seeking fertile mates. Some would fight and kill for what they wanted. Some would fight just to survive. And some would fight and die, wondering why men fought.